Llyfrgelloedd Caerdydd
www.caerdydd.gov.uk/llyfrgelloedd
Cardiff Libraries
www.cardiff.gov.uk/libraries

KU-050-828

ACC. No: 02352183

SPECIAL MESSAGE TO READERS

This book is published under the auspices of

THE ULVERSCROFT FOUNDATION

(registered charity No. 264873 UK)

Established in 1972 to provide funds for research, diagnosis and treatment of eye diseases. Examples of contributions made are: —

A Children's Assessment Unit at Moorfield's Hospital, London.

•

Twin operating theatres at the Western Ophthalmic Hospital, London.

•

A Chair of Ophthalmology at the Royal Australian College of Ophthalmologists.

•

The Ulverscroft Children's Eye Unit at the Great Ormond Street Hospital For Sick Children, London.

You can help further the work of the Foundation by making a donation or leaving a legacy. Every contribution, no matter how small, is received with gratitude. Please write for details to:

**THE ULVERSCROFT FOUNDATION,
The Green, Bradgate Road, Anstey,
Leicester LE7 7FU, England.
Telephone: (0116) 236 4325**

**In Australia write to:
THE ULVERSCROFT FOUNDATION,
c/o The Royal Australian and New Zealand
College of Ophthalmologists,
94-98 Chalmers Street, Surry Hills,
N.S.W. 2010, Australia**

Jeanne Whitmee originally trained as an actress and later taught speech and drama before taking up writing full time.

SUMMER SNOW

The end of the war brings unwelcome changes for Mary Snow. Her husband, Paul, announces his intention of returning to his acting career — but without the encumbrances of a wife and child. Returning to her home town with her daughter, Mary finds picking up the threads of her pre-war life a challenge, which is not improved by the old antagonism between herself and her sister. Bringing up a child alone also has its problems. But Mary finds a job, and a new romance begins to blossom for her. Six-year-old Vivien shows a talent for the stage, inherited from her father, and life looks promising again. Then the past unexpectedly rears its head — with devastating consequences. Can Mary win through?

Books by Jeanne Whitmee
Published by The House of Ulverscroft:

ORANGES AND LEMONS
THE LOST DAUGHTERS
THURSDAY'S CHILD
EVE'S DAUGHTER
BELLADONNA
KING'S WALK
PRIDE OF PEACOCKS
ALL THAT I AM
THE HAPPY HIGHWAYS

JEANNE WHITMEE

SUMMER SNOW

Complete and Unabridged

CHARNWOOD
Leicester

First published in Great Britain in 2005 by
Robert Hale Limited
London

First Charnwood Edition
published 2006
by arrangement with
Robert Hale Limited
London

The moral right of the author has been asserted

Copyright © 2005 by Jeanne Whitmee
All rights reserved

British Library CIP Data

Whitmee, Jeanne
   Summer snow.—Large print ed.—
Charnwood library series
1. Single mothers—Fiction
2. Love stories
3. Large type books
I. Title
823.9′14 [F]

ISBN 1–84617–431–7

Published by
F. A. Thorpe (Publishing)
Anstey, Leicestershire

Set by Words & Graphics Ltd.
Anstey, Leicestershire
Printed and bound in Great Britain by
T. J. International Ltd., Padstow, Cornwall

This book is printed on acid-free paper

1

The train journey seemed endless. Five-year-old Vivien was bored and fretful and Mary had run out of games to play and patience with which to play them.

'For heaven's sake, sit down and stop fidgeting,' she snapped. 'Look out of the window and count the cows or something.'

'Aren't any cows,' Vivien said petulantly. 'Only fields. When will we be there?'

'*Soon.* I keep telling you.'

'I'm hungry.' Vivien's lower lip trembled and Mary relented. The child looked grubby and tired. They had been travelling since early that morning and now it was almost teatime. It would be at least another forty minutes before they reached Ferncliff-on-Sea. She couldn't afford a meal in the restaurant car and the sandwiches she had packed for the journey had been eaten hours ago. She held out her arms.

'Come here and have a cuddle,' she invited. 'Try and have a little bye-byes, then when you wake up we'll be there.'

Reluctantly Vivien allowed her mother to pull her on to her lap and hold her close. Her thumb crept into her mouth and for once Mary ignored it.

'What's she like — my grandma?' Vivien mumbled through a mouthful of thumb.

'She's nice,' Mary told her. 'She's kind. You'll

1

like her house. You can see the sea from the bedroom windows and she's a very good cook.'

Two large brown eyes, heavy with sleep, looked up at her. 'Will she like me?'

'Of course she will.'

'Why haven't I seen her before?'

Mary sighed. 'Because we've been living a long way away and we weren't allowed to travel to the seaside when the war was on.'

It wasn't a total lie. It was true that visits to the south-east coast were restricted during the war, but it was possible to get a special permit if you had relatives living there. The reasons they had never visited Mary's mother were far too complicated to explain to Vivien. She glanced down at the child and was relieved to see that she had dropped off to sleep at last.

Mary leaned her head back against the prickly fabric of the seat and closed her own eyes, allowing her thoughts to drift back to that other train journey; a very different one. The memory of it had now assumed a surreal dreamlike quality so that sometimes she wondered if it had ever actually happened.

She and Paul had been so happy and excited that day. It had seemed so romantic, eloping; just the two of them against the world. A world set on its ear by Hitler and his Nazi storm troopers.

★   ★   ★

Paul Snow had arrived at the Theatre Royal, Ferncliff, in the spring of 1939. He was twenty, the same age as Mary, when they first met.

2

Although she had started work in the post office when she left school, Mary sometimes used to help out with collecting and washing glasses in the theatre bar on Saturday evenings where Dora Flynn, her mother, was manageress.

The first time Paul came into the bar to collect drinks, ordered for the cast in the interval, she was completely bowled over. He was tall and dark with melting brown eyes the colour of treacle toffee. It was love at first sight for her. And miraculously, Paul seemed to feel the same way.

She learned that he was what was known as an ASM. It stood for 'assistant stage manager' and sounded very grand but, as Paul told her, all it really meant was general dogsbody; running errands, sweeping up and making tea, begging special props from local tradespeople in return for a couple of complimentary tickets. All the jobs, in fact, that no one else wanted to do. Occasionally Paul would get to play a small part. Once he'd been a body that fell out of a cupboard and in another play he had to dress up in different outfits and walk past a shop window to simulate passers-by. They used to laugh about it, but Paul assured her earnestly that he was constantly watching the actors and learning what he called 'his craft'. One day he would be a famous actor, he vowed. His name up in lights in the West End and everyone asking for his autograph.

She loved to hear him talk like that. All that summer they would spend their Sundays together, walking on the cliffs or the beach and making dreamy plans about the marvellous future they would one day share.

Her sister, Erica, a year younger, had tried her hardest to spoil things for her right from the start. She worked behind the counter at Woolworths and she'd always been resentful because Mary had been allowed to stay on at school an extra year, which enabled her to get a better job. She hadn't got a boyfriend of her own either and when their mother expressed her disapproval of Mary's developing relationship with Paul, warning that he wasn't the type to settle down with a wife and family, Erica agreed enthusiastically, her hands on her hips and her green eyes flashing triumphantly. But Mary ignored it all. With every passing week she fell more in love with Paul. She knew without a doubt that he was the one she wanted to spend the rest of her life with. Erica was only jealous as usual and what could their mother possibly know about love? Dora was old — almost *forty*. She and their father had parted years ago. Because her marriage hadn't worked she thought Mary and Paul's wouldn't either. It was sad, of course, but Mum's life was over whilst Mary's was just beginning.

All that spring and summer there was talk of war and the danger of invasion everywhere. Groups of people stood about talking gravely in pubs and shops and on street corners about this terrible man called Hitler and his obsessive determination to make the German people the Master Race. The cinema newsreels showed the great rallies in Berlin, the build-up of Nazi power chilling the blood of all who saw them. But Mary was oblivious to it all. She could think of nothing but Paul, counting the days impatiently all week till Sunday, when they would be together.

Then, in September, Hitler's troops invaded Poland and Mr Chamberlain, the Prime Minister, announced gravely on the wireless that they were at war. Suddenly everything seemed to go mad. Ugly brick air-raid shelters began to appear at the end of each street. The beach and prom were closed off, walls of sandbags and barbed wire entanglements everywhere. Some people even said there were mines hidden under the sands. The cinemas closed, the Theatre Royal too, which meant that Mum was out of a job. Dora quickly found herself a cleaning job to feed them all and set her two daughters to work every evening sewing blackout curtains for all the rooms in their little terraced house.

It all seemed so unreal. Mary could not believe that the things she saw happening on the newsreels would ever happen here at home. Erica, on the other hand, saw things more pragmatically. She had already applied to join the ATS, seeing it as her passport out of a dead-end job and a boring life.

But reality struck Mary with a cruel force just a couple of weeks later when Paul appeared unexpectedly one morning at her window in the post office. His face white and shocked, he pushed an official-looking envelope across the counter to her. She stared at it, then up at him.

'It's my call-up papers,' he explained.

It was almost time for her lunch break and he

waited for her outside. They went to a small park nearby and sat on a bench.

'When do you have to go?'

'Very soon,' he told her.

'How soon?'

'Next Monday.'

'Oh no!'

'I had to have a medical like everyone else but I never thought I'd hear this quickly.' He unfolded the letter. 'I have to report to Catterick Camp at eight o'clock on Monday morning.' He pulled another piece of paper out of the envelope. 'Look, they've even sent a travel warrant.'

They stared at each other; two pairs of eyes full of bewilderment and misery.

'I can't bear the thought of leaving you,' Paul said.

'Neither can I.'

They were silent for a moment, their hands tightly clasped, then Mary looked up and said, 'What if I came too?'

'But — I'll be in the army.' Paul shook his head. 'They won't . . . ' He looked at her, his eyes widening as a daring idea occurred to him. 'If we were to get married . . . '

Mary's heart leapt. 'Oh, *Paul!*'

He shook his head. 'But you're still under-age. Would your mother give her permission?'

'Yes. Yes, I'll *make* her!'

'We could travel up to Yorkshire on Friday evening and get married on Saturday morning by special licence. Then we'd have all of Sunday together.' His cheeks pink with excitement, he grasped her other hand and held them both against his chest. 'Will you, Mary? Will you really marry me?'

She threw her arms around his neck, tears shining in her eyes. 'Oh, Paul, you *know* I will!'

But of course it wasn't to be that simple. Dora refused flatly to give her consent. 'You're still a child,' she protested. 'We're at the start of a war — an even worse one than the last. God alone knows where it'll all end. He'll be sent off to fight and you'll be left — chances are with a little one on the way too.'

Tears slid down Mary's cheeks. 'But I *love* him, Mum. We can't be apart — we can't! It'll *kill* me!'

'No, it won't,' Dora said with maddening calm. 'Look, if you're dead set on marrying him why don't you wait till his first leave? It'll give you time to get a few bits and pieces together. You haven't thought any of this through properly. Where are you going to live, for instance? And what would you live on? You've got a good job here at the post office and it's going to be an important one with the war and everything. If you chuck it all in now . . .'

Mary guessed that what Dora was really afraid of was losing both her daughters in one fell swoop. But this was *her* life — *her* future — and she was all the more determined to marry Paul, with or without her mother's blessing.

She decided that if her mother would not give her written permission she would have to lie about her age. It was only a few months till her twenty-first birthday anyway. No one would ever know. She managed to find her birth certificate and it was simple to change the last 9 of 1919 into an 8.

When Paul left for Yorkshire that Friday evening Mary was with him. She had packed a small suitcase and smuggled it out of the house that morning, leaving a brief note for her mother. She had told no one where she was going but all day long her stomach had churned with excitement, and once Paul had met her out of work and they were on their way she could hardly contain herself.

The train was packed to bursting with soldiers and their bulky kit bags. The windows were painted over with blue paint so that only a faint glimmer of light came through, but she and Paul stood together in the corridor, pressed tightly against each other, their arms entwined, happy, excited and oblivious to the discomforts.

The cost of the special licence, the cheap wedding ring and the room at the small hotel they checked into for the weekend took almost all of the money Paul had, but Mary had her unopened wage packet in her handbag and she was sure she would be able to get herself a job before too long.

The memory of that weekend was vague and dreamlike. She and Paul spent most of the time clinging to each other and trying hard not to think of the imminent parting that would be all the more painful now that they had consummated their love.

Monday morning came and Paul left for the camp. He learned that as a married man he would be allowed to sleep out after his initial five weeks' square bashing so Mary looked around for rooms for them.

She found a job in the local post office. Many of the men had been called up so there were plenty of vacancies. Finding rooms was another matter. The town was packed with other army wives and evacuees. It was as though the whole country had been stirred up like some gigantic pudding and strewn around in large indigestible portions. All she could find was a dingy bed-sit in a large old house in the poorer part of the town. The bathroom and kitchen were shared with the occupants of the other four rented rooms. It wasn't ideal but Mary told herself it would do for now. The important thing was that she and Paul could be together. She sent a telegram to her mother.

Paul and I married. Will write soon. Mary

Paul found the training hard. Each night he came home with painful blistered feet and aching limbs. Often he was so tired he could scarcely speak and fell asleep almost at once. Then as October came in there were rumours of an imminent embarkation to France. Soon the rumours were confirmed and Paul learned that he and most of his fellow conscripts were to go. In mid-October, with his training still incomplete, Paul left on a convoy of lorries packed with troops for an undisclosed coastal destination. The convoy was to travel at night to avoid the German bombs. No one had any idea how long they would be gone.

They parted tearfully. Paul begged her to go home to her mother and Mary nodded noncommittally. She couldn't bring herself to tell him that she was almost certainly expecting their child. Her pride wouldn't let her admit that her mother's prophecy had come true. The thought of admitting defeat and running home like a wounded puppy was unthinkable. She would brave it out and wait for Paul to come home to her. The letter she wrote to Dora gave nothing away.

Dear Mum

Paul and I have a nice flat here in Catterick and I have found a good job at the post office. Paul looks very handsome in his uniform and seems to like the army life. I have made friends with my work mates. I hope that you are both well. Has Erica joined up yet? If not please tell her that I wish her good luck. The people are friendly here, but there are a lot of strangers in the town just like everywhere else, I suppose. Have you taken any evacuees in, Mum? I'll write again soon. Love Mary.

Dora wrote back:

Dear Mary

I was very shocked by what you did, running away like that. I think it was very silly and underhand and all I hope is that you don't live to regret it. I feel you have betrayed me and everything I stand for. It's not the way I brought you up to behave. I would like to say that your home is always here if you want to come back but I have three little evacuees from London, poor mites, and so no space left. Anyway, you are a married woman now. You have made your bed Mary and so must lie on it and live your life as you have chosen. Your sister has joined the ATS and seems to be enjoying it. I'm not allowed to tell you where she is stationed, but I will pass on your address to her when I write.

I remain your very disappointed Mum.

Erica never wrote and Mary did not write to her mother again. The letter had both chastened and angered her.

Agonizing weeks passed between Paul's letters. When they did arrive they came in batches, heavily censored, thick blue pencil scored through anything that would give away his whereabouts. Because of it the letters often made little sense but Mary was happy to get them anyway. At least they were proof that he was still alive.

Christmas was lonely and the winter that followed long and bleak. She told Paul about the baby in a letter soon after Christmas. She didn't receive his reply until March, but he sounded pleased and excited.

If it's a girl shall we call her Scarlett?

Mary smiled to herself over the letter. They had been to see *Gone With the Wind* just before Paul had gone away and he had been entranced by the film, but Mary felt that if she had a girl she would prefer to name her Vivien after the actress who played the part. It was more of a *proper* name somehow.

She worked on at the post office for as long as she could, only giving up in the final weeks when her feet swelled and her back felt as though it would break.

The first pains began soon after she woke one hot and sultry morning in June. Mary waited as long as she dared and then took herself to the hospital on the bus in the height of a thunderstorm. Once there she took another twelve hours to deliver her daughter. Vivien Pauline Snow was born in the early hours of 25 June. She weighed seven pounds four ounces and had Paul's large dark eyes and thick brown hair. As Mary held her to her breast and looked down at the tiny perfect face, she wondered fleetingly if Vivien Pauline would ever know her father.

★　★　★

'Ferncliff-on-Sea!' *Ferncliff-on-Sea!*

The jolt of the halting train and the strident call from the platform brought Mary to her senses and she quickly shook Vivien.

'Wake up, lovey. We're there!' She stood and

12

reached up to the luggage rack for their cases. Rudely awakened and unceremoniously dumped on the seat, Vivien rubbed her eyes and pouted.

'I want to go back to sleep.'

'Later!' Mary grabbed the child's hand. 'Come on, love, we have to get off quickly now before the train starts again.'

They stood on the platform as the train steamed out and Mary looked around her. Nothing had changed. It all looked just the same. She wondered if the buses still stopped at the end of Gresham Terrace. She hoped so. Vivien was in no shape for a long walk and she certainly couldn't carry her.

By the time they alighted from the bus, the little girl was clearly exhausted, complaining at every step as they walked from the bus stop along the terrace of neat little houses. Number twenty-seven looked the same. The front door was still painted green and the brass gleamed with daily polishing. The front-room window still had looped-back frilled curtains, and scarlet geraniums still bloomed in the terracotta urn by the door. Mary knew her mother hadn't moved. She had been able to check through her job at the post office. She had written to say they were coming but had received no reply to her letter. She refused to think about the consequences if Dora refused to see her. As she took a clean handkerchief from her bag and bent down, Vivien automatically poked out a small pink tongue. As best she could Mary wiped the sooty railway grime and tear-stains from her daughter's face, thrust the soiled hanky into her pocket and rang the doorbell. She held her breath and cast a sideways warning glance at Vivien.

A movement from inside made her catch her breath with apprehension and a moment later the door opened. For the first time in almost five years Mary came face to face with her mother.

Dora looked the same. There were fine lines now around her eyes and mouth, but basically she was unchanged. Mary could almost have sworn that she wore the same cotton print dress she'd been wearing the day she and Paul had left. For a long moment neither of them spoke, then Vivien broke the tension.

'I'm Vivien. Are you my grandma?' she asked shyly.

Dora looked down at the child for the first time and her face crumpled, her eyes filling with tears. '*Oh*, you little pet,' she said, reaching out her hands. 'You pretty little dear.' She gathered the child to her and looked accusingly at Mary over her head. 'Why have you waited all this time to tell me I had a granddaughter?' she asked.

Mary took a deep breath. Where did she begin? But before she could reply Vivien spoke. Looking up at her grandmother, her big brown eyes wide with innocence she said, 'My daddy's dead.'

2

Vivien provided a merciful ice-breaking diversion for Mary and her mother during that first hour. Dora quickly rustled up Vivien's favourite, egg and chips, though by the time it was ready the little girl was almost too tired to eat it. The priority for both Mary and Dora was feeding the exhausted child and putting her to bed.

In the little back bedroom that Mary and her sister Erica had once shared, Mary undressed and settled a heavy-eyed Vivien, hastily searching the half-unpacked suitcase for the beloved teddy. Kneeling by the bed to tuck the bear in beside her daughter, she whispered gently, 'Vivvy, why did you tell Grandma that your daddy was dead, sweetheart?'

Vivien looked up at her and briefly removed her thumb from her mouth. 'You said he wasn't coming back,' she said. 'An' that's what it means. I know because Patsy Smith told me. Her mummy said that when her daddy got killed in the war.'

Slightly shaken by the child's matter-of-fact acceptance, Mary sat back on her heels. Vivien was only five. What could she know of the finality of death, especially when she had heard it spoken of so often during her short life? She hardly knew her father anyway. Paul had served in almost every major campaign throughout the war. After the initial shock he had taken to army life well and by the end of 1941 he had risen to the rank of lieutenant.

After Vivien's birth in 1940, Mary had managed to find a small furnished bungalow to rent on the outskirts of the town and had moved in to make a home for her new little family. But Paul's leaves had been few and far between. He was wounded at Dunkirk and spent several weeks in a military hospital. He didn't even see his baby daughter until after her first birthday. After that, on the rare occasions that he came on leave, the child seemed to see his presence merely as a disruption to her secure little daily routine.

Mary looked at Vivien again and saw that she was asleep. As she rose to her feet she wondered whether it might be better to let Dora go on believing that what Vivien said was true. It would save her an awful lot of awkward explanation. And after all, she hadn't deluded herself into believing that they would be welcomed with open arms. Coming home was never meant to be a permanent arrangement.

Downstairs Dora was in the kitchen, putting together a meal. In the adjoining living-room the table was laid for two; a jug of water and two glasses stood in the centre of the pristine white cloth. There were raffia tablemats and gingham napkins. Mary smiled to herself. Clearly Dora had not allowed the war to lower her standards.

'It would have been a help to know what time you were arriving,' Dora called out from the kitchen. 'Still, never mind, you're here now. You'll just have to take pot luck.' She bustled into the room with two steaming plates. 'I thought as I had the chip pan on we might as well have the same as Vivien,' she said, setting the plates down. 'Luckily a neighbour at the end of the road keeps chickens. I let her have all my kitchen waste and she keeps me in eggs.' She sat down and shook out her napkin. 'Come on, girl, tuck in. You look half starved.'

'I am.' Mary seated herself. 'I made sandwiches for the journey, but we ate them at lunchtime. That seems ages ago.'

They ate in silence for a moment or two, Dora shooting glances in her daughter's direction from time to time. Finally she said, 'You're looking well in spite of everything.'

Mary looked up. 'You look well too, Mum.' She laid down her knife and fork. 'Mum. I wouldn't have blamed you if you'd refused to see us.'

Dora did not look up. 'Turn away my own flesh and blood? As if I could.'

'I'm sorry about everything.'

'Well, if I tell the truth I did wonder at your sudden change of heart. I know why now, of course.'

'I hope you don't think I'm making a convenience of you.'

'If you can't turn to your own mother in times of trouble, who can you turn to?'

'I never wanted to lose touch but the time just went on and . . .'

Dora held up her hand. 'Finish your tea, girl. We'll talk later.'

Throughout the rest of the meal Dora chatted

as though the long silence between them had never existed.

'We didn't get much bombing here,' she said. 'I had three little evacuees. Two little sisters from Mile End, Daisy and Molly, and their baby brother, Johnny. Only four, he was, and missing his mum something terrible. She came and took him home after a while but the girls stayed on all through the blitz and after. Dear little mites, they were. Not a bit of trouble. Of course we were constantly aware of the invasion threat along this coast, but somehow I had faith. I never believed it'd really happen.'

'What about your job?' Mary asked.

'Oh, the Theatre Royal opened up again after a week or two and I kept the bar going, when we could get anything alcoholic to sell, that was. I did my bit of war work too — joined the WVS. That kept me busy in my spare time. We had a lot of Canadian airmen stationed here. The big hotels on the cliffs were requisitioned and they were stationed in those. Lovely lads; well, most of them anyway.'

She got up and fetched the pudding: gooseberries and custard in the fluted green glass dishes that Mary remembered so well. As she resumed her seat she looked at Mary and said, 'I know it's not much of a comfort, but you're not the only young wife to be widowed before your time, more's the pity. There must be thousands of women picking up the smashed bits of their lives and starting again. Well, you know you're welcome to stay here as long as you like, you and the little one, bless her. I do wish you'd written to tell me about her, though. I've missed all her baby years.'

Mary swallowed hard. 'I'm sorry about that, Mum — and for everything.'

Dora nodded. 'There's a lot I want to know, of course, but there's plenty of time for talking. The main thing is to get that little one settled. It must be such an upheaval for the poor little scrap. Started school, has she?'

'Yes. Just finished her first year. She was five in June and she started school after Easter.'

Dora took a spoonful of her dessert, glancing up sideways at Mary. 'There's only one thing I would like to know. Were you ever actually married?'

'Of course we were!'

'How? I never gave my permission and you were under-age.'

Mary sighed. 'I had to lie about my age, Mum. I altered the date on my birth certificate. You gave me no choice.'

Dora bridled. 'Don't you go putting the blame on me. There's always a choice in such matters.'

'It was the beginning of the war, Mum. Plenty of others were doing the same thing.'

'That doesn't make it right. It's against the law.'

'Paul and I loved each other. He was going away. What would you rather we'd done? You told me to wait till his first leave, but he was posted even before his basic training was over.'

Dora was thoughtful. 'So you were left to have the baby alone?' she said quietly. 'When you wrote you never even said you were expecting.'

19

'I didn't want — '

'You didn't want to hear me saying 'I told you so',' Dora finished for her. 'Well, I can't say I blame you. Did Paul's parents know they had a little granddaughter?'

'No. I never even got the chance to meet them. They were both killed in the Coventry blitz.'

Dora shuddered. 'God rest them. But you could have come home after the baby was born — even if it was just for a visit?'

Mary sighed. 'The letter you wrote me seemed pretty unforgiving. Anyway, I knew you had no room.'

'That's true enough, but we could have managed somehow,' Dora said. 'As for being unforgiving, I was still hurt and shocked that a daughter of mine could go behind my back like that.' She sighed. 'But there, it's all water under the bridge now and we've got that little one to think of. We'll have to make the best of things and try to look to the future. I just thank the Lord that I still have a family when so many haven't.' She got up and began to gather the used plates together. Mary stood up too.

'Let me help. I'll wash up.'

'We'll do it together, girl.'

In the tiny kitchen everything was just as Mary remembered it. The dresser shelves with their blue and white gingham frills that matched the curtains. The willow pattern plates, and the cups hanging from their little hooks. Under the window was the deep white sink that still wore its gingham skirt, hiding the shelves of soap and cleaning materials.

As they washed up Mary looked out of the window into the back yard. 'You've made a little vegetable patch,' she said, surprised.

Dora smiled. 'Dig for Victory, they told us. So I took up five of the paving slabs out there and grew a few salad things: a couple of tomato plants, some lettuce and radish, a few onions, even some runner beans growing up sticks. You'd be surprised how much I got off that little patch. Those little London kids had never eaten things fresh cut from the soil. I think they thought it all grew right there in the shops.'

Mary felt a sudden rush of love for her mother. She'd always been a strong, resourceful woman. She'd had to be, abandoned by a faithless husband and left to bring up two children on her own. Now that Mary was a mother herself she could imagine something of the pain her teenage defiance and rejection had given Dora. Her return home had been so much easier than she'd expected it to be, easier than she deserved. Now she regretted the years they'd spent apart, vowing there and then to try to make up for the long estrangement.

It was only later, in the quiet of her old room, that she remembered the deception she'd unintentionally created. It was no way to begin picking up the threads of her relationship with her mother, but there was no reason why Dora ever need know the facts. The truth was that Vivien had taken the wind out of her sails with her sudden announcement on the doorstep. Mary didn't quite know why she hadn't contradicted the child there and then. But thinking about it, perhaps it was kinder to Vivien to let her go on thinking that her father was dead.

* * *

His last leave had been in March. Mary had made special plans and preparations, excited and apprehensive at the same time. She was determined to make it perfect, to try and revive the romance and the joy they had once shared.

The war years had taken so much from them. After five years they should by now have grown together like a proper married couple — to have become almost like two halves of the same person. Instead they seemed to have grown apart. Worst of all, she sensed that instead of making their union complete, baby Vivien had for some inexplicable reason driven a wedge between them.

It was the first leave Paul had had since before D-Day and it was for seven days. Mary queued patiently for hours to get some little off-ration extras. She filled all her vases with daffodils picked from the garden and cleaned the bungalow until the scuffed furniture gleamed and the whole place was fragrant with the scent of polish. But when he walked through the door Paul hardly seemed to notice. He looked handsome in his officer's uniform, but he seemed weary and preoccupied as though his thoughts were a thousand miles away. Mary asked him if he thought Vivien had grown and proudly showed him the first crayoned pictures she had brought home from school, but he nodded abstractedly, casting only a cursory glance at them.

In the days that followed he was irritable and touchy. He was cool with Mary, even turning his back on her in bed, yet he seemed to resent the time she devoted to Vivien. He barely touched the food she so lovingly prepared for him and every time Mary suggested an outing or a walk he refused, saying that he was too tired. Things finally came to a head on the day before his leave was up.

Mary suggested taking Vivien to the park and once again Paul showed no interest. 'You go. I'm fine here with the paper.'

'This is your last day! What's the *matter* with you, for heaven's sake?' Mary erupted, her patience finally snapping. 'I've been looking forward to your leave for so long. I've done everything I can think of to make you happy, but nothing's right for you. What *do* you want?'

'I want my freedom.'

The words, coldly and deliberately spoken, hung in the air between them like a cobweb, thick and heavy. Mary stared at him, her heart missing a beat. 'What do you mean, your freedom?' she whispered.

Paul had been sitting in a chair; now he got up and began to pace the room. 'Every time I come home we seem to grow further apart,' he said.

'And that's *my* fault?'

He turned to look at her. 'No, of course it isn't. Mary, we were so young when all this began. A couple of starry-eyed kids eloping romantically in the face of enormous difficulty. In the years since then reality has stepped in in a big way. So much has happened.'

'You think I don't know that?' she snapped. 'You think it's been easy for me? I had to carry Vivien and give birth to her all by myself. I fell out with my family to marry you. When I came out of hospital I had no one to turn to and nowhere to live that was fit to bring a child to, so I had to find this place — and budget to pay for it. Do you think it was easy on an army wife's money? Do you think I wanted to have to give up work and struggle to make ends meet?'

He shook his head. 'I know. It must have been hard for you. Having a baby was an unforeseen slip-up.'

'A *slip-up*! It's our daughter you're talking about.'

He frowned, shaking his head irritably. 'I didn't mean it like that.' He turned to face her. 'Mary — you can have no idea what fighting a war is like. I know it was a struggle here at home. My own parents were killed in the Coventry blitz, remember? But over there . . . ' His eyes clouded. 'You can have no idea. I've seen things that no one should ever have to see. Friends blown to bits, death and destruction, turmoil everywhere you looked. Hell on earth is the only way to describe it.'

'But it's almost over now,' she protested. 'We can start to build our life together at last. You and me and Vivien — we have so much catching up to do.'

But he was shaking his head. 'No. Mary, listen, there's no easy way to say this but when the war ends I'm not coming home.'

'Not . . . '

'I want it to end — *us* — our marriage.' She opened her mouth. 'No, hear me out. You know how much I wanted to become an actor when we first met. I've wanted it ever since I can remember. The army was fine. In many ways I enjoyed it; the comradeship and the solidarity. But now all that will soon be over. I've come through some of the worst conflict ever known to man. I feel that my survival has to have a purpose and it's certainly not working nine till five every day in some dead-end job and cleaning the car on Sundays.'

'So what are you going to do?'

'I feel I'm meant to pick up my acting career again.'

She almost laughed. One would think he had some sort of religious vocation. It was on the tip of her tongue to remind him that he never *had* an acting career — that playing dead bodies and walk-on parts, sweeping the stage and making the tea hardly added up to a career. He'd probably forgotten everything he'd learned by now anyway. She forced down her irritation and took a step towards him. This was her husband, the man she had loved for seven years. She couldn't let him go without a fight.

'All right. If that's what you want. Vivien is at school now. I can get a job. I'll work to support us all until you find work.'

'You're not listening, are you?' He pulled away

from her and sighed. 'Please don't make this any more difficult than it is. Don't you see, I have to do it alone, Mary. I can't have . . . encumbrances.'

'*Encumbrances*!' She flinched. 'Is that how you see us?'

'What we had has gone, Mary,' he told her. 'I don't mean to sound brutal, but it has to be said and I think you know as well as I do that it's true. We don't love each other any more. Not in the way we should and it wouldn't be fair to either of us to stay together after the war, be together all day, seven days a week. It wouldn't last more than a few months. And that wouldn't be fair to Vivien either.' He smiled wryly. 'As it is, at the moment she doesn't even realize that I'm her father so she won't miss me.'

Panic filled Mary's chest, making her heart thump. 'I won't give you a divorce!'

He shrugged. 'That's your decision. I'll send money whenever I can.'

'Oh! That's good of you!' She stared at him. It was as though she were looking into the face of a stranger. Then she saw that he was indeed a stranger. The Paul Snow she had fallen in love with before the war had been a wide-eyed boy on the brink of manhood, with dreams and aspirations. This Paul was a man trying to battle with nightmares and demons; a man who believed that the only way to dispel them was to attempt to climb back into the world he had known. Tragically, it was a world in which she no longer had a place. Suddenly she was angry.

'And what am I supposed to do?' she asked.

'You can do anything. I mean that, Mary.

26

You're an intelligent woman. You can go back to the work you did before, or learn a new skill. You're still young and attractive. There's plenty of time for you to meet someone else. Marry again.'

'You seem to forget that I have your daughter to bring up.'

'You could always go home,' he said. 'Let your family help you. Unlike me, you still have a family.'

'We are your family!' she shouted. 'Vivien and me!' She stared at his impassive face. 'I can't believe you're ducking out of your responsibilities like this. Do you know how . . . how *feeble* it makes you look?'

'All I know is that it's what I have to do.'

'You're just chasing a dream. *You'll* never have a career in the theatre!' she sniped. 'You haven't acted for years and only bits even then. I think you have an over-inflated opinion of your talent!' Fear and rejection were making her spiteful now. She wanted to hurt him as much as he was hurting her. But it seemed that nothing she could do or say could touch him. It was as though he wore a suit of solid steel armour against her jibes.

'I know what this is all about. There's someone else, isn't there?' she threw at him. 'All this rubbish about acting is just a smoke-screen. You've met someone else and you haven't the guts to tell me the truth.'

'The Ministry of Information is planning to make an epic documentary film,' he told her, not even addressing her accusation. 'It's to be a

27

drama, based on true facts from the war. Several big stars will be in it. The film company came to our unit and asked if anyone had acting experience. I volunteered. They auditioned me and I got a part. It's only small but it's a foot in the door, Mary — a start.'

His excitement was tangible; it lit him from within like a shining aura and just for a moment she hated him for it. 'I see. Congratulations,' she said. 'So you want to be rid of us so that you can go your own way — follow this fantasy life of yours?'

'You make it sound so tawdry.'

'It *feels* tawdry.'

'Then I'm sorry.'

'So am I.'

When she wakened the following morning she found he had gone. She lay there, thinking of all her mother's warnings and hating the fact that after all this time Dora had been proved right. Then the practicalities began to dawn. Once the war was over and Paul was demobilized she could no longer rely on regular money. If she were to keep a roof over their heads and food in their mouths she would have to work. Who would take Vivien to school and collect her each day — give her her tea? Employing someone to do it would cost money she could not afford and anyway she hated the thought of a stranger hearing about Vivien's day before she did. How could she ever trust anyone else with her child? Then there were her doubtful prospects as an employee. Who would offer her work after five years out of the workplace? She would be hopelessly out of touch and rusty.

As the days went by she was convinced that Paul would change his mind. She could not make herself believe that he could be so selfish — that their marriage was really over. They had been so much in love. Each morning she looked eagerly for the postman, sure that there would be a letter asking for her forgiveness. She told herself that Paul's restlessness and discontent was the result of war-weariness and exhaustion and that he would surely come to his senses when he saw his comrades returning to their families.

But no letter came and as week followed week, hope began to die slowly and painfully in her breast. May came and with it, victory in Europe. There was such an atmosphere of happiness and optimism in the air as street parties were held and flags hung out of windows. So far Mary had made no attempt to find a job and she guessed that with the men filtering back into the workplace it would now be even harder than before.

As the end of Vivien's first school term approached, she knew that something must be done. Paul's words came back to her, *You could always go home*. Suddenly she was filled with nostalgia, remembering the little terraced house high above the sea at Ferncliff. She recalled lying in bed and listening to the cry of the seagulls, coming home from school to the smell of her mother's baking; the fun they used to have at Christmas time, even though money was always short. Maybe Paul was right. If her mother would accept her again after all that had happened maybe she owed it to Vivien — and to herself — to go home whether she was welcome or not. At least it would be somewhere to start from. That evening she sat down with pen and paper to write the letter she had vowed never to write.

Dear Mum

Now that the war is over I'd love to come home for a visit. I hope that you and I can bury the hatchet and be a family again. I'll come next week if it's all right. On Monday, probably arriving late afternoon. If I don't hear from you I'll take it you're willing to see me.
Love Mary

There had been no reply.

★ ★ ★

When she awoke the first thing she was aware of was the cry of seagulls. Something she hadn't heard for a very long time. The familiar sound raised her spirits. Maybe everything would work out after all. She looked across at the other bed and saw that it was empty. Getting up, she pulled on her dressing gown and went downstairs.

Vivien was sitting at the kitchen table in her pyjamas, her bare feet swinging under her chair as she chattered away nineteen to the dozen to her grandmother.

'Good morning. I hope you slept well.' Dora turned from the stove where she was frying bacon.

'Like a log, thanks, Mum.' She looked at the kitchen clock and saw with a shock that it was after nine o'clock. 'You should have wakened me, and you shouldn't be giving us your bacon ration.'

'She said she'd like a bacon sandwich,' Dora said. 'And if you don't mind, madam, I'll do as I like with my own bacon ration!'

'When I woke up I remembered what you said about the sea,' Vivien said. 'So I got up and looked out of the window — and I *saw* it!' She giggled excitedly. 'It's all blue and shiny! After breakfast can we go down and see it properly, Mummy? I've never seen the sea before.' She reached eagerly for the thick sandwich her grandmother passed across the table to her and sank her teeth into it.

'I don't know if you're allowed on the beach yet,' Mary said.

'Oh, the beach is open again all right,' Dora said. 'They've been clearing the defences, the barbed wire and all those ugly concrete blocks for a few months now.'

'Can we go, Mummy? *Can* we, please?'

'If you like,' Mary said with a smile. 'But don't bolt that sandwich or you'll get tummy ache.'

'Now.' Dora looked at her daughter. 'What can I get you?'

'A cup of tea is all I want, thanks,' Mary said.

Dora tutted. 'No wonder you look as if a puff of wind'd blow you away, girl,' she remarked.

31

'We'll have to see if we can't put some meat back on your bones.'

The remark amused Vivien so much that she almost choked on her sandwich and Mary had to pat her back.

'Off you go and get dressed,' she told her. 'I'll come up soon and then we'll go down to the beach.'

'Have you made any plans?' Dora asked when the child had gone upstairs.

'Well, I'll have to get a job,' Mary said.

'I see. So you intend to stay on in Ferncliff then?'

Mary blushed. 'Well, yes, as soon as I've found something I'll look for a place for Vivien and me, and I'll pay my way, Mum. I don't want you to think . . . '

Dora held up her hand. 'No need for that, girl. This is your home and always will be for as long as you need it. So — what kind of work are you looking for?'

'I don't know,' Mary admitted. 'I haven't worked since before Vivien was born and I don't fancy the post office any more.'

Dora poured two cups of tea from the big brown teapot and sat down, looking thoughtful. 'Mmm, I don't suppose an army widow's pension goes very far,' she said.

Mary said nothing. She was still receiving her allowance but how long that would continue, she had no idea. She had no illusions about the kind of money Paul was likely to earn as a jobbing actor, even if he remembered his responsibilities, which seemed doubtful.

Dora slid into the chair opposite. 'The town council are doing their best to get the tourist trade up and running again,' she said. 'A lot of the little guesthouses have already opened again and they're doing good business. First thing the fellers coming out of the services want is a holiday with their wives and kiddies.'

'Yes. I suppose they do.'

'I've been approached about opening up and running the beach café.'

'Oh?' Mary looked up. 'How did that come about?'

'Councillor Bill Major is a regular at the theatre. I've got to know him well over the years and he put my name forward.'

'That's a bit of luck. So when would that be?'

'Well, they'd like it to be this summer, before the season's over if possible. It's almost ready and the money they're offering is good.'

'I see.'

'The trouble is,' Dora went on, 'The council wants my decision as soon as possible.'

'But you want to do it?' Mary was wondering what all this had to do with her.

Dora paused. 'The thing is, I don't want to let the Royal down,' she said. 'The management there have been good to me. I've been open and above board about the situation and I promised I wouldn't take the café job unless I could find them a reliable replacement to take over the bar.'

Mary frowned. 'Mum, what does all this have to do with me?'

'It's obvious, isn't it? I thought you might be interested.'

'Oh!'

'I'm pretty sure the job could be yours if you want it,' Dora said. 'I daresay they'll want to interview you but if I say you're OK they'll take my word. What do you reckon?'

Mary's spirits rose. 'Well, I haven't done bar work before but I daresay I could soon learn.'

'Course you can. I'll show you the ropes. I could even work with you the first week or so.'

'I'll have to find a school for Vivien,' Mary said.

'Cable Street Elementary is still going strong,' Dora said, smiling. 'You and Erica liked it there well enough.'

Mary smiled. 'So we did.'

'And Mrs Hapgood is still headmistress, believe it or not.'

'Maybe I'll take Vivien in to see her this afternoon.'

'I'm sure she'd like that. And it would be ideal, Mary. If you were to take over the bar at the Royal you'd be here for Vivien in the daytime. And I'd be here for her in the evenings.'

Mary's heart lifted. Maybe things were looking up for her after all.

3

'But I've already *been* to school!' Vivien looked up at her mother, her brown eyes bewildered.

They were on their way down to the sea-front. The morning was warm and sunny like the summer mornings Mary remembered from her childhood. A gentle breeze blew in from the sea and the sky was a clear cloudless blue.

'That was in Yorkshire,' she told Vivien. 'Now you have to go to a new school here.'

Vivien shook her head. 'I'd rather stay at home with you.'

'You can't, darling. Everyone has to go to school.'

'Why?'

'Because you have to be educated.'

'What's ed-u-cated?' Vivien pronounced the new word carefully.

'It's learning all sorts of things so that when you're older you can get a job and earn a living.'

'How long do I have to stay at school then?'

'A long time. Till you're almost grown up.'

The child was silent for a moment as she digested this devastating piece of news. Then, 'If I go, will my friends be there? Peter and Sheila and Heather?'

'No, Vivvy. They are still at the other school.'

'I'm not going then!' Vivien thrust out her lower lip. 'It won't be nice. I'll hate it!'

'No you won't. Your Auntie Erica and I went to Cable Street School when I was a little girl. It's lovely. You'll see. Anyway, all children must go to school. It's the law.'

They'd arrived at the pier head and Mary saw that her mother had been right: although the pier, demolished at the outbreak of war, would need rebuilding, the beach and promenade looked almost back to normal. About fifty yards out to sea the steel invasion defences still poked up out of the water, but there were notices up everywhere to say that it was safe to bathe. Holidaymakers were already enjoying the smooth, golden sand. Little family units dotted the beach; fathers getting acquainted with children born while they had been away, couples getting to know one another anew. Honeymooners gazing into each other's eyes. Mary turned her head away, her heart twisting painfully at the sight.

The builders were still working on the refurbishment of the beach café, but already one or two of the small kiosks were open for business. Vivien cheered up at the sight.

'Can I have an ice cream?'

Ice cream was still a new and exciting treat for Vivien. When it was last available she had been a baby.

'And can I paddle?'

Mary laughed. 'Yes, all right, come on.' On the way to the beach she'd telephoned to make an appointment to see Mrs Hapgood during the lunch break. They still had an hour to kill till twelve. She looked down at her little daughter, trotting purposefully towards the nearest ice-cream kiosk. She seemed to have forgotten her aversion to school for the time being, thank goodness.

Armed with their top-heavy vanilla cornets, they made their way down the steps on to the sands. It seemed to Mary that everywhere she looked there were happy little family groups. What had she done, she wondered, to drive Paul away. She must have been sadly lacking in some vital wifely quality to make him want to abandon her and their child. She watched as Vivien, her cotton print dress tucked into her knickers, paddled on the edge of the water, dancing and shrieking with delight as the frothy little wavelets washed over her toes. She ran back to Mary,

'Can I take the rest of my clothes off and get wet all over?'

'Not today. We'll have to get you a bathing costume and come down another day.'

'I want to learn to swim like those children over there.' Vivien pointed to where a father was holding his little daughter's chin out of the water whilst an older brother doggy-paddled beside them. 'Will you teach me?'

Mary shook her head. 'I can't swim, but I will come in with you.'

Vivien pouted. 'That's no good. Why haven't I got a daddy to teach me? Why does he have to go and be dead?'

Appalled, Mary snatched Vivien's hand and pulled her towards her. She was mortified by the compassionate glances cast in their direction. 'Be *quiet*, Vivien!' she said more sternly than she intended. 'Don't make a show of us. People are looking.' She began to pull the child's skirt out of her knickers and smooth out the creases, brushing the sand from her legs. 'Put your shoes and socks back on now. It's time we were going.'

★　★　★

'Of course, we break up for the summer holidays at the end of next week,' Mrs Hapgood said. 'But I'll be happy to reserve a place for Vivien in September.' She smiled at Vivien, who was standing half behind her mother's shoulder, biting her lip. 'Perhaps you'd like to come to our sports day on Friday and meet some of your new friends,' she suggested.

Vivien did not reply and Mary gave her a little nudge. 'We'd love to. That would be lovely, wouldn't it?' Vivien nodded unenthusiastically. Mary added, 'Say thank you to Mrs Hapgood.'

'Thank you,' Vivien mumbled, gazing at the floor.

'And just think,' Mrs Hapgood went on, 'when you start in September you won't be in the babies' class any more.'

This seemed to cheer Vivien up and the ghost of a smile lifted the corners of her mouth. Mrs Hapgood stood up, a portly figure in her blue knitted jersey suit and white blouse. She came out from behind her desk. 'Now, would you like to come and see the classroom where you'll be?' She offered Vivien her hand. 'I'll show you the rest of the school too and introduce you to your new teacher.' She smiled at Mary. 'I think you'll see a lot of changes since you and your sister were here.'

★   ★   ★

That evening Vivien was full of chatter as the three of them sat for their evening meal.

'Mrs Hapgood let me choose the desk where I'll sit,' she told her grandmother excitedly. 'It's in the front. My new teacher's name is Miss Granger and she's ever so pretty. And I'm going to have a peg in the cloakroom with my name on it, where I can hang my coat. And there are goldfish in a big square glass thing and lovely pictures of birds and trees and things.'

Dora smiled across the child's head. 'I take it your visit was a success,' she said.

Mary nodded. 'It was touch and go but Mrs Hapgood knows how to win kids over. She always did.' She reached into her bag. 'I've been to the food office and I've got some emergency ration coupons to tide us over until our ration books are transferred.' She handed her mother the buff-coloured coupons. 'It shouldn't take long.'

'I wonder how much longer we're going to need these,' Dora said, tucking them into her apron pocket. 'It'd be nice to see pre-war stuff back in the shops again and be able to buy as much as you wanted without standing for hours in a queue.' She sighed. 'Not much sign of it yet, though. Some say that we'll have rationing for at least another year, maybe longer. We won't get very fat on what we get now, will we?'

'Does Mrs Hapgood get more rations than us?' Vivien asked.

Dora looked surprised. 'No, dear. We all get the same.'

'So why is she so fat then?'

'Vivien! That's rude,' Mary admonished. 'We don't say things like that about people.'

'But she is,' Vivien protested, wrinkling her nose. 'And she's got a moustache.'

'*Vivien!*'

'A ginger one.'

Dora stifled a giggle, quickly turning it into a cough. 'Oh, dear me,' she said, changing the subject. 'I almost forgot.' She reached into her pocket and brought out a telegram in its orange-coloured envelope. 'This came this morning. It's from Erica. She's coming home tomorrow.'

Mary felt slightly crestfallen. She looked at her mother. How would her sister feel at finding her at home again? They hadn't been in touch since the war began. 'For good or just on leave?' she asked.

'For good. She's out of the ATS, apparently.'

'You're going to be very overcrowded. Maybe Vivien and I should — '

'Not at all. We'll manage,' Dora said firmly. 'There's plenty of space in my room for another bed. I've got a little camp bed up in the attic that I used when the evacuees were here. We'll move Vivien in with me, and you and Erica can share just like you used to.'

Mary had misgivings. She and her sister had been good friends when they were children. It was only when they began to grow up that the rivalry had sprung up between them. Erica, with her ginger hair and freckles, had shown an unattractive jealous streak at that time. Mary wondered if the war and being in the ATS had mellowed her. She hoped it had.

★　★　★

Dora came home from the theatre that night with an invitation for Mary to go to the Theatre Royal the following afternoon to be interviewed by Mr Lorimer, the manager. Feeling nervous, she got up early next morning and pressed her best navy blue suit, ironing a white blouse to wear with it. All her clothes were quite old. She'd had no spare money for new ones for some time, but when she'd sponged and pressed the jacket and skirt it looked fresh and smart.

It felt strange to be walking into the foyer of the little theatre in Grove Street again. It hadn't changed. The box office just inside the swing doors had its shutter down when she arrived just before two. There was no one about and she stood for a moment looking round.

The foyer smelled just as she remembered it, a sophisticated mixture of coffee and cigar smoke, which evoked nostalgic memories of visits to the pantomime at Christmas and other occasions when she and Erica had been allowed a visit to the theatre for a treat. She had thought then that it was the most exciting smell in the world.

The floor was still carpeted in dark red — now slightly threadbare — and photographs of the

41

resident company still adorned the walls. She examined them all, but none of the actors was familiar to her. Suddenly she looked at her watch and realised with a small shock that it was two o'clock and that Mr Lorimer would be waiting.

The manager's office was reached by a door next to the box office, giving access to a narrow staircase. At the top of the stairs Mary knocked and a voice from within called out to her to enter. As she entered the office she saw with surprise that the man sitting behind the desk was not the grey-haired Mr Lorimer she remembered. This one was quite young, no more than thirty. He smiled and rose to meet her.

'Mrs Snow, good afternoon. I'm David Lorimer.' As he offered his hand, he noticed her bemused look. 'Perhaps you were expecting to see John Lorimer, my father.'

She smiled. 'Well, yes, I was.'

'He has retired. He handed over to me when I came out of the RAF last month. I think he was only too glad to hand over the reins. Please have a seat, Mrs Snow.'

Mary sat down on the chair opposite as he resumed his own seat. He was a good-looking man, about six feet tall and well built, with gentle brown eyes and thick dark hair. He wore a well-cut grey suit and immaculate white shirt and she found herself picturing him in his RAF uniform. To her embarrassment she blushed when he looked up and caught her speculative gaze.

'Your mother has told me a little about you,'

he said. 'I understand that you're a war widow. I'm sorry.'

'Thank you.' Mary cleared her throat. 'Perhaps I should warn you that it is some time since I worked. Not since the birth of my daughter five years ago, in fact.'

'That's really no time at all.' David Lorimer looked up. 'And before that you worked as a counter clerk for the GPO.'

'That's right.'

'So obviously you are used to handling money. That's the most important part.' He laughed at his own attempt at jocularity and Mary joined in nervously.

'Er . . . quite. I should tell you though that I've never done bar work before.'

'We have two very good barmaids who'll handle that side of things,' he assured her. 'Except when we're very busy, of course. Your main job will be overseeing the staff during opening hours, keeping the stocks up, cashing up at closing time and making sure that the wages and the accounts are paid and that the books are up to date. Your mother has offered to work with you for a week or so to show you the ropes, as it were, and I'm sure that she'll be there to advise you any time you feel you need help.'

'Yes, of course.'

'Under the circumstances I'm sure that the take-over will be smooth and seamless.' Noticing her hesitation, he leaned forward. 'But it's important that you feel happy, Mrs Snow. Do you think you would enjoy working here, managing the bar for us?'

Mary felt like saying that she had little choice in the matter — that she needed to work as she was now the sole breadwinner of her little family — but it seemed churlish to snub the man's obvious concern, so she smiled and nodded.

'Oh, very much so, thank you.'

He smiled. 'Then I have pleasure in offering you the position, Mrs Snow. Shall we say you can begin on Monday next?

Mary walked home thoughtfully. Working at the Royal would be a complete change of lifestyle to what she had been used to. She hoped she'd be able to live up to David Lorimer's expectations of her. As soon as she opened the front door of number twenty-seven Gresham Terrace she heard Vivien's excited chatter and as she walked into the living-room she saw her daughter sitting on the lap of the sister she hadn't set eyes on for almost six years.

Erica had changed quite a lot. The carroty-red hair that Mary remembered had darkened to a rich auburn and Erica's freckles seemed to have vanished. Her teenage plumpness had slimmed down to a slender shapely figure too. In fact she looked quite glamorous. When Erica saw Mary she slid Vivien off her lap and stood up.

'Mary!' She smiled and held out her arms. 'Our kid after all this time! Come here.'

Mary took a step towards her and her sister's arms went round her in a warm hug.

'I'm sorry about what happened, love,' Erica whispered in her ear. 'Mum's told me. Are you all right?'

Mary nodded. 'I'm fine. And I've just been offered a job.'

'At the theatre? Mum was just saying. So you're taking over the bar from her. That's terrific.' Erica looked round and reached out her hand to Vivien. 'And what about this little poppet? She and I have been getting on like a house on fire, haven't we, sweetheart?'

Vivien grasped Erica's hand and pressed herself against her side. 'Auntie Erica can swim and she says she'll teach me to if it's warm enough tomorrow,' she announced, gazing up at her new aunt adoringly.

Over tea Mary voiced her concern about starting work at the theatre under Dora's supervision the following week. 'I said yes but I wasn't thinking. If we're both out every evening, Mum, I'll have to find someone to baby-sit Vivien,' she said.

Erica smiled. 'Look no further,' she said. 'I'll be around in the evenings. She'll be fine with me, won't you, darling?'

Vivien nodded enthusiastically.

'You'll be looking for work too now, I expect,' Mary said.

She saw the look that passed between mother and sister and Dora said, 'You'd better tell her your news.'

'I'm getting married,' Erica announced. She held out her left hand, displaying an expensive-looking diamond ring. 'He's a captain in the Eighth Air Force.'

'An American?'

'That's right. Captain Bob Phillips. We're to

be married at the end of next month and when he goes home to the States I'll be going with him — or soon after,' she added.

'How exciting. Is he stationed near here?'

'That's the best bit. He's on the base at Kettborough. It's only ten miles away so we'll be able to see quite a lot of each other and I want to be married in the parish church here.'

'That's if the vicar can fit you in,' Dora said. 'You'd be surprised at how many weddings are happening with the fellers coming home. You'd better go and see him first thing tomorrow.' She looked at her daughter. 'I must say I'd have appreciated a bit more time to prepare,' she complained. 'Fancy springing it on us all like this.'

'Oh, you don't have to worry,' Erica said airily The reception will be on the base and catered for by the USAF. You wouldn't believe the food they can get. All we have to do is send out the invitations.'

'What about your dress?' Mary asked. 'And bridesmaids?'

'Oh, I've got my dress,' Erica said. 'I'll show you later. As for bridesmaids, I've asked one of my ATS friends and now that I've met her I think that little Vivien here would make a beautiful little flower girl.'

Vivien clapped her hands in delight. 'Oh!' She looked at her mother. 'I can, can't I, Mummy? Say yes!'

They all laughed. 'Of course,' Mary said. 'We'll have to see about making you a special dress.'

'I can do that,' Dora offered. 'I'll get my sewing machine out and we'll hunt for some pretty material.' She looked at her elder daughter. 'But most important of all — when do we get to meet this Captain Bob of yours?'

'I've invited him to lunch on Sunday,' Erica said. 'He can't wait to meet you. He's very keen on family life. He's got three sisters and a brother at home in California. They all help run the family peach farm. They sell their fruit to all the big canning firms — Del Monte, Libby's, Heinz.'

'It sounds very prosperous,' Dora remarked.

'Oh yes, plenty of cash.'

Mary stole a look at her sister and saw the old familiar smug look she remembered so well. Trust Erica to fall on her feet, she told herself, swallowing down the sudden resentment that stuck in her throat like a stone from one of Captain Bob's peaches.

★   ★   ★

Dora managed to get a lean piece of topside for Sunday lunch. She bought fresh runner beans from a friend with a kitchen garden and made her celebrated Yorkshire pudding. For dessert she made apple pie because she had heard that Americans were particularly fond of it.

Captain Bob Phillips arrived dead on the dot of one o'clock and when Erica led him proudly into the living-room where they were all waiting to meet him, Mary could scarcely conceal her gasp of admiration. She had listened to Erica's

47

ecstatic descriptions of him with her tongue in her cheek. Surely no man could be that perfect, that handsome or chivalrous. But Bob Phillips seemed to be all of them. He had film-star looks, the bluest eyes that Mary had ever seen and wavy fair hair that he wore brushed smoothly back. After shaking hands all round — even with a delighted Vivien — he handed Dora a large brown paper carrier bag. She blushed.

'For me?'

'Courtesy rations,' he told her. 'We are all too aware of how short of food you folks are so when you're kind enough to invite us over to eat it's only fair we bring along some little luxuries to help out.'

Peering into the bag, Dora gave a little squeak of pleasure. 'Tinned fruit!' she exclaimed. 'Pears and peaches and fruit salad. *And* chocolate biscuits. There are packets of sweets in here too. Oh, how kind of you. There must be a whole year's worth of points coupons in here!'

Captain Bob beamed. 'Just enjoy, ma'am. It's my pleasure.'

Dora's meal was a great success, especially the Yorkshire pudding on which Bob complimented her until she blushed bright pink. Vivien, sitting opposite him at the table, stared with large round eyes, completely mesmerized by the big handsome man in the smart, well-cut olive uniform. Later, as Mary was putting her to bed, she asked non-stop questions about him.

'Why does he talk like that, Mummy?'

'Is America a long way away?'

'Do peaches really grow on trees? I thought

you could only get them in tins.'

'When Auntie Erica goes to live there can we go and stay with her for the holidays?'

'If he comes again will he bring some more sweets and chocolate biscuits?'

Mary eventually settled her down to sleep in the little bed in Dora's room and when she came downstairs she found Dora alone.

'He said to say goodbye,' she explained. 'He's taken Erica out for a spin in his jeep,' she said. 'I expect they want to be alone for a while.' She raised an eyebrow at Mary. 'So — what do you reckon?'

Mary sat down. 'He seems very dashing. Handsome too.'

Dora sighed. 'Mmm, handsome is as handsome does,' she said. 'I'm not sure I trust all that charm.'

Mary smiled. 'That's Americans for you. They're not as buttoned up as we are. I thought he was very polite, and he obviously thinks the world of Erica.'

'Mmm.' Dora folded her lips into a tight line, which meant that she intended to keep her own counsel on the matter.

It was late when Erica came in. Dora had already gone up to bed, but Mary waited up for her, going through to the kitchen to put the kettle on when she heard her sister's key in the front door.

'Have a nice evening?' she asked as she came back into the living-room.

Erica flopped down into a chair. 'It was OK,' she said. 'What did you think of him?

'Very attractive,' Mary told her. 'Vivien is completely smitten. It's a good job she isn't older or you might be in danger of losing him to her.' She went back to the kitchen to make the tea and came back to see her sister looking pensive. 'Everything all right?' she asked.

Erica sighed. 'For some reason Bob wants to wait till we're back in the States to get married,' she said. 'I've tried to explain to him what it means to me to get married in the church where I was christened, to have my family and friends there, but he doesn't seem to understand.'

'I expect he's thinking that he'd like his family at the wedding too.'

'It's not just a question of family,' Erica went on. 'There's the practical side of things. Wives will get priority when it comes to travelling over there. As a mere fiancée it could take ages to get a passage.'

Mary frowned. 'Have you explained that you've got your dress and everything?'

'He says it isn't important, that I can take it with me.' Erica gave her auburn curls a little shake. 'I'll talk him round, though, you see if I don't. He's got a couple of days' leave next weekend and he's booked a hotel for us along the coast at Seabourne. I think I know how to get round him once we're alone together.' She smiled her smug little smile. 'I know all his little weaknesses. I should by now.'

Mary raised her eyebrows. 'You've already slept together?'

'Of course we have!' Erica laughed. 'Have you had your head in the sand all through the war,

Mary? There's been no time for old-world courtship, you know. It's been a case of take all you can before it's snatched away.' She opened her handbag and took out a cigarette, looking over the flame of her lighter as she lit it. 'I've lost count of how many lovers I've had, if you want to know.' She laughed at Mary's shocked expression. 'Don't look at me like that! It helps to know that you're compatible. Anyway, don't tell me you and Paul didn't.'

'No, we didn't as a matter of fact.'

'What, not at all? All those long Sunday afternoon walks. Don't tell me you never found some convenient little corner for a — '

'No. I told you.'

'If you say so.' Erica shrugged. 'But you still ended up with a kid and no husband, didn't you?' She bit her lip. 'Oh God! Sorry, kid, I didn't mean it to come out like that.'

'Don't worry about it,' Mary said, hiding her hurt. 'I suppose you're right anyway.'

Erica regarded her sister thoughtfully. 'Was it a good marriage?' she asked. 'I've never seen anyone as much in love as you were. I was fiendishly jealous, but of course you knew that.' She inhaled deeply of her cigarette. 'I've often wondered if it lasted.'

'It wasn't much of a marriage at all,' Mary confessed. 'The war saw to that. Paul was abroad so much that we hardly saw each other and when we did we were almost like strangers. I suppose the truth is, Mum was right. We were too young.'

'It must have been lonely for you.'

'It was, especially when I was expecting Vivien

51

and after she was born.'

'And now, after all you've been through, it's over. Poor Paul. And poor you,' Erica said. 'But at least you're still young enough to start again.'

Mary said nothing. Erica had echoed Paul's sentiment almost word for word and she resented it no less for being repeated.

'If you don't mind me saying so,' Erica went on, 'you really ought to do something about your hair and clothes.'

'Really? You think I'm frumpy, do you?'

'Oh come on, don't get uppity. I'm only trying to help. You must admit that you're hardly the height of fashion, are you?'

'Neither would you be if you'd had to manage and bring up a child on what I've had!'

'Well, the ATS doesn't exactly shower you with diamonds,' Erica countered. She stubbed out her cigarette. 'Why don't you let me take you shopping for a new outfit for the wedding?'

'The wedding that might not take place?'

Erica smiled her secret smile. 'Oh, it will,' she said. 'Trust me. It will.'

★ ★ ★

Mary's first week at the theatre wasn't nearly as bad as she'd expected and by the end of it she felt she was beginning to get the hang of things. The two barmaids, Rose and Jessie, had been at the Royal for years. They were two motherly ladies who had known and respected Dora for many years and were more than willing to help her daughter get to grip with the day-to-day bar work. Dora took her through the books and introduced her to all the suppliers, making sure they all knew that she would be in charge from now on.

'Don't take any nonsense from them,' she advised. 'Get a firm delivery date and make them stick to it. I've never stood for any messing about and they know it. They might try it on, knowing you're new. Just start as you mean to go on and they'll respect you for it.'

The beach café was now finished and Dora was eager to start her new job. They were to do light meals as well as trays of tea for the beach and she was busy sorting out suppliers and taking on staff. During the week that followed she was too busy to help at the theatre but Mary found her confidence growing with each day.

Erica had offered to sit with Vivien in the evenings, but she seemed to have taken over the days as well. The two had formed a firm bond, with Erica behaving more like an older sister than an aunt. For her part, Vivien was having the time of her life spending the long sunny days at the beach where, to her delight, Erica was teaching her to swim. She splashed about fearlessly in the shallows in the little red bathing costume and water wings that Erica had bought her. Mary, listening each day to her daughter's excited account of the fun they had had, began to be a little resentful and afraid that the child was becoming spoilt; a worry that she voiced. Erica shrugged off the accusation.

'That's what kids are for,' she said flippantly.

'Anyway, she deserves it, poor fatherless little mite.'

Mary often wondered what she'd started, letting her family believe that she was a widow. Sometimes it seemed so wicked to pretend that Paul was dead, almost like blasphemy. Then at other times it seemed perfectly reasonable. It was what he wanted, after all, she told herself; to disappear from their lives without trace. He had no intention of coming back. If Vivien ever found out that her own father had abandoned her like an unwanted kitten she would be so hurt, and if Erica knew that Paul had walked out on them she would despise Mary for not being able to hold on to her husband. No such thing would ever happen to Erica. She would never let it. Proof of her impressive powers of persuasion came when she returned from her weekend with Bob looking smug and announcing triumphantly that he had finally agreed to a wedding at St Mary's in Ferncliff in four weeks' time.

Immediately it was all systems go as plans went ahead for the wedding. Dora shopped around and managed to find some pretty material, pink rayon with tiny floral sprigs, for Vivien's bridesmaid dress. She bought a pattern and brought out her sewing machine at once to make a start on it. The little girl was beside herself with excitement. She was to have rosebuds in her hair and carry a basket of pink and white roses.

Erica's dress had been made by the friend who was to be her bridesmaid. It was made from ivory brocade material, originally intended for curtains, which meant that no clothing coupons were needed. Both Dora and Mary had to admit that it made a sumptuous gown. The long tight sleeves were decorated from wrist to elbow with tiny pearl buttons and the full skirt sprang out from the waist, cut to a point at front and back. The collar was stiffened to stand up at the back and edged with tiny pearls. Erica looked beautiful in it and Mary remembered with a pang her own hurried register office wedding and the cheap little dress she had worn.

'Bob will wear his uniform, of course,' Erica told them proudly.

On the morning of the wedding the atmosphere at 27 Gresham Terrace was electric. All the neighbours were watching from behind their front-room window curtains to see the bride emerge. As there was no male member of the family to give Erica away, Dora was to do it. She wore a hyacinth-blue suit and a pretty navy straw hat decorated with daisies. At ten to eleven she stood proudly in the hall, waiting with Erica for the car that would take them to the church.

Vivien was hopping excitedly from one foot to the other, asking every few seconds when the car would arrive. She was to go to the church first with the chief bridesmaid, Erica's friend, Jenny. Their car arrived and Mary squeezed in with them so that she could be there to calm Vivien down and arrange her dress in the church porch. When they arrived, the last of the guests were just straggling in. Mary smoothed the creases from Vivien's skirt and tidied away a loose strand of hair.

'You're quite sure you don't need to go to the toilet?' she whispered.

Vivien shook her head indignantly. 'No, Mummy. I'm not a baby.'

Erica had announced that she intended to be at least five minutes late, so Mary was not surprised when the vicar came out to the porch. He smiled, looking uneasily at his watch.

'I think my sister is taking advantage of the bride's prerogative to be late,' she said with a smile. 'But I'm sure she'll be here very soon.'

The vicar nodded. 'Yes, yes, I'm sure she will.' He laid a hand on her arm and drew her aside. 'I'm afraid that the problem is, the bridegroom hasn't arrived yet,' he said. 'If your sister does arrive first, perhaps you'd ask her driver to drive round again.'

'Yes.' Mary looked at his furrowed brow. 'Does this often happen?' she asked.

He shrugged. 'There's hardly a wedding that doesn't have a hitch,' he said. 'I'm sure everything will be all right.'

Mary watched him walk back into the church. Through the open door she could hear the organ quietly playing and the gentle buzz of conversation from the guests. A feeling of disquiet began to stir in her stomach. Vivien pulled at her sleeve.

'Mummy, when's Auntie Erica coming? When will the wedding start?'

'Soon, darling,' Mary muttered, looking anxiously up and down the road.

A few minutes later the car carrying Erica and her mother arrived at the gate. Mary ran

56

forward. Bending down at the front window she said, 'There's been a slight delay. Could you please drive round a little longer?'

Erica leaned forward. 'What kind of delay?' she asked. 'What's happened?'

'Nothing to worry about,' Mary said, hoping she sounded reassuring. 'I'm sure everything will be in place by the time you get back.'

When the car had gone she slipped inside the church and stood on tiptoe to see the front pews where Captain Bob Phillips and his best man should be seated. They were still empty. Her heart sank. The wedding was supposed to take place at eleven. It was now almost twenty past. Surely Bob should be here by now?

It seemed like no time at all before the car was back. Erica and her mother got out and walked the short distance to the porch. Erica looked at Mary hopefully.

'Everything all right now?'

'The driver said he had another booking,' Dora explained. 'He couldn't spare any more time.' She raised an eyebrow at Mary. 'Everything is all right, isn't it? We can go ahead?'

Mary was just searching for the words to tell her sister what had happened when the vicar appeared again.

'Ah, Miss Flynn.' He cleared his throat. 'Have you had any communication from your future husband?'

Erica looked from one to the other. 'No. Why, should I have done?'

'It's .. er . . . just that he seems to be cutting it rather fine,' the vicar said.

'You mean — he isn't *here* yet?' The colour left Erica's face.

'No, I'm afraid he isn't. Perhaps you could telephone. There could have been an accident — anything could have happened.'

'No! He'll be here,' Erica insisted. 'Any minute now. We'll wait.'

The vicar looked uncomfortable. 'As you say, of course. The problem is that he is almost half an hour late now and I do have another wedding at twelve o'clock. I really do need to know . . . ' He trailed off. 'You are most welcome to use the telephone in the vestry. I can take you round to the other door.'

Erica handed Mary her bouquet and followed the vicar round to the back of the church. Dora and Mary exchanged glances and Vivien tugged at Mary's sleeve.

'How much longer?' she wailed. 'Where has Auntie Erica gone?'

'Just try to be patient,' Mary told her. She looked down at her daughter and saw the tell-tale signs as the child wriggled and squirmed.

'Vivien. Do you . . . ?'

'*Yes!*' Vivien looked up at her, her cheeks pink. 'I do need the toilet now, Mummy. Sorry.'

'It's all right.' Mary took her hand, almost glad of the diversion. 'Come on, we'll find somewhere.'

As they came back round the side of the church, Mary saw Erica getting into a taxi. She looked at her mother.

'What's happened?'

'There isn't going to be a wedding,' Dora said, her mouth drawn into a tight line. 'The vicar has kindly offered to make an announcement to everyone. I think the best thing we can do is get home to Erica as soon as possible. She'll be needing us.'

4

It was only a short walk back to Gresham Terrace but by the time they got home Vivien's hair was awry and her face stained with tears of disappointment. As Dora closed the front door, she turned to Jenny.

'I'm sorry it's all ended like this,' she said.

'Don't worry about me,' Jenny said. 'It's poor Erica we have to think of now.'

'You can use my bedroom to get changed,' Dora offered. 'I'll put the kettle on. I think we could all do with a cup of tea.' She looked at Mary. 'I'll see to Vivien. You go up to Erica. See what you can do.'

In the little bedroom they shared, Mary found her sister lying face down on the bed, her beautiful wedding gown crumpled. She was clutching a sodden handkerchief and sobbing quietly. Mary sat down beside her.

'Do you want to talk about it?' she asked gently.

Erica turned her head on the pillow. 'All I want is to die,' she sobbed.

'No, you don't.' Mary reached out a hand and stroked her sister's hair. 'Why don't you get up and take your dress off?' she said. 'Come on, let me help you.'

Erica silently sat up and swung her feet to the floor. Mary helped her unhook the dress and slip it off. She quickly slipped the dress on to a hanger and hid it at the back of the wardrobe.

Wrapped in her warm dressing gown and with a clean handkerchief in her hand, Erica sat down again on her bed.

'He's gone,' she said bleakly.

Mary frowned. 'Gone? Gone where?'

'Back to the States. I rang his office on the base and asked to speak to him. The young sergeant who answered said he flew home yesterday afternoon. He obviously didn't know who I was or that Bob was supposed to marry me today.'

Mary frowned. 'Did he explain why Bob had gone?'

'Oh yes. He said . . . ' Erica took a deep breath. 'He *said* that Captain Phillip's *wife* was ill.'

The two sat looking at each other in stunned silence for a moment, then Erica went on, 'It seems that *Mrs* Phillips is in hospital with appendicitis. Bob was given compassionate leave so that he could fly home to be with her.'

Mary reached out and put her arms round her sister, holding her while her body shook with fresh sobs. 'And you had no idea he was married?' she asked gently.

'Of *course* I didn't!' Erica snapped. 'Do you think I would have arranged a wedding — turned up at the church done up like a dog's dinner — just for the pleasure of being jilted in front of all those people?'

'I'm so sorry.'

'I must be the laughing stock of Ferncliff at

this moment.' Erica raised her swollen face to look at her sister. 'It serves me right. That's what you're really thinking, isn't it? I've been swanking away and rubbing your nose in the fact that you've lost your husband.' She blew her nose. 'All that talk about going to live in California, the peach farm and everything. You must have hated me.'

'Of course I didn't hate you. I was happy for you,' Mary said.

'Yes, I bet you were too,' Erica sniffed. 'Because you're a better person than me, a much nicer person. You always were. Prettier, slimmer, sweeter natured. Do you have any idea how maddening that is? When we were growing up I wished I could be just like you, but I knew I never would so I had to go one better whenever I could.' She held up her hand against Mary's protest. 'It's true. You know it is. I thought I'd grown out of those spiteful little juvenile ways after all these years, but I hadn't. I actually *liked* the fact that I'd got one over on you. How despicable is that?'

'Stop it!' Mary hugged her close. 'Stop punishing yourself. We all have feelings of envy. We wouldn't be human if we didn't. Yes, I envied you your happiness. I admit it. But I wouldn't have wished this on you.'

'You don't deserve what happened to you,' Erica said. 'But I do. Now I'm being punished for all those nasty mean thoughts I had.'

'Listen.' Mary shook her gently. 'Bob lied to you in the worst way possible. He's a liar and a cheat. But worst of all he's a coward. No one deserves treatment like that. You're better off without him.'

Erica swallowed hard and dabbed her face. 'I think I'll have a bath,' she said. 'I need some time to think what to do.'

'Do?' Mary asked. 'All you can do is to live this down; put it behind you and move on with your life. Show people that you're not beaten.'

'Oh I intend to!' Erica's eyes glinted. 'But someone's going to have to pay for what's happened today. I'm not carrying the burden of it all alone.'

There was a tap on the door and Jenny looked in. She had changed into her outdoor clothes and carried a tray with three cups of tea on it. 'Can I come in?'

She put the tray down on the dressing table and looked at Erica. 'I've got a suggestion to make,' she said. 'Why don't you come home with me for a few days?'

'Home with you — to Nottingham?'

Jenny smiled. 'Well, that's where I live. I've got a little flat. It's not much but there's only me there. I've got a week off work too. We could do anything you fancied — have some fun. You could even look round for a job and settle there if you liked it.'

'You think I want to run away and hide?' Erica said briskly. 'I've done nothing to be ashamed of.'

'I'm not suggesting you have. A break would do you good, though, and by the time you come home — if that's what you want — people will have forgotten.'

Erica looked thoughtful. 'I'm sorry, Jenny. It's kind of you to offer but . . . '

'Why don't you go?' Mary broke in. 'Just for a few days. A change of scene would help. I know it would.'

'I'm all packed and ready,' Jenny said. 'And your mum is getting a meal ready. Throw a few things into a case and we can catch a train later this afternoon. Do say yes.'

Later that afternoon Mary went to the station with Erica and Jenny and saw them off on the train. Erica still looked pale and shocked but she'd bravely disguised the ravages of her tears with make-up and the old glint of determination was back in her eyes.

As the train pulled out, she leaned out of the window. 'I'll be back in a week and then we'll see,' she said. 'Bob Phillips hasn't heard the last of me. Not by a long chalk!'

★ ★ ★

While Erica was away Vivien was impossible. She missed her Auntie Erica and the lovely days they had enjoyed together on the beach. Even though the weather had broken and it rained non-stop all week, she still thought that if Erica had been there the sun would have shone. One evening Mary's patience was driven to the point when she lost her temper and, lifting up the child's dress, she slapped her legs hard.

Vivien howled loudly. 'Ow! Auntie Erica wouldn't do that!' she sobbed.

'She would if she was here to see how naughty

you are. She'd be ashamed of you! Go upstairs,' Mary commanded. 'You're a horrid little girl and I'm sick and tired of your tantrums. You can go to bed.'

'But it's only teatime!'

'I don't care. You're not getting any tea today. I've had enough. I think you need some time to think about how naughty you've been.'

As Vivien reluctantly climbed the stairs, bawling loudly, Dora looked at her daughter. 'I can't say I blame you. She really has tried your patience this week, but it's understandable, I suppose. She was so looking forward to being a bridesmaid, poor little scrap.'

Already regretting her action, Mary's throat tightened and tears pricked her eyes. 'I don't know what came over me. I've never smacked her before. Shall I go and get her?'

'No.' Dora shook her head. 'Let her be till you've both calmed down. This business over Erica's wedding has upset us all. You were right when you said she needed time to think about her behaviour.' She looked thoughtful. 'You know, it might help if she had things explained to her. I know she's only a child but she's an intelligent little thing. She needs to understand.' Seeing her daughter's distress, Dora touched her arm. 'Don't worry. You can make it up with her later with a little treat of some kind.'

Mary gave Vivien half an hour to be by herself then she went upstairs with a bar of chocolate she'd slipped out to buy with the last of her sweet ration. When she saw her daughter's unhappy little face, her heart melted.

'Are you a good girl now?'

Vivien nodded.

'What do you say then?'

Vivien sniffed, her lower lip trembling. 'Sorry, Mummy.'

'That's a good girl.' Mary sat on the bed beside her and gave her a hug. When she produced the bar of chocolate Vivien's eyes lit up. Mary broke a square off and popped it into her mouth. Vivien sucked thoughtfully for a moment.

'I'd almost learned how to swim,' she said wistfully. 'And I wanted to walk down the church behind Auntie Erica in my lovely dress. Why did it all go wrong, Mummy?'

'Auntie Erica's fiancé, that's Bob, needed to go back to America.'

'Why?'

'Someone in his family was ill.'

'Is he coming back? Will we have the wedding then?' Vivien asked hopefully.

'No, darling. He and Auntie Erica have changed their minds now,' Mary told her. 'People do sometimes. But I'm sure there'll be another chance for you to be a bridesmaid one day. And you can always wear the dress when you get invited to parties. Grandma will shorten it for you if you like.'

'Will the sun ever shine again?' Vivien asked forlornly.

Mary's heart lurched. She knew the feeling only too well. 'Of course it will,' she said. 'If not tomorrow then the day after. You'll see. And when it does maybe you and I can learn to swim together.'

* * *

Erica came home a week later looking more like her old self. 'I'll have to look for a job,' she announced after she had unpacked.

'Have you any idea what you'd like to do?' Mary asked. 'There isn't much going here in Ferncliff. It's mainly the holiday trade. Didn't you fancy staying in Nottingham with Jenny?'

'Oh! Lovely to see you too! Thought you'd got rid of me, did you?'

'No! I just meant . . . '

Erica laughed. 'I'm only teasing. Nottingham was OK, but I've got unfinished business here.' She smiled to herself and wouldn't be drawn any further.

Mary felt uneasy. What did Erica have in mind, she wondered. She hoped it wasn't something that would land her in trouble.

Erica scanned the 'situations vacant' in the local paper and spotted an advertisement for an usherette at the Savoy, the town's largest cinema.

Dora looked doubtful. 'Is that really the kind of thing you want?' she asked.

'It'd suit me fine for now,' Erica said. She slipped an arm round Vivien and squeezed her. 'I'd have my mornings free to take this little lady out. And just think, I'd get to see all the films free of charge.'

'The same films about twenty times a week, remember!' Mary pointed out. 'You'll be sick

67

and tired of them.' She looked at her sister. 'I would have thought a job in one of the dress shops would have suited you better,' she said. 'When you came shopping with me you saw clothes I would never have thought of wearing. You've got a real flair for fashion.'

'We'll see,' Erica said with a smile. 'I don't intend to be an usherette for ever. And I shan't let the grass grow under my feet, don't you worry.'

Erica got the job at the cinema. She brought her uniform home to show them — a dark green dress with gold braid and buttons and a jaunty little pillbox hat. She put it on for them and paraded up and down the living-room like a model.

'What d'you reckon, then? Would I win Miss Ferncliff 1945 in it?'

They all laughed but Mary's laughter was tinged with concern. She knew her mother was relieved that Erica seemed to have got over the pain of Bob's betrayal but Mary sensed a certain brittleness in her sister's manner. She knew she was far from recovered and that she had something up her sleeve, though she could not imagine what.

★ ★ ★

On 6 August the news broke of the atomic bombs dropped on Nagasaki and Hiroshima. A week later Japan had surrendered and the war in the Pacific was finally over. There were celebrations again and the town of Ferncliff prepared for a late season of holidaymakers as more servicemen came home.

Mary settled in well at the Theatre Royal. At the end of her first month David Lorimer made a point of coming into the bar to see her, complimenting her on her first month's takings and the efficiency of her book-keeping.

'I hope you are happy here,' he said.

Mary nodded. 'I'm enjoying it very much. I'm conversant with the prices of all the drinks now, thanks to Rose and Jessie, and I'm getting quite good at pulling a pint.'

'Oh! You enjoy serving, then?' He looked surprised.

'Yes, very much. After years of being nothing but a housewife and mother it's nice to talk to adults and meet new people.'

He looked thoughtful. 'I've been wondering — my secretary is retiring shortly. Miss Frazer worked with Dad for twenty-five years and I think she's been finding it difficult, getting used to my strange new ways.' He gave her a tentative smile. 'Would you consider standing in until I've found someone to take her place?'

Mary was surprised. 'What about my work here?'

'Oh, it would only be part-time — mornings only. So it wouldn't interfere with the bar, and it would mean more money of course.' He took in her doubtful expression. 'But it was only an idea. Just say if you'd rather not.'

She shook her head. 'It's not that. I was thinking of my little girl.'

'It wouldn't be for a couple more weeks,' he

said. 'Won't she be at school by then?'

'Well, yes.' Mary's heart lifted. The extra money would come in useful and she had always liked office work. 'I think I'd like that, Mr Lorimer. If you just let me know when you'd like me to start.'

He smiled. 'I'll let Miss Frazer know. I'm sure she'll be relieved.' He turned and then looked back over his shoulder. 'Oh and by the way, can we drop the formality? It's David.'

She felt herself blushing. 'Well — yes.'

'And I may call you Mary?'

'Of course.'

As he disappeared through the swing doors, Jessie came in from the storeroom her homely face wreathed in smiles. 'Aye-aye! Looks like you're well in there,' she remarked with a wink.

Mary blushed. 'He doesn't like to be formal, that's all.'

Jessie gave her a nudge. 'He fancies you, more like.' She laughed. 'Don't look like that. You're a very pretty young woman.'

'I thought he was probably married,' Mary said.

'I heard he was engaged but while he was away his girl got tired of waiting and ran off with a Yank.' She lowered her voice. 'Speaking of which — how's your sister?'

The news of Erica's jilting had spread far and wide. Mary shrugged. 'She's fine,' she said. 'Getting on with her life.'

Jessie pursed her lips. 'Humiliation like that takes some getting over,' she said, shaking her head. 'Poor lass. But she'll win through.'

Vivien's first morning at school was traumatic. At the school gates she clung to Mary's hand tearfully and begged to be taken home again. Mary had to harden her heart but she left her with grave misgivings. Suppose she didn't settle, didn't like it, couldn't make friends? What would she do? She needn't have worried. When she went to collect her at half past three, Vivien trotted out of school clutching the hand of another little girl, her face alight with enthusiasm.

'This is Vicky,' she said. 'She's my best friend. Can she come home to tea with me?'

Mary smiled. 'Another day, when Vicky has asked her mummy,' she said.

Vivien parted reluctantly with her new friend and chattered all the way home about what she had done during the day.

'We made raffia mats,' she said. 'Only mine kept falling to bits. We fed the rabbits and we went outside to play rounders.'

'That sounds nice.'

'Vicky fell over and hurt her knee, but I lent her my hanky to bandage it up. That's when she said we could be best friends.'

'And what about your teacher?'

Vivien nodded. 'She's nice. She showed me how to do add-ups and take-aways with the counters and she said I was clever to know all my letters and numbers.'

'That's good.'

'Vicky's daddy is a sailor.' Vivien looked up at

her. 'He's coming home soon. I told her my daddy was dead.' She frowned. 'Mummy — will you get me another daddy?'

Mary shook her head. 'You can only have one daddy.'

Vivien shook her head. 'No, Peter's had two. His first one died and his mummy got him a new one.'

Mary remembered that she was talking about a boy they had known in Yorkshire whose father had been killed at Dunkirk. His mother had married again a year later. She looked down at Vivien. 'It happens sometimes, but not to us,' she said. 'It's just you and me now. But you've got Auntie Erica and Grandma.'

'Vicky's got a skipping rope,' Vivien said. 'Can I have a skipping rope?'

★   ★   ★

It was a week later that Erica came home from the evening shift at the Savoy with a certain look in her eye. Mary knew the look only too well and she couldn't wait till they were alone in their room to question her.

'Come on, what have you been up to?'

Erica affected innocence. '*Me*? Up to? I don't know what you mean.'

'I know that look. Come on, tell me.'

Erica pulled on her nightdress. 'Look, don't tell Mum but I went over to the base this morning.'

'The base? You mean . . . ?'

'Yes. The American base. I went to see Bob's

friend, Major Jeff Harding. He was his CO.'

Mary was aghast at her sister's daring. She would never have had the nerve to do anything so audacious. She climbed into bed and sat with her arms round her knees. 'So what happened?'

'Not a lot so far, but we'll see what develops.'

'What did you say to him?'

'I told him I was suing Bob for breach of promise. He told me coolly that I hadn't a leg to stand on as Bob was not a citizen of this country and therefore not accountable to the British legal system.'

'What did you say to that?'

'I told him I knew where his family lived and I'd write and tell them what Bob had done. I said I had about a hundred witnesses to prove the story of how I was jilted at the church.' She smiled grimly. 'That shook him. Do you know, he actually didn't know that Bob had let me go ahead with the wedding arrangements. Oh and by the way, there was never any reception food ordered. Bob never had the slightest intention of being in this country on that day.'

'So what did the Major say to that?'

'Well, I could see he was shocked. He asked me not to write to Bob's family, said he was appealing to my better nature. I told him that Bob Phillips had choked all the life out of my better nature on what should have been my wedding day.'

'Is that what you intended to do, write to his family?'

Erica blew out her cheeks. 'Course not. I never really had the address. I was bluffing. I could see he was knocked for six, though, so I struck while the iron was hot. I said I'd go to the papers — local *and* national — and tell my story. I said I'd send a photograph of me in my wedding dress as proof along with one of the invitations. I pointed out that no American airman would get served in any shop or pub in Ferncliff if the story got out and I put the finishing touch on it by saying that I'd see to it that Bob Phillips' wife got a copy of the newspaper articles *and* my own personal story.'

Mary gasped. '*Erica*! What was his reaction?'

'He thought about it for a minute, then he asked me what I wanted to keep quiet.'

Mary's eyes opened wide. 'What you *wanted*? What a cheek. As if any . . . '

'And I said two thousand pounds ought to do it.'

Mary stared at her sister. 'You said *what*?'

'Well, I think I'm due some compensation, don't you? Why should I be shamed and humiliated in front of all my friends and family and all for nothing? All the things that man promised me — the lies he told. He took advantage of me, Mary. Why should he get away with it?'

'So, are you going to get it, the two thousand pounds?'

Erica shrugged. 'Don't know. He said he'd think about it and get in touch. And I said he better had. Now I'll just have to wait and see.'

A few days later Erica received an unsigned letter asking her to be at The George, Ferncliff's largest hotel, at 10.30 the following morning. In

74

the lounge she found the Major waiting for her. He wore civilian clothes and handed her a plain envelope. Then, without a word, he turned on his heel and left. Erica repaired to the Ladies, where she opened the envelope. Inside she found £2,000 in used five-pound notes. With the money was a note, again unsigned, on which was written a brief message:

> This is unofficial. Please don't attempt to get more. It could only make life difficult for you.

Ignoring the veiled threat, Erica stuffed the envelope and its contents into her handbag and went home, satisfied that justice had been done.

★ ★ ★

After the euphoria of VJ Day and the influx of servicemen and their families on Ferncliff, winter seemed to descend suddenly. The beach and the busy streets were almost empty. The café, the ice-cream kiosks and the bucket and spade shops put up their shutters for the winter months and the rest of the town settled down to wait for Christmas.

Mary had settled into the part-time job as David Lorimer's secretary well. Her typing was a little rusty to begin with but she soon increased her speed and the book-keeping, box-office returns and wages were straightforward. David allowed her more and more authority as the weeks went by and she took a pride in fending off unwanted visitors and dealing with the more trivial matters to save him time and trouble.

The theatre was putting on a traditional pantomime that year, so rehearsals took place on some afternoons as well as mornings. Sometimes Mary would creep in and sit at the back of the circle to watch. It was planned to engage some local children for the chorus and she wondered whether Vivien would like to audition, but so far she hadn't mentioned it to her. She was growing concerned by Erica's behaviour. She had taken to walking round with that tight little smile on her face again and Mary knew that usually meant she was up to something. But when questioned, Erica refused to say anything. Mary wondered whether there was a new man in her life, though she doubted it. Erica had sworn that she would never trust another man as long as she lived. From now on, she said, she would treat them all as they deserved to be treated.

Dora, with time on her hands now that the beach café was closed, was making elaborate preparations for the coming festive season.

'Do you know, I spent most of the wartime Christmases on my own,' she told them. 'Apart from when the evacuees were here. Damned lonely it was, too, toasting the King's speech with my glass of elderberry wine and a solitary mince pie.'

Erica pulled a face. 'Come on, Mum, you'll have us getting out the violins in a minute.' She gave Dora a quick hug. 'We'll make up for it this year, just you see if we don't.'

Vivien had expressed a wish for a doll that

opened and shut its eyes and said 'Mama' when held upside-down. Erica laughed.

'I reckon I'd say 'Mama' if you held me upside-down!'

One afternoon Mary took Vivien to the theatre with her to watch a rehearsal. The pantomime was *Babes in the Wood* and Vivien sat wide-eyed and entranced throughout. Mary had discovered that the producer would be holding auditions for local children the following Saturday morning. As they walked home, she asked Vivien if she had enjoyed the rehearsal.

'Ooh yes. It was lovely.' Vivien nodded excitedly.

'How would you like to be in it?' Mary asked.

Vivien stared up at her. '*Me?* Could I?'

Mary explained carefully what an audition was. 'Next Saturday lots of children will be coming along to the theatre. They'll be asked to sing or maybe dance — whatever they want. And the best ones will be chosen to be in the pantomime.'

Vivien's eyes were like saucers. 'Will I be the best?'

'Well, we'll have to see.'

'What shall I sing?'

'Why don't you sing that song you like, what's it called 'Cruising Down The River'.' The song had come out earlier that year and Vivien knew all the words and was always singing it. She began now, her little girl's voice sweet and pure.

'Cruising down the riv-er on a Sun-day after-noon . . . ' When she had finished she looked up at Mary. 'Will they like it?' she asked.

'I'm sure they will. But being in a pantomime is quite hard work so you've got to be sure you want to do it.'

'Oh, I *do*!'

'And you mustn't be too disappointed if they don't choose you.'

Vivien smiled. 'Oh, I think they will,' she said, her chin held high.

Mary smiled to herself. Vivien had a lot of Erica in her at times.

On Saturday afternoon they went along to the theatre. Under her best coat Vivien wore her bridesmaid dress, which Dora had shortened for daywear, and a pink ribbon in her hair. When her turn came she walked confidently up the steps on to the stage and sang her song, accompanied by the movements Erica had taught her. She ended with a curtsy, which made Mary smile.

When all the children had been seen, the producer read out the names of the twelve children he had chosen. Vivien sat on the edge of her seat, her lower lip between her teeth and her eyes round with expectancy. Hers was the last name to be read out. She clapped her hands and turned to Mary, her face alight with excitement.

'That's *me*! I'm going to be in it, Mummy! I'm going to be an — an *actor-ess*!'

Rehearsals for the pantomime began a few days after the auditions. The children were to play the parts of woodland creatures. Six little girls were chosen to be butterflies and perform a little ballet. To her delight Vivien was one of them. The little group were to wear pretty gauzy costumes with butterfly wings and Vivien talked about it non-stop, almost forgetting her anticipation of Christmas and the baby doll.

Christmas was a great success. It was the first family Christmas any of them had enjoyed for a very long time. Dora had decorated the house with paper chains and bought a Christmas tree. To decorate it she dug out the box of coloured glass baubles, which had lain unused at the back of a cupboard since before the war.

Everyone enjoyed Dora's sumptuous dinner. She had been saving dried fruit and putting aside a little of the butter and sugar ration for weeks to make a cake and even though the marzipan was made of soya flour, everyone agreed that it tasted just like real ground almonds.

Mary had booked tickets for the three of them to see the pantomime in the week following Christmas. They had good seats in the centre of the front stalls and when Vivien came on with the little group of butterflies they quite stopped the show. Mary felt nervous and proud at the same time.

'I think you should let her start dancing classes after this,' Dora said in the interval. 'You can see she's got real talent. She must get it from her father.'

Mary laughed. 'Thanks, Mum!'

Dora shook her head. 'You know what I mean. It's the stage thing. She's obviously inherited it.'

'Well, as long as she doesn't let it go to her head,' Mary said. 'I'm glad it'll be over before school begins again.' But secretly she agreed with her mother. If Vivien had talent of the artistic kind, it certainly didn't come from her. The thing was, did she encourage it or try to damp it down? If Paul was anything to go by, it turned people into selfish egotists.

Later, at home, when Mary had seen a heavy-eyed Vivien to bed and joined her mother and sister in the living room. Erica suddenly produced a bottle of sparkling wine.

'I know it's not champagne, but it's the nearest I could find,' she said, opening the bottle with a pop.

Dora looked at her. 'What's all this in aid of?' she asked. 'Christmas is over.'

Erica was grinning from ear to ear as she handed round the glasses. 'For me it's just starting,' she said. 'I want us to drink a toast to my new venture.'

'New venture? What are you talking about?' Dora was starting to look alarmed.

'You know the little dress shop in Maple Street?'

'Dianne's?' Mary said. 'The one where I bought my outfit for your — ' She broke off.

'My wedding, yes,' Erica put in. 'Well, say hello to the new owner.' She held up her glass. 'From the beginning of next month, Dianne's will be Erica's. I'm going into business.'

'Where did you get money like that from?' Dora asked.

Erica shrugged. 'Oh, savings, plus a bank loan,' she said airily. She gave Mary a sly wink and raised her glass again. 'I've got you to thank for the idea,' she said. 'Thanks, sis. Ten per cent off everything you buy from now on! And guess what's going in the window the day I open.'

Dora looked bemused. 'No, what?'

'My bloody wedding dress!' Erica said, tossing down the last of her wine. 'Cleaned and pressed and looking like new. I'm hoping it'll be the first thing I sell! A symbol of my new independence. Who needs men?' She refilled her glass. 'Sod the lot of them!'

★   ★   ★

Vivien went back to school after Christmas very reluctantly. She had loved being in the pantomime and school life seemed very dull compared with wearing costumes and make-up and dancing for an appreciative audience every evening. The weather didn't help. January came in with squally rainstorms and freezing temperatures. Dora did her best to keep the little house warm, but as there was only one open fireplace in the house it was a losing battle and they all took hot-water bottles to bed every night.

Erica was impatiently working out her notice at the cinema. She was eager to begin her new venture and planned to open with a sale. Each weekend she spent some time at the shop, sorting out the stock.

'You should see some of the frumpy stuff they've got stashed away in the back,' she told Mary. 'They must have had a lot of it since before the war! I pointed that out to them when I went to look the shop over and I got them to lower the price because of it.'

'Do you think they'll take clothes off coupons soon?' Mary asked.

Erica shrugged. 'Who knows? All I do know is that I can't wait to get started.'

'Did you really get a bank loan?' Mary asked.

Erica lowered her voice. 'What do you think? No, my compensation money was enough with a bit left over to buy some new stock if I'm lucky. But not a word to Mum about that.' She looked at Mary. 'Before I move into the shop I'd really like to redecorate the place. You wouldn't like to give me a hand, would you?'

'I will if I can, but I don't get much time,' Mary said. 'I'm working in the office in the mornings and I'm in the bar six evenings and two afternoons.'

'Well, I'm still working at the Savoy,' Erica said. 'So if you could give me an hour at the weekends it would be wonderful.'

In the end all three women turned their hands to paintbrushes, painting the walls of the shop a pretty pale pink. Dora shampooed the carpet and managed to find some material to make curtains for the changing cubicles. In a short time the little shop was transformed and Erica was at last on her last few days at the cinema.

It was on the day before her last that she came home with a request for Mary.

'I want you to come to the Savoy tomorrow,' she said. 'Come in the afternoon.'

Mary was surprised. 'Whatever for?'

'The programme changed yesterday and I want you to see this film.'

Mary laughed. 'I have to pick Vivien up from school in the afternoons,' Mary said. 'I haven't really got time to go to the pictures.'

'Just come. It's important.' Dora came into the room at that moment and Erica threw her sister a look that clearly indicated secrecy. Later, upstairs in their room Mary pressed her for an explanation.

'What's so special about this film you want me to see? What's it called?'

'*Bombers' Moon*. It's a war film.'

'Aren't they all?' Mary said wryly. 'Either that or historicals. Can't they think of anything else to make films about these days?'

'Just come, that's all I ask,' Erica said. 'You won't have to pay. You can use my complimentary ticket. Sit at the back of the circle and I'll try and sit with you once the programme's started. OK?'

'Oh, all right then,' Mary agreed. 'But I warn you, it had better be good.'

Dora agreed to collect Vivien from school the following day and Mary went along to the cinema in time to catch the 2.30 showing. As directed by Erica, she sat in the back row of the circle, keeping the end seat free so that Erica could join her, which she did soon after the lights were lowered. They sat through the newsreel and the supporting film, by which time Mary was beginning to fidget. Erica had to get up several times to show latecomers to seats with her torch, but at last the main film began. As the credits began to roll, Erica once more slipped into the seat next to Mary. It was a story about the RAF and began on an aerodrome in Suffolk. About ten minutes into the film, there was a scene in the village pub where a crowd of servicemen were gathered. Suddenly Erica nudged Mary.

'*There!* Look. The airman buying drinks at the bar.'

Mary's heart almost stopped. There was no doubt about it. The man at the bar was unmistakably Paul. And as if to verify the fact, the camera homed in on him at that moment as he spoke:

'*Come on, lads. This round's on me!*'

A feeling of panic threatened to choke Mary. Her heart was thumping and her mouth was dry as she started to get out of her seat. Erica grabbed her hand and held it firmly. 'Sit down!'

'Let me go,' Mary whispered.

'It's *him*, isn't it?' Erica said. 'I was right.'

'*Please*, Erica let me go. I feel ill.'

Erica looked at her sister's stricken face and released her grip. 'OK, come on then. We'll go to the café.'

'But you're working.'

'It's my last day. So they'll sack me. What the hell!' Erica got up and led the way out of the auditorium. The cinema café at the rear of the circle was empty and they chose a table at the far end. Erica ordered two cups of tea and sat down opposite her sister, clearly waiting for an explanation. When Mary offered none she said,

'You already knew he was alive, didn't you?'

'Of course I did.'

'So what happened?'

Mary sighed. 'He came home shortly before the war ended. He said our marriage was a mistake and that he wanted to be free — free to pick up his acting career again.' She shrugged. 'Seems he's done just that.'

Erica lit a cigarette. 'I already had my suspicions,' she said. 'Soon after I came here to work they showed a Ministry of Information film about life in the army. I was pretty sure I saw Paul playing a bit-part in that, but I couldn't be sure. It's a few years since I last saw him. Anyway, it could have been made before he was killed, so I didn't say anything. This film was made recently, though, so there was no mistaking it.' She sat back in her chair and drew thoughtfully on her cigarette. 'What made you tell us he was dead?'

'I didn't, really. It just sort of happened. On the day we came home Vivien suddenly announced to Mum that her daddy was dead. I'd explained that he wasn't coming home any more and she just assumed that I meant he was dead.'

'Poor little scrap,' Erica said. 'He's a selfish bugger, leaving you like that. He doesn't deserve a lovely little daughter like Vivien.' She looked at her sister. 'Does he send you any money?'

'No.'

'No? Are you mad? I take it you're getting a divorce.'

'I told him I wouldn't.'

'Don't be a fool. If you get divorced he'll have to support Vivien at least.'

'I don't need his help. I'm earning quite good money now,' Mary said stubbornly. 'Anyway, I don't suppose he's earning very much. I'd rather be independent.'

'What are you thinking about? Pride is all very

well but it's only what you deserve. You stood by him all through the war, kept a home going for him to come back to, had his child, and then he treats you like this. Why should he get away scot-free? If it was me I'd be squeezing every penny I could out of him.'

'I just want to forget we were ever married,' Mary said.

'But you can't, can you? Not when you've got Vivien as living proof.'

'Now that I've let Mum think he was dead all this time, I can't really go back on it.'

'You could. She'd understand.'

'It's Vivien, though. I've thought about it since. How do you think she'd feel if she knew her father had walked out on her — didn't want her? It could scar her for life. She's better off believing he's dead.'

'You're thinking of our dad, aren't you? Did it scar you for life?'

'Not really.'

'No, and it won't scar Vivien, either. Come clean, Mary.'

But Mary shook her head. 'I can't. Don't ask me.'

'OK, OK.' Erica sighed resignedly. 'By the way, I noticed from the credits that he's changed his name. He's calling himself Paul Summers now.'

'Really? I suppose that's all part of his fresh start.'

'He's got quite a good part in this film,' Erica said. 'He's not at all bad either. Do you want to go back and see the rest?'

'Are you joking? *No*!'

Erica looked at her sister for a long moment. 'Aren't you afraid it might all come out some day?'

'There's no reason why it should.'

'You might want to marry again.'

Mary gave her sister a rueful look. 'So might you.'

Erica stubbed her cigarette out forcibly. 'Not a chance!'

'My sentiments exactly!' Mary looked at her sister. 'You will keep this to yourself, won't you?'

'Of course, it that's what you want,' Erica said. 'The same goes for my little pay-off from USAF. Or wherever it came from.'

Mary nodded. 'It's a deal. We won't mention it again, right?'

Erica nodded. 'If you say so.'

5

The first of May was the date selected for the official opening of the beach café and Dora's step was light as she made her way along the sunlit promenade. It felt as though life was almost back to normal and she couldn't wait for the summer season to begin.

It was a beautiful spring morning. The sea was calm and blue with tiny frothy wavelets breaking on the smooth yellow sand. And although it was only 8.30 there were already a few early holidaymakers walking along the shoreline, shoes in hands as they enjoyed the cool water trickling over their toes. The sight gave Dora's heart a lift as she made her way towards the café. Although last year the season had started late, Ferncliff had enjoyed good business with all the servicemen returning to enjoy a late holiday. And from what she had heard, this year already promised to be even better. The fortunes of the little seaside town were looking up at last.

To the casual observer, Dora Flynn was a good-looking woman in early middle age. At forty-nine she showed no outward signs of the difficulties life had thrown at her. Her hair was still the same rich brown it had been when she was twenty, and her figure, though slightly heavier, was slim and shapely. But in spite of appearances, life had not been easy for Dora. She met Michael Flynn at a dance when she was just twenty-one and fell in love with him at first sight. Within five weeks he had swept her off her feet and proposed. Nothing her distraught parents could say would change her mind and they ran away together to his native Ireland, severing her family ties for ever.

But Dora was soon to regret her girlish impulse. Inside six months the romance of their elopement was dead. Mike, all Irish charm and good looks, had turned out to be a work-shy drunk and a bully who thought nothing of using his fists to take out his frustrations on his wife when things did not go his way.

In the first two years of the marriage Dora had given birth to two little girls. Tied to the home with them it seemed there was no escape from Mike's drunkenness and violence and she was often in despair. To make ends meet she took in casual work at home — dressmaking and addressing envelopes. She found a cleaning job where she was allowed to take the babies with her, but that came to an end once they were running about and getting into everything. She scrimped and saved, hoping against hope that Mike's behaviour would improve and they would one day have enough money to escape from the two miserable rooms they called home and rent a little house of their own. Then one night Mike came home incandescent with rage. He had gambled everything he had on a horse and lost it. He blamed her — smashed everything in sight and beat her so badly that at last she decided she could take no more.

From that night she began to make her plan.

Her case stood packed and ready, out of sight at the back of the wardrobe, and the money she had saved was hidden where Mike would not find it. Choosing a night when he was too drunk to know what was happening, she seized her chance. Creeping out of the flat, she walked to the station with her single suitcase and her two sleepy little girls and boarded a train for Cork to catch the night ferry. Once in England she bought a ticket to Ferncliff-on-Sea, a place chosen at random that she had seen advertised on a railway poster. Once there, she set about finding work and a place to stay that she could afford out of the small amount of money left in her purse.

She found work in one of the town's backstreet boarding houses where the owner took pity on the bedraggled little trio and allowed them to live in on the top floor in a tiny attic bedroom until Dora could find somewhere permanent. The work was sheer slavery and it was a constant battle, keeping the girls quiet and out of sight, but she knew she had to stick at it to keep a roof over their heads.

For the first six months she was constantly looking over her shoulder, sure that Mike would track them down and force them to go home with him. In those first weeks she seemed to see him everywhere she looked. A glimpse of a big man with red hair would leave her shaking with apprehension; a voice behind her with an Irish accent would make her spin round, certain she would see him standing there; an obstreperous drunk staggering out of the pub at closing time was enough to make her knees tremble and her heart thud. But as the weeks turned into months and nothing happened, she gradually began to relax. Perhaps Mike was relieved to be rid of them after all.

As soon as Mary and Erica were old enough, Dora got them into the local school. It gave her more working hours and she saved as hard as she could from her wages, eventually finding a small flat for the three of them. The girls were growing up fast; Mary looked like her with brown hair and hazel eyes but Erica was the image of her father with the same flashing green eyes and auburn hair. She also had his charm and wit and, unfortunately, his quick temper. When the girls were younger Dora had sometimes worried about Erica's jealousy. She had shown that she could be spiteful and shrewish, but the war years seemed to have ironed that fault out of her and Dora was hopeful that her younger daughter had now grown into a responsible, well-balanced young woman.

She had always let the girls believe that she and their father had parted amicably — that the marriage had failed through no one's fault. She was ashamed to tell them that their father was a violent bully and that she was terrified of him. She didn't want her girls growing up with that kind of picture of marriage.

The girls were nine and ten when Dora saw the little house in Gresham Terrace advertised to let. Although she was afraid that she might not be able to afford the rent, she replied to the advertisement. To her delight the rent was affordable and the three of them moved in. At long last they had a real family home of their own and room to spread themselves out. Soon afterwards Dora saw that the job as manageress of the bar at the Theatre Royal was vacant. Although she had plenty of experience of bar work she had no real knowledge of management and she didn't hold out much hope of getting the job. However, she applied and was called in for an interview. John Lorimer had taken to her on sight and to Dora's delight he offered her the job there and then. They had remained good friends ever since.

From that day the luck of the little Flynn family seemed to change. The girls grew into teenagers. Mary, the more academic of the two, stayed on at school until she was sixteen and got her school certificate, something that the less able Erica resented. It was to cause friction between them and for a time the girls went through a quarrelsome period, forever bickering and falling out. When Mary met Paul Snow, the situation became worse. Jealousy made Erica shrewish and spiteful and it took all Dora's tact and patience to keep the peace between them. But then the war began and everything changed. It seemed to Dora that all she had striven for over the years was about to be taken from her.

Mary's defiance in eloping with Paul affected her more than she had ever admitted. Mary had always been the easier of her two daughters and Dora felt bitterly hurt and let down when they ran off together. It was like history repeating itself and secretly Dora felt she was being made to pay for her own headstrong action all those years before. She dreaded the thought that her daughter might suffer the same fate that she had, but in spite of all her warnings and pleadings Mary refused to give Paul up. There were times when it seemed to Dora that she no longer knew the headstrong, determined young woman who had taken the place of her compliant daughter.

Erica joined the ATS and was stationed so far north that she hardly ever got home. The little house in Gresham Terrace was suddenly silent and empty. Even the evacuees went home in the end, leaving her feeling deserted and wondering how her life could have gone so badly wrong.

Mary's sudden return last year had meant everything to her. When she received the brief letter she had been overjoyed. It was the second chance she had prayed for. It was sad that Mary had to be widowed before she turned to her mother again, but the important thing was that she had wanted to come home. And little Vivien was a surprise and a wonderful bonus. Now, not only did she have both her girls back with her again, but she had a delightful little grand-daughter and an interesting new job here at the beach café as well. Life was good.

Dora unlocked the front door of the café and stepped inside. The cleaners had already been in and the whole place smelled clean and fragrant with Sunlight soap and furniture polish. She stood for a moment and took a deep, contented breath. Then she hurried through to the kitchen and took off her coat. There was a lot to do if she was to open for business by half past ten.

The delivery van arrived with freshly baked bread and another with a supply of fish, which they stowed away in the big new refrigerator. This season the café was to offer light lunches as well as teas and trays for the beach. Doreen, the cook, arrived and rolled up her sleeves to start peeling the huge mound of potatoes that awaited her. Later Kath and Doris, the two waitresses, arrived and changed into their gingham aprons to begin laying the tables. Dora took the board from the cupboard and found the chalk. TODAY'S MENU, she wrote on both sides, then beneath it a list of everything on offer. Taking it out to the front, she opened it up and positioned it on the pavement so that it could be seen by people coming from both directions.

She was just turning away when she saw him. Wearing a tattered army greatcoat, unshaven and grubby, he was rummaging in a litter bin on the opposite side of the promenade. Normally the bins were emptied by eight o'clock. This morning the refuse lorry was late. Dora wondered whether to call out to him to go away. Already there were quite a few people on the beach. This was hardly the kind of image that Ferncliffe needed. If only the refuse lorry had been on time, it would not have happened. Annoyed, she decided to go inside and telephone the council to complain. Then the man turned towards her and she drew in her breath sharply. His hair was long and grey, the stubbly beard the same colour, but there was something about his eyes and the way he held his head that almost stopped her heart. She shrank back against the door and quickly turned to go inside, but not before he had spotted her.

'Hello there, missus,' he hailed her. 'Would you have a bite to eat going spare?'

Dora swallowed hard. 'Wait there and I'll see.' She hurried through to the kitchen and cut a crisp crust from one of the new loaves, spread it with margarine and jam and called to one of the waitresses.

'Kath, there's a tramp outside. Take him this.'

The girl stared at her. 'Give him that and he'll only be back for more,' she said.

But Dora shrugged. 'Never mind. Tell him not to come back if you like, but I can't see anyone go hungry.'

Kath shot Doreen a look and took the bread. 'OK. If you say so.'

Doreen looked at her. 'Are you all right, Mrs Flynn?' she asked. 'You look as if you've seen a ghost.'

Dora forced a smile. 'I'm fine,' she said. 'And we'd better get the urn filled up if we're to open for coffee.' But the words still echoed in her head: '*Hello there, missus. Would you have a bite to eat going spare?*' That voice. That accent. After all this time — more than twenty years. Surely it couldn't be? She shrugged off the notion. It was sheer fancy because he had been on her mind this morning. What would he be doing here in Ferncliff? Her imagination must be working overtime.

★   ★   ★

Erica's had survived the winter but only just. Most people seemed to wear the same winter clothes year after year and save their clothing coupons for summer wear. As Erica opened up the shop that morning and pulled the dust covers off the rails, she thought again about applying for a bank loan with which to buy new summer stock. The garments she had were way behind the times and hopelessly out of fashion. She was reluctant to ask for a loan. The interest was high and she hated the thought of getting into debt. She still had some money left in the bank but there was the shop rent to find and the overheads to pay. She didn't dare let her account get too low.

True to her word, she had made her wedding dress the centrepiece of her first window display on the day she had taken the shop over. To her surprise, it had sold almost at once. A young starry-eyed girl had come in with her mother and enthused over the cut and material. The dress had fitted her perfectly and Erica had made a satisfying profit from the sale. She put the money in the till with a triumphant smile. How ironic that the sale of her dress was the first money she had taken. It was the first good thing to come out of the sorry affair of her jilting.

Jenny was due to arrive later this morning for a short holiday and Erica was looking forward to seeing her. It would be the first time the two had met since she had stayed with her friend after the catastrophic wedding day. She closed the shop briefly at lunchtime and went to meet Jenny's train. They talked non-stop all the way back to the shop and when they arrived Erica opened the door with a flourish.

'Ta-raaa! Welcome to Erica's.'

Jenny stepped inside and looked round excitedly. 'Wow! It's great, Erica!' she said. 'You're so lucky. How did you manage to afford it?'

'Wasn't easy,' Erica said evasively. 'Still isn't. I might have to get a bank — *another* bank loan to buy some new stock. I can't see the summer visitors being very impressed by the dreary stuff I've got upstairs.'

'No? Let's go and have a look,' Jenny suggested.

Upstairs in the stockroom, she cast a critical eye over the collection of summer dresses that Erica had inherited from the previous owner.

'Mmm, I see what you mean,' she said. 'This military style — square shoulders, short skirts and patch pocket — is definitely out.' She was examining the hems. 'I suppose we could let some of these down. Hemlines are definitely dropping.' She looked at Erica. 'You know, I could alter most of these to bring them more up to date.'

Erica brightened. 'Could you really? But I couldn't let you do that. You're here on holiday.'

'I don't mind,' Jenny said. 'I enjoy sewing and I daresay your mum would lend us her sewing machine.'

Later, as they shared a sandwich lunch in the tiny back room downstairs, Jenny looked thoughtful. 'I've just had a thought. There's a factory at home where you can buy seconds.

Nothing drastic — frocks and skirts with uneven hems, badly matched patterns and so on.'

Erica pulled a face. 'Oh, I don't think . . . '

'No, the thing is, I could put them right for you,' Jenny went on. 'I've done it for myself before now. They turn out all the latest styles and sell their perfect stuff to the big West End stores. I could fix them up and you could legitimately sell them as perfect. The mark-up would be well worth it.' She leaned forward, warming to her idea. 'Not only that, if you were buying in bulk we could negotiate an even lower price.'

'Do you really think so?'

'I'm sure. I know the woman who runs the seconds shop. Tell you what — it's open on Sundays. If you were to come back with me next weekend we could go and have a look.'

'It sounds good, but it wouldn't work with you in Nottingham and me here, would it?' Erica pointed out.

'Mmm.' Jenny looked thoughtful. 'You know, I wouldn't need my arm twisting too hard to make the move down here.'

'Are you serious?' Erica began to smile. 'You'd actually move here to Ferncliff lock, stock and barrel?'

'To be honest I'd love to,' Jenny said. 'I'm keen to make a fresh start, like you were.'

'But what about what's-his-name, Geoff?'

Jenny sighed. 'Geoff was demobbed a couple of months ago and things just didn't work out between us.'

Erica knew that Jenny had been writing to Geoff all through the war. They'd known each other since their schooldays and it had been taken for granted by both their families that they'd marry after the war. 'Why not? What happened?'

'Much the same as what happened to so many other couples,' Jenny said. 'When he came home we tried but we just didn't seem to have anything in common any more. The war — being apart for so long — I suppose it changed us both. No one's fault.' She forced a smile. 'I'm just so grateful that we didn't get married on one of his leaves like so many others did.'

'Well, you know I'd love to have you living closer,' Erica said. 'And it'd be great to have you working with me. The trouble is, I can't really afford an assistant at the moment.'

'I was coming to that.' Jenny smiled. 'I've still got the money I was saving up for my wedding. I won't need it now, so would you consider taking on a working partner?'

Erica brightened. 'Do you mean it?'

'Certainly do.'

'There could be a problem with living accommodation,' Erica warned. 'We're already crowded at home and it's really hard to find a room or a flat anywhere once the season begins.'

Jenny looked round her. 'How many rooms upstairs?'

'Three,' Erica said. 'The stockroom and two more. And there's a little kitchen.' Her face cleared. 'I believe it used to be a flat.'

'Then it could be again!' Jenny laughed. 'And what could be better than having an alteration hand on the premises?'

At the end of the week Erica travelled back to Nottingham with Jenny and they visited the factory shop. Jenny negotiated a price with the manageress that was mutually agreed upon. Erica could hardly believe her luck. She was delighted with the selection of fashionable summer clothes, some of them needing only minor alterations. Now she wouldn't need that bank loan after all.

Erica caught the late train back to Ferncliff and Jenny promised to pack and return as soon as she could.

Two weeks later the flat above the shop had been cleared and furnished with pieces Jenny and Erica had managed to find at local auction sales. Dora had produced some curtains and promised to help Erica decorate the flat at weekends whilst Jenny worked on the alterations. The little shop was a hive of activity over the weeks that followed but at last both the flat and the new summer stock were finished. Now all they had to do was wait for the summer customers.

6

By July Ferncliff was buzzing with summer visitors. Every hotel and guesthouse was full. The beach café was doing excellent business and Erica was delighted with her sales figures. She and Jenny had made several more Sunday trips to Nottingham to replenish their stocks and Jenny worked hard at her machine in the stockroom, straightening hems and putting right other small flaws. Erica's was making quite a name for value and top fashion garments.

Vivien's first year at Cable Road Elementary School was coming to a close and Mary was beginning to worry about what to do with her in the holidays. She worked at the theatre office from nine till one and then in the bar from six till ten. On four afternoons she was free but on Wednesdays and Saturdays the bar was open in the afternoons for the matinée performances. She voiced her problem to David a week before school broke up.

'Well, I daresay Rose and Jessie could manage the matinées on their own during the summer break,' he suggested. 'Could you find someone to look after Vivien in the mornings?'

Mary nodded. 'I'm sure I'll think of something,' she said, feeling far from convinced. Both Erica and her mother were working all day now and she couldn't think of a solution at the moment, but it wasn't David's problem.

'You could always bring her into the office with you,' he said.

Mary looked up quickly. 'Oh, I don't think that will be necessary. You don't want a child under your feet.'

He smiled. 'As a matter of fact I've been wondering when I was going to get to meet Vivien,' he said. 'I saw her in the panto, of course, but we've never actually met.'

'Meeting her is one thing. Having her here in the office for four hours every morning for six weeks is something else.'

He nodded. 'It wouldn't bother me, but I'm sure it would be really boring for her.' He paused. 'We could ask her, though.'

'Ask her?'

'Yes. On Sunday, perhaps. I've been wondering how you'd feel about going out for the day. We could have a run along the coast in the car and find somewhere for lunch.' He looked at her expectantly.

Mary blushed. 'Oh. It's very nice of you to ask us . . . '

'It's not at all nice of me,' David interrupted. 'I've been looking for an excuse to ask you out for ages. What would be nice would be for you to say yes.'

She smiled. 'All right, then. I'd love to. I'm sure Vivien would enjoy it too. She hasn't been in a car very often. It will be a treat. But suppose we have a picnic instead of lunching out? I'll bring it,' she added quickly.

He smiled. 'That sounds perfect. Sunday then. I'll pick you up — around ten o'clock?'

When Erica heard that Mary and Vivien were going out with David on Sunday, she couldn't resist making sly remarks.

'A *picnic*? And you're taking the food! What kind of date is that?'

'I've told you. It isn't a *date*. Anyway, he wanted to take us somewhere for lunch,' Mary told her. 'The picnic was my idea.'

Erica laughed. 'You always were a soft touch. What's wrong with lunching in style?'

'I'm sure Vivien will enjoy a picnic more.'

'And what about poor David? I suppose he'll just have to put up with it.'

Dora, who was bustling back and forth as she prepared supper, shook her head at her daughter. 'Really, Erica, just leave it, can't you? I think it'll be really nice for Mary and Vivien to get out for the day.'

When she'd gone Erica crossed the room to where her sister was sitting. 'I suppose he knows you're still married,' she whispered.

Mary looked up at her sister. 'You promised not to mention that again.'

Erica shrugged. 'He'll have to know sooner or later, won't he?'

'Not necessarily. He's only my employer.'

'At the moment, he is. But now that you've started dating him . . . '

'For the last time, I am *not* dating him. He suggested it would be nice to meet Vivien if I'm going to have to take her into work with me during the holidays.'

Erica, who had been fussing with her hair at the mirror, turned sharply. 'Taking her to work with you? There's no need for that. She can come to the shop with me. There are two of us there to keep an eye on her and she'll love it.'

'Oh, I don't know . . . '

'Too late anyway. I've already asked her if she'd like to and she's thrilled.'

Mary bridled. 'You could have asked me first!'

Erica grinned unrepentantly. 'If I had you wouldn't be going out with his lordship on Sunday, would you?'

⋆　⋆　⋆

Sunday was one of the hottest days of the year. By eight o'clock it was already 70 degrees. Mary was up early, packing up the picnic lunch. Dora had managed to find a tin of salmon and one of corned beef at the Co-op and willingly parted with the precious points coupons she had been saving so that Mary could make sandwiches. She was delighted that she and David were getting along so well together and secretly harboured hopes that the friendship might develop into a romance. With this in mind she had carefully coached Vivien when she and her granddaughter were alone together.

'You will be polite to Mr Lorimer when you're out with him on Sunday, won't you?'

Vivien was becoming rather precocious, the result of living with three adult women. 'Of course I will, Grandma,' she said.

'He's a very nice man and he is your mummy's boss, so you won't interrupt when

104

they're talking, will you? You know you do that sometimes.'

'No, Grandma.' Vivien looked at her with innocent brown eyes. 'Has Mr Lorimer got any little girls?'

'No, dear. He isn't married.'

Vivien brightened. 'So do you think he might marry Mummy?'

Dora gasped. 'Good gracious, no!' she protested. 'And you mustn't say things like that.'

'Why not?'

'Because — because it's bad manners. Just you enjoy your day out and mind what you say.'

★   ★   ★

At ten minutes to ten, Mary was ready. She wore a dress she'd bought from Erica's, the first new dress she'd bought herself for ages. The pretty pale blue cotton suited her colouring perfectly and Dora complimented her.

'You look lovely, dear. It's time you started going out and enjoying yourself again. Have a lovely time.'

Erica was pulling a face at her behind her mother's back, but Mary ignored it and smiled. 'Thanks, Mum.'

The picnic was packed in Dora's old picnic basket, unused since before the war and dredged out of the attic for the occasion. There were sandwiches and fresh tomatoes, slices of Dora's homemade cake and plenty of fresh fruit as well as a flask of tea. Mary had also packed Vivien's swimming costume and a towel.

Vivien hopped from one foot to the other, running to and from the window every few seconds.

'What kind of car is it, Mummy? What colour?'

'It's grey.' Mary lifted the net curtain to peer out. 'And here it is.' She quickly straightened the bow in Vivien's hair and bent to pull up her white ankle socks. 'Come on then. And best behaviour, mind.'

Erica came with them to the front door. 'Off you go then, and don't do anything I wouldn't do,' she said with a sly wink.

David got out to greet them. He wore stone-coloured slacks and a blue open-necked shirt. It was the first time Mary had seen him in casual clothes and he looked different, more relaxed and quite handsome. His car was a pre-war Hillman and as they drove he told Mary that he had put his name down for a new one.

'They've started producing them again, but it could be at least four years before mine comes up.'

'As long as that?'

He nodded. 'I don't have the kind of occupation that gives me priority, unfortunately. Still, this little bus is still in pretty good condition.'

Vivien's voice piped up from the back seat. 'By the time you get your new car I'll be ten,' she announced proudly.

He laughed. 'So you will. You're very good at sums, aren't you?'

'Yes. How old will you be?'

'*Vivien!*' Mary turned to glare at her daughter

but David was still laughing.

'Ancient,' he told her. 'In my dotage.'

'What's dotage?'

Mary shot him an apologetic look. 'Sorry,' she said.

'I go to dancing classes,' Vivien told him. 'Every Saturday morning.'

'I know. Your mummy told me.' David smiled at her through the rear-view mirror. 'But I've seen you dance, remember? In the pantomime last Christmas.'

'Oh, I'm heaps better than that now,' Vivien said airily. 'I can do tap and ballet. On my toes too.'

'Gosh. I'm impressed.'

'What's impressed?'

'It means I think you're very clever.'

'Yes, Miss Harris says so too. She's our teacher.'

Mary turned and gave her daughter a warning look. 'Vivien, just be quiet for a little while now,' she said. 'Why don't you look out of the window at the scenery?'

'What's seen-ry?'

David chuckled. 'I can see we're in for a lively day.'

*   *   *

They drove along the coast to a little cove where an easy route down a rocky cliff path gave on to an almost deserted beach. Vivien managed the descent easily, but Mary's high-heeled sandals gave her a few problems. At the bottom of the

107

cliff David held out his arms.

'Here, let me help you.' He lifted her the last few feet, his hands firmly on her waist. As she landed on the soft sand her face was close to his and he smiled down into her eyes. 'Thanks for coming with me today, Mary.'

She shook her head. 'No, thank you for asking.' She was acutely aware of his body close to hers, the scent of the cologne he used and the warmth of his hands, still on her waist. It was so long since she'd been this close to a man and even then there had only ever been Paul, who in the end didn't want her. She found herself growing hot with confusion and embarrassment. 'I — I'd better see what Vivien's up to,' she said, easing away from him. 'She's apt to run straight into the water if I don't stop her.'

Changed into her little red swimming costume, Vivien played happily in the shallows for a while, but it wasn't long before she was back, asking for company.

'Aren't you coming in too?' she asked, standing challengingly in front of them as they sat on the sand. 'Auntie Erica was teaching me to swim last summer and I can nearly do it.'

David got to his feet. 'As a matter of fact I do have my trunks on underneath,' he said. 'Give me a minute and I'll be with you.' He disappeared behind some rocks and emerged a few minutes later in navy blue swimming trunks. He reached out his hand to Vivien. 'Come on, let's see what you can do then.'

Mary watched as they ran down to the water's edge together, Vivien's hand trustingly in his. If

108

only Paul could have been a proper father to Vivien. Did he ever think about her, she wondered. Would he some day regret letting his daughter go without ever really knowing her?

'Mummy! Mummy! I did it. I swam!' Vivien hurled herself at her mother's feet. 'I did three whole strokes.'

David caught her up, laughing as Mary looked up enquiringly at him. 'It's true, she did,' he said, dropping down beside her. 'We'll have her setting off for France in no time.'

'Well done, both of you,' Mary said. 'But now I think we must all be ready for some lunch.'

After they had emptied the picnic basket Vivien ran off happily to play at the water's edge. David lay back on the sand.

'I always thought I'd be married with a family of my own after the war,' he said. 'I was engaged.' He glanced up at her. 'I expect you've heard what happened.'

'Not really,' she hedged, shaking her head.

'I'd be very surprised if you hadn't. Bad news usually travels fast.' He gave her a cynical smile. 'It was a very familiar story. Betty met an American serviceman while I was away and preferred him. It's as simple as that.'

'I doubt if it is,' Mary said softly. 'It must have been very hard for you.'

'I admit it doesn't do a lot for the self-esteem.' He looked up at her, narrowing his eyes against the sun. 'But it can't be nearly as hard as having the person you love killed,' he said. 'That must be terrible. So final.'

Mary said nothing. She hated the deception

she had unwittingly created and especially she hated lying to this man. She would have given anything at that moment to pour the truth out to him, but something held her back. The deception had gathered momentum like a snowball over the past months. So many people believed that Paul had been killed that it was impossible now to tell the truth without looking suspicious. Turning her head she looked to where Vivien was playing. 'I've got her,' she said. 'A good family and a job I love. I'm lucky.'

'And I'm lucky to have you,' he told her. His hand reached out for hers and gave her fingers a brief squeeze. 'My mother died when I was ten,' he told her. 'Dad puts on a brave face but I know he's been lonely all these years. He's always been very fond of your mother and I believe he hoped that one day they might make a go of it together.'

His words surprised her. 'Really? I'd no idea.'

'I doubt if she had either,' he said. 'She probably saw him more as a father figure. After all, he is about twelve years older.' He smiled. 'He was so pleased that her daughter was taking over from her when I took over at the Royal. You must come and meet him sometime.'

'I'd like that.'

He looked at her. 'I haven't told you yet how nice you look today.'

Mary blushed and began to busy herself putting things away in the basket.

'Not that you don't always look nice.' He shook his head. 'Damn! I can't even pay you a compliment without messing it up, can I?'

'No!' She reached out to touch his hand. 'It's

me. I'm still very . . . '

'I know. You don't have to explain.' He laughed and shook his head. 'We're a pair, aren't we?'

Vivien joined them. 'Is there any more to eat?'

Mary shook her head. 'No, and I think it's time we started for home,' she said. 'It's school in the morning.'

Sitting in the back of the car Vivien said suddenly, 'The summer holidays start next week. We don't have to go to school for six whole weeks,' she said. 'I'm going to help Auntie Erica at her shop every morning.'

David glanced at Mary. 'So you won't be bringing her into work with you after all?'

'They arranged it all between them,' Mary told him. 'I know today was so that you could get to know her. I hope you don't think it's been a waste of time.'

'Don't say things like that!' The look he threw her made her colour. 'This has been one of the most enjoyable days I've spent for a long time,' he said. 'And very far from a waste of time. In fact I was going to ask you if we could do it again sometime.'

'That would be lovely.'

'Soon?'

'If you like.'

'Right.' The car was turning into Gresham Terrace. 'I'll hold you to that.'

As they got out of the car Mary asked if he would come in, but he shook his head. 'I've got some paperwork at home that needs attention. I'll see you at the office in the morning, though.'

'Yes. In the morning.' As Vivien ran on indoors, Mary gathered up their belongings and the picnic basket. 'Thank you so much for today, David,' she said. 'I — Vivien and I, we've really enjoyed it.'

He reached out to touch her arm. 'Thank you for coming. And by the way, I really meant what I said. That blue suits you perfectly.'

7

As summer turned to autumn and the visitors began to thin out, Ferncliff settled down for the off-season. At Erica's, Jenny and Erica were beginning to stock up with the latest winter styles.

The girls had made their monthly trip to Grayson's Fashions Ltd early in September and picked out the styles they thought would be popular with the women of Ferncliff for the coming season. Erica knew that as the winter season progressed there would be the usual crop of formal evening functions. The Licensed Victuallers' dinner and dance, always a grand occasion, would be held as usual at the Pavilion Ballroom, and the slightly smaller Hoteliers' Association were already advertising their dinner and dance, which would be held this year at the newly opened Minsmore Country Club.

At Grayson's Erica made straight for the evening-wear, choosing several sumptuous ball gowns. She knew that the local hoteliers' wives and landladies looked forward to competing with one another for the most glamorous outfit. Black and pastel shades seemed to be in vogue this year, with strapless bodices and wide tulle skirts decorated with plenty of sequins and sparkle. She visualized her window, dressed with just one stunning gown lit by the spotlight she had recently had fitted. Jenny argued that it might be a mistake to spend most of their budget on evening-wear but Erica was adamant.

'The poor old dears have been slaving over hot stoves in pinnies all summer,' she said. 'This is their glamour time. Their chance to come into their own. They'll buy the frocks all right. And if they get their pictures in the local paper it'll be a free advert for us. Don't worry, we'll still have enough left over for some seconds you can alter.'

Back at the shop Jenny worked hard on the collection of wool suits and separates they had bought, straightening hemlines and realigning patterns and buttons. She was skilful enough to be able to straighten the hems of flared and pleated skirts, a task that most dressmakers found too daunting to tackle. Jenny was a gem and Erica was the first to admit that she was lucky to have her. She had made the little flat above the shop into a cosy little home and, as she had pointed out, it was certainly an advantage, having a resident alteration hand. Often, if a garment needed altering Jenny could have it ready for the customer on the same day — an advantage that often secured a sale.

★　★　★

At the Theatre Royal the winter programme was being drawn up. Instead of the summer variety shows, touring plays were being booked, filling the weeks when the resident company was in rehearsal. In the winter the local people had time to go to the theatre and gripping dramas and thrillers were always winners at the box office.

The Christmas pantomime was being planned too and Vivien had already formed her own ideas about the part she intended to play in it.

Mary tentatively mentioned it to David as they took their mid-morning coffee break together one morning. 'I'm afraid Vivien has set her heart on appearing again this year,' she told him, almost apologetically.

'It's to be *Dick Whittington*, as you know,' he said. 'So there will just be the usual chorus of children. I daresay Vivien's dancing school will be arranging that so she's bound to be in it anyway.'

Mary smiled. 'I'm afraid she's got bigger ideas than that. She's got it into her head that she wants to play the cat,' she told him. 'I've tried to tell her that it's a part for an acrobat or someone with special skills, but she won't listen.'

David looked thoughtful. 'She's a very supple little girl,' he said, remembering watching her turning cartwheels on the beach. 'I wonder . . . I always feel that it looks wrong, played by an adult — too large. A dainty little cat would be nice. Leave it with me. I'll have a word with Elaine Sheppard, the company's dance director.'

Much to Vivien's excitement a date was made for her to be auditioned. Mary took her along to the theatre, pointing out that an audition only meant a kind of test and that she mustn't take it for granted that she would be chosen. But Vivien had already made up her mind.

'I've been watching the cat next door,' she announced with a smile. 'I can do all the things

115

she does. I'll be good enough, just you wait and see.'

Mary sat in the empty auditorium, watching as Elaine Sheppard auditioned Vivien, carefully explaining what she wanted her to do. Dressed in the little tunic she wore for dancing classes and her little ballet shoes, she rolled and purred, pounced at imaginary mice and sat washing her ears and whiskers. She leapt and jumped with a lightness and agility that amazed Mary. At last Elaine laughed and clapped her hands.

'That was lovely, Vivien. Thank you very much. I think you'll make an excellent Tommy the cat.' She turned to smile at Mary. 'I'll draw up a rehearsal schedule and let you have it soon.'

On the way home Vivien took Mary's hand and looked up at her. 'Told you,' she said with a smug little smile.

★ ★ ★

At the beach café the shutters went up in mid-October and for the two weeks that followed Dora supervised its thorough end-of-season cleaning. It had been a wonderful autumn, all blue and golden with sunshine. There had been quite a few late visitors and coach parties and at Dora's suggestion the café had stayed open for two weeks longer than planned. They had stopped serving full meals but had offered snacks and teas as well as ice-cream and had done really good business. When she balanced the accounts at the end of the season, Dora was surprised and pleased by the profit they had made.

The following Sunday morning she took the books along to John Lorimer for their annual audit. John had taken on the franchise on the café on behalf of the town council when he retired from managing the theatre. John still lived in the bungalow he had shared with his late wife in Minsmore, a pleasant suburb of Ferncliff. As he ushered Dora through to the lounge, he took a quick glance at the ledger.

'My goodness, these figures look wonderful,' he said. 'But then I knew you were the right person for the job when I recommended you to Bill Major.' He indicated a comfortable arm-chair. 'You don't have to rush off, do you, Dora? Stay and tell me all your news. I've missed seeing your smiling face every day.' He went to a corner cabinet and took out the sherry bottle and two glasses, looking at her enquiringly. 'You'll have a drink with me?'

Dora nodded and sat down in the armchair by the French windows. 'So, what have you been up to all summer?' she asked.

'Not a lot.' He smiled wryly. 'It's not all it's cracked up to be, this retirement lark. To tell you the truth I'm beginning to think I was a bit too hasty in handing over the management of the Royal to David.'

'Well, you don't look so bad on it,' Dora told him. She meant the compliment sincerely. John Lorimer looked nothing like his sixty-two years. He was still lean and upright and his hair, although silver, was still thick and wavy.

'You do all the donkey work at the café,' he was saying, 'so nothing for me to do there.' He smiled wryly. 'Never thought I'd look forward to poring over dusty old accounts, but it's the highlight of the year for me nowadays.'

She laughed. 'Get away with you. I don't believe a word of it. Anyway, it looks as though you've put in a lot of good work out there in the garden.' She looked out at the lush green sweep of the lawn and late flowering shrubs.

John shook his head. 'Only so much gardening you can do without getting bored,' he said. 'But boredom obviously isn't on your agenda what with the café and both your girls home again, not to mention that lively young granddaughter of yours.'

Dora smiled as she sipped her sherry. 'She's a proper little character, but I daresay you'll have heard all about her.'

'I have. That son of mine and your Mary seem to work together well.'

'Yes.'

'I hear they've had one or two little outings together.' He peered at her. 'That *is* all right with you, isn't it?'

'Oh yes. It's just — well, you know she lost her husband in the war.'

'Of course, poor girl, but you needn't worry about David. I think I can safely say that he's becoming very fond of her and he's not the fly-by-night type to trifle with a girl's affections if that's what's worrying you.'

Dora hid a smile at the old-fashioned expression. 'Not at all. Anyone can see he's a perfect gentleman. It's not easy for any man to take on another man's child, though. But I'm sure that he and Mary are well aware of that.'

John laughed. 'Listen to us! Talking about them as though they're a couple of kids. I'm sure they're both old enough to work things out for themselves.' He held out his hand for her glass. 'Here, let me top that up for you.'

Dora allowed him to take her glass to the cabinet and refill it, taking the time to make up her mind whether to tell him about the thing that had been troubling her.

When he resumed his seat he gave her a quizzical look. 'Unless I'm very much mistaken, Mrs Dora Flynn, there's something on your mind,' he said.

She took a thoughtful sip of her sherry and looked up at him. 'You're right. John. There is something.'

'So — are you going to tell me about it?'

She sighed. 'There's been a man all summer — a tramp, I suppose you'd call him — at the café, begging for food.'

John frowned. 'Have you reported it? The council frowns on that kind of thing. Not at all the image . . . ' He stopped and looked at her. 'He hasn't been bothering you, has he?'

She shook her head. 'No, at least not in the way you mean.' She took a deep breath. 'I've never told you anything about my background, have I, John?'

'No.' He held up his hand. 'None of my business. I know everything I need to know about you. I like to take people as I find them.'

'I know you do, but this — it has a bearing on it. I met Mike when I was just twenty-one. The war was just over — the first war, that is. Mike was Irish and he was over here working on a building site. He was handsome and fun and I fell head over heels in love with him. My parents didn't approve but I'd come of age so we ran away together. I haven't seen or spoken to my parents since. We went to live in Ireland and it wasn't long before I found out that under all the charm he was a drunk and a bully. I stuck it for two years, being beaten black and blue on a regular basis, but things got so bad that I began to fear for the girls. To cut a long story short, I left him. Mary and Erica were only tiny at the time and they don't remember anything about it and I've never told them.'

'I see.' John looked puzzled. 'So what does this have to do with . . . ?'

'This tramp?' Dora paused. 'I just can't get it out of my head that it's *him*, John. I know it's highly unlikely, and he certainly showed no sign that he recognized me, but there's just — just this *feeling*.'

He reached across and covered her shaking hand with his own. 'Dora, my dear, this is really eating away at you, isn't it?'

'I can't sleep for thinking about it. He looks as if he's living rough, probably under the pier or somewhere. I know I shouldn't have but I've been giving him the odd snack. Now that the café's closed and the winter's coming on I've been wondering what he'll do.'

He shook his head at her. 'You're too soft-hearted, my dear. Surely if he was your ex-husband he'd have recognized you.'

Dora looked down at her hand with its worn wedding band. 'The thing is, John, he's not my 'ex',' she said quietly. 'We were never divorced.'

John paused for a moment, then went on, 'There are places chaps like him can go, you know. No one has to sleep rough if they don't want to. Anyway, some of these tramps prefer the open road and living free. He'll probably move inland for the winter — get some work on a farm where they'll give him food and shelter. He'll be all right.' Seeing her expression, he stopped. 'This isn't what you want to hear, though, is it, Dora?'

She bit her lip. 'I was thinking — you know people — know how to find things out.'

'You want me to try and find out who this man is?' He looked shocked.

'Just for my peace of mind, I thought . . . '

'All right, Dora. Because it's for you I'll try and do what I can but it might not be easy. I haven't even seen the man myself. You'll have to give me his full name and a detailed description of what he looks like.'

'I can do better than that.' Dora opened her handbag and took out a faded snapshot. 'This was taken on our wedding day. And this — ' She passed him a second snap. 'I took my camera to work with me one day and took this. He turned just as I was taking it. He looked a bit startled and I thought he might stop coming, but he didn't. He was back again next morning.'

'I should think he was when he was getting free grub,' John said wryly. He compared the two snapshots. 'I can't see the slightest similarity

121

between these two men. What makes you think this man might be your husband?'

'I don't know. It's just . . . something.'

John looked at the second snap again. 'Well, he's certainly unkempt. Could be anyone under all that hair. And the greatcoat looks a couple of sizes too big as well.' He looked up at her. 'And what if I were to find out that he was who you think he is?'

'I haven't thought that far.'

'Well, perhaps you should. You say he was violent.'

'He was.'

'You're not planning to get in touch with him again then?'

'I — I don't know.'

'Forgive me, my dear, but wouldn't it be better to let sleeping dogs lie? After all, he'd be none the wiser. And you have to think of your girls, remember. If he knew you were here, with his daughters, in a comfortable home, he might start making all kind of demands on you. As you were never divorced he'd still have certain rights.'

Dora shook her head. 'I'd just like to *know*, John, to put my mind at rest. I'll think about what to do then.' She looked at him. 'Will you help me, please?'

His face softened. 'When you look at me like that how can I refuse?' He shook his head. 'But I can't help feeling we might be opening up a can of worms.'

★ ★ ★

Rehearsals for *Dick Whittington* got under way. Mary had misgivings about Vivien's part in it. She was afraid the heavy rehearsal schedule would disrupt her schoolwork. Erica disagreed.

'She's only a baby,' she said. 'Let her enjoy herself while she's still young. Plenty of time for exams and all that boring stuff later.'

'She's been doing really well. I don't want her to miss schooling and fall behind,' Mary pointed out. 'At her age she'd find it hard to catch up afterwards.'

Erica shrugged. 'If you ask me book learning is highly overrated.' She raised an eyebrow at her sister. 'After all, look at you. You were always getting higher marks than me at school, always studying your socks off, I remember. Proper little swot. Yet here I am with my own flourishing business and you — well, to be brutally honest you're not much more than a glorified barmaid.'

Mary coloured hotly. 'I am *not*! And just how did you get the money to start your business, may I ask?'

Dora, who had just come in, put her head round the door. '*Girls*, really! I could hear you before I put my key in the door! Time you realized that you're a couple of grown women and not school kids any more. What kind of example is this to set Vivien?'

'Vivien's at the theatre, Mum,' Mary said.

Dora began to take off her coat. 'Just as well!'

When she had gone upstairs Erica glowered at her sister. 'I'm not the only one with a secret, our Mary,' she hissed. 'And don't you forget it. I richly deserved that money and I've put it to

123

damned good use. One word to Mum about it and I'll spill your little can of beans too, so be warned.'

'All right, as long as you remember that Vivien is *my* daughter, not yours. And I won't have you putting ideas into her head. Right?'

'OK, have it your way, but I'm warning you. The time will come when she'll have her own ideas. In fact she's already got them and if you don't stop putting your foot down and spoiling her fun she's going to start thinking of you as the enemy.'

Mary was already worried about how head-strong Vivien was becoming. Living with an indulgent aunt and grandmother, she was getting far too much of her own way. The thought of her becoming the kind of spoilt child that no one liked concerned her deeply. She voiced her fears about it to David late one Saturday night about a week later as they cashed up together in the office.

'She used to be such a sweet little girl,' she said. 'So easy and obedient. Now she argues over every little thing. And she's so full of herself. I'm beginning to feel I'm losing control of her and it's frightening.'

David smiled. 'She's getting older, that's all. You are no longer her only influence. There are her schoolmates, her teachers — others here at the theatre. It happens to all kids once they go out into the world. They see that there are other points of view and start forming opinions of their own.'

'Surely she's pretty young for that. And

anyway, it doesn't mean they know what's best for them, does it?'

'I daresay she misses her father.'

His words brought Mary up sharply. 'She hardly knew Paul,' she said.

'Nevertheless, she's missing out on a male influence in her life,' he said. 'Girls need a father as much as boys. Maybe more so in some ways.'

'Well — that's something that can't be helped.'

He turned to look at her. 'You know, when I was a boy I used to wish Dad would remarry so that I could have a mother again.'

Mary refused to look at him. 'Did you?'

'Have you ever thought of remarrying, Mary?' he asked quietly.

They had been seeing each other out of working hours ever since the summer seaside outing and Mary sensed that his feelings for her were growing stronger. She had resolutely refused to acknowledge her own feelings and so far she had held him at arm's length, but every time they were alone together it grew more and more difficult. She knew it was a situation that couldn't last but refused to think about what would happen when things came to a head between them. Now it looked as if it had and she was faced with a choice. She took a deep breath.

'I can't marry again,' she told him.

'Why not?'

'Because I'm . . . ' She bit back the words, on the very point of telling him the truth. Imagining the look of shock and disappointment on his face, she lost her nerve. If she told him that she'd been living a lie all this time she'd surely lose him, lose everything: her job, her self-respect and her happiness.

'Because you're still in love with your husband?' he ventured. When she didn't reply he moved across to her. Hands on her arms, he raised her to her feet and looked into her eyes. 'Tell me the truth, Mary. It's important to me. I really need to know. Do you think you could ever feel what you felt for him again? Do I mean anything at all to you?'

'David — of course you do. You've been so good to me and Vivien and I . . . '

'You know damned well that's not what I mean.' He shook her gently. 'Oh, Mary!' Suddenly he pulled her close and his mouth came down on hers in a kiss powered by his hunger. As he crushed her to him, the pent-up desire he had controlled for weeks was palpable in every tensed muscle of his body. She tried hard to remain detached but it was no use. The feelings she had kept at bay for so long overwhelmed her and she gave in, melting against him, her knees turning to water and her heart thudding. The intensity of the kiss left her breathless. David looked down at her, his eyes dark with longing.

'I think you've just told me what I wanted to know,' he said. 'So what makes you so sure you can't marry again?'

'I — I can't rush into anything,' she said, hating herself for her own weakness.

'I understand that and I wouldn't expect you to.' He cupped her face in his hands. 'I love you, Mary,' he said softly. 'You must have realized that by now. I thought it would never happen to me again but it has. All I want to know is, do you — could you ever feel the same?'

She reached up to touch his face. She too had never foreseen loving again like this. He was so very dear to her. The thought of hurting him was like a pain. 'Yes, of course I feel the same, David. But I . . . ' His mouth silenced the rest of the sentence.

'That's all I need to know,' he whispered as he held her close. 'I'll never rush you into anything, darling. Just as long as I know you love me I'm happy to wait.' He smiled. 'Providing it isn't too long.'

Mary lay awake for a long time that night. This was the worst dilemma she had ever faced. If she told David the truth she was sure to lose him. But if she didn't tell him how could she allow their relationship to continue? She longed for nothing more than to be David's wife, for Vivien to have a father for the first time in her life. Living as a family in a home of their own would be so perfect. It would be a fresh start; the life she had always dreamed of. But it couldn't happen without everyone knowing she had lied about Paul being dead.

* * *

Erica and Jenny had done well at the shop. The ball gowns had sold well and, once in the shop, the customers had looked through the rails at the day wear, remarking at the reasonable prices. Their profits had mounted nicely and they planned to have a sale after Christmas, before stocking up with Grayson's spring fashions.

It was just a few days before Christmas and Erica's was going through a quiet spell. Vivien had broken up from school and was spending the day with her aunt at the shop. She was busy with her crayoning books in the back room just after lunch when the shop bell tinkled. Erica had gone upstairs to have a word with Jenny, who was altering a dress for a customer. Vivien got up from her chair and peeped out into the shop. A man stood there, looking around him. Seizing her chance to be grown up, she stepped out and, mimicking her Aunt Erica's best 'saleswoman' voice, she said, 'Good afternoon, sir, can I help you or are you just looking?'

The man looked surprised to see such a diminutive sales assistant. 'I'm looking for Miss Taylor,' he said. 'Miss Jennifer Taylor.'

Vivien shook her head. 'This is my auntie's shop,' she said. 'She's called Erica Flynn.'

'I see. And no one else works here? Apart from you, of course,' The man smiled down at her.

'Oh, I don't work here. I'm an actor-ess,' Vivien told him proudly. 'I'm going to be in the pantomime at the Theatre Royal. It starts on Boxing Day. I'm Dick Whittington's cat, Tommy.'

'Are you really? I'd like to see that.'

Vivien was about to tell him where he could obtain tickets when the door that led to the stairs opened and Erica came in. 'Did I hear the shop bell?' She stopped when she saw the man. 'Vivien, why didn't you call me?' She smiled at the customer. 'I'm sorry about that. Are you looking for something special, sir?'

'I'm looking for Jennifer Taylor, but the young lady here says she doesn't work here.'

Erica smiled. 'I think Vivien has only ever heard her called Jenny,' she said. 'Yes. Jenny is my business partner.'

'Oh!' The man looked crestfallen. 'She may have mentioned me to you. My name is Geoff Markham. Jenny and I used to be engaged.'

Erica stiffened, acutely aware of Vivien standing at her side, wide-eyed with curiosity. She turned to the child. 'Go and play with your crayons, Vivien, there's a love.'

Vivien turned and went slowly and reluctantly towards the back room. She was still hovering, pretending to button her shoe, as Erica said, 'I'm sorry but Jenny isn't here at the moment.'

'When will she be back?' Geoff asked.

'I've no idea. Probably not today at all.'

Geoff looked disappointed. 'Do you happen to know where she's gone?'

Vivien could hardly believe her ears. She had always believed that grown-ups never told fibs. 'She's upstairs in her flat,' she piped up. 'She's working on her sewing machine.' She looked accusingly at her aunt. 'I thought you knew, Auntie.'

Erica was torn between anger and frustration as she looked at the reproachful brown eyes. 'I thought I told you to go and play, Vivien,' she snapped. Turning to smile at Geoff, she said, 'I'm sorry about that. She must have come back while I was busy.' She saw Vivien's mouth beginning to open again and moved swiftly towards her. 'Off you go, Vivien. Now!' She pushed the child inside and closed the door firmly. The shop bell tinkled again and a woman came into the shop and began looking through the rails. Geoff looked at Erica.

'May I go up?' he asked. 'I'd like to surprise her.'

Erica looked hesitantly at the customer who was beginning to show signs of losing interest. 'I'll be with you in just a moment, madam,' she called.

'Look, I'm holding you up,' Geoff said. He moved to the door leading to the stairs. 'Is it through here? May I?'

Erica gave in with a sigh. 'Oh, I suppose so.' She watched him disappear through the door with a feeling of foreboding. It seemed that every time a man walked into her life it spelt trouble.

★　★　★

At four o'clock Mary arrived to pick Vivien up. The bar closed after the matinée interval, leaving her free to go home and give Vivien her tea before the evening performance.

'Get your things together, Vivien. Mummy's here' Erica called out.

'Has she been good?' Mary asked.

'As a matter of fact she's been a bit naughty,' Erica complained. 'Chipping in when I was talking to someone and making me out to be a liar.'

Mary frowned. 'Really?' As her daughter emerged from the kitchen with her coat on, she

130

shook her head. 'Auntie Erica says you've been naughty.'

Vivien pouted. 'No, I haven't. I only said that Jenny was upstairs when the man came.' She looked up at her aunt. 'You said you didn't know where she was and I did — so I told him.'

Mary looked at her sister. 'What's all that about?' she asked.

'You know I love having her here,' Erica said, 'but you'll have to tell her not to butt in and interfere in things she doesn't understand.'

Mary looked down at her daughter, who had truculence written all over her face. 'Have you got all your things?'

'Yes.'

'Come on then. If we hurry we might get home before it starts raining again.' Mary turned to her sister. 'Sorry, Erica. See you later.'

As they walked down the street together, Mary looked down at Vivien. 'Do you want to tell me about it?' she asked.

Vivien's lower lip came out again. 'She told a fib,' she said. 'Fibs are naughty aren't they?'

Mary sighed. 'Sometimes — just *sometimes* — we have to tell very small fibs,' she said. 'When it would hurt someone to tell the truth. for instance. They're called white lies. What *is* naughty is to contradict when it's about something you don't understand.'

'But the man only wanted to see Jenny,' Vivien insisted.

'But you shouldn't really have been listening, should you?' Mary took her daughter's hand and squeezed it. 'Tell you what, just say sorry to

Auntie Erica when she gets home and forget it,' she advised. 'That's much the best.'

⋆ ⋆ ⋆

Erica's closed at six. When the cashing up had been done, the door locked and the blinds pulled down for the night, Geoff had still not reappeared. A feeling of deep uneasiness was nagging at Erica and at last, unable to bear the suspense any longer, she decided that she would have to go up and find out what was happening for herself.

She climbed the stairs and knocked on the flat door. After a pause she heard Jenny call, 'Come in.'

Geoff was sitting with his arm around Jenny's shoulders on the settee, looking for all the world as if he owned the place. Erica felt irritation twanging her nerves.

'You were so quiet I wondered if you'd gone out,' she said.

Jenny jumped up, her face flushed. 'Good heavens, is it that time already? Geoff was just going, weren't you, Geoff?'

He unwound his six feet from the settee and stretched. 'I suppose I must.' He looked at his watch. 'I've left it a bit late to look for somewhere to stay.'

Erica looked at him coolly. 'Oh, you're not going back to Nottingham tonight then?'

Before he could reply, Jenny broke in. 'I've finished that alteration. I think the customer said she wanted it first thing tomorrow so I'll press it when I've had my tea.'

Geoff was pulling on his overcoat. 'I'll go,' he said.

'Oh — I'll have to come down and let you out.' With a quick glance at Erica, Jenny hurried after him. When she returned Erica was standing by the window, waiting for her.

'Well, what did *he* want?' she demanded.

Jenny looked uncomfortable. 'He — wants me back,' she said. 'He says he missed me, that we made a terrible mistake. He's asked me to marry him.'

Erica gave a harsh laugh. '*Huh*! He'll be lucky! I hope you told him where to go.'

'No. No, I didn't.' Jenny bit her lip.

'All a bit sudden, isn't it?'

'Not really. He's been writing to me for some time now.'

'But if you didn't get on before, what makes him think you will now?'

'Things were difficult when Geoff first came home. He couldn't get a job and felt bad because he couldn't provide for me. The war had changed us both. It was a question of getting to know one another all over again and that wasn't easy. But being apart has made us see things more clearly. Now Geoff has a job with good prospects. He says life isn't complete without me.'

'*Very* romantic! And you?'

'I — I feel the same. I still love him.'

'I can see what's happened here.' Erica narrowed her eyes. 'You've been to bed with him, haven't you? You've let him . . . '

'I think that's *my* business,' Jenny interrupted. 'The fact is, Erica, I've never really stopped loving Geoff,' she said. 'I've missed him terribly.'

'First I've heard of it!' Erica snapped.

'We don't all wear our hearts on our sleeves.'

'You're a fool, Jenny. I thought you'd learnt your lesson when you saw what happened to me.'

'Not all men are cheats and liars, Erica. Perhaps if you weren't so embittered . . . '

'I'm not embittered, just wise to the way men try to pull the wool over our eyes.'

'Not this man. Geoff's not like that and never was. And seeing him today; coming all this way to see me, begging for us to get back together, just made me realize that I can't let him go.'

Erica stared at her. 'I don't believe this! You're *joking*!'

'No.'

'So you'd give up your career — for *him*?'

'It's hardly a career, is it? I can do what I do here anywhere.'

'So what about me? What about Erica's and all we've built together here? I offered you a job and a home when you wanted to escape. Does that count for nothing?'

'I know and I'm really sorry about it, but it can't be helped. It's my life!' Jenny pleaded. 'Mine and Geoff's. We want to be together.'

'How lovely for you!' Erica said. 'So you're just going to walk away from it all.'

'The favours weren't all one way, Erica. I think I've put quite a lot into the partnership apart from the money I invested,' Jenny pointed out. 'I have helped you get on your feet.'

'Yes, OK and I'm grateful. I suppose I'll just have to try and find another *alteration hand*,' Erica said spitefully.

Jenny paused. 'Erica — look, I'm sorry but there's something else. I'm afraid I'm going to need my money back,' she said. 'I'm asking you to buy me out.' Seeing the shocked look on Erica's face, she added, 'There's no hurry. I can wait — for a while.'

Erica sat down heavily on the settee. Suddenly she saw her dreams of a prosperous future dissolving before her eyes. They'd started to do really well. This Christmas they'd gone into the black at the bank for the first time since they opened. She'd even thought of buying the shop next door when the lease ran out and extending — maybe even opening another branch some time in the future. If she had to pay Jenny back what she'd put into the business she'd be back where she started. *And all because of some bloody man!*

8

Christmas was more than usually busy at Gresham Terrace. The theatre was closed for the first three days of Christmas week for pantomime rehearsals and all Mary's time was taken up with ferrying 'Tommy the Cat' to and from the theatre. Vivien seemed to be in a permanent state of excitement and each night it was a struggle to get her calmed down and settled for sleep.

Christmas Day was meant to be quiet. Dora had made up her mind that the four of them would spend it happily together, enjoying each other's company as well as the festive fare she had been preparing for weeks. Sadly it didn't turn out to be quite what she'd planned.

The main problem was Erica. She was in a black mood. She had been bad-tempered for days and neither Dora nor Mary had the slightest idea why. When asked if she was all right she would snap back with a tart remark or simply remain silent. On Christmas Day she hardly touched her dinner and refused Dora's succulent pudding and mince pies; something quite unprecedented.

As the sisters washed up in the kitchen, leaving Dora playing with Vivien and her new toys, Mary made up her mind to end the deadlock.

'Look, Erica, just what is the matter with you?'

she demanded. 'You've been unbearable for days now, taking it out on the rest of us as though we've done something wrong. I think you owe us an explanation.'

Erica threw down the tea-towel she was using. 'Mind your own sodding business, can't you?' she snapped. 'I'm sick and tired of living here, all of us on top of each other. I can't call my life my own any more. Haven't you got enough problems of your own? Why don't you all go and jump off a bloody cliff!'

Shocked at the outburst, Mary turned and saw the angry tears in her sister's eyes and the way her lower lip was trembling. '*Erica*!' She quickly dried her hands. 'What is it? You're really upset. Come on, why don't you tell me? I'm sure you'll feel better if you do.'

The kind words were too much for Erica, who covered her face with her hands and burst into noisy sobs. 'What is it about me? First I'm left at the altar by that pig Bob and now my best friend is about to chuck me!'

'Chuck you? What do you mean?' Mary put her arms round her. 'Oh, don't cry, love. It can't be as bad as all that.'

'It *is*!' Erica swallowed hard. 'I'm going to lose the business.'

'Lose it! *Why*?'

'Because of *her* — Jenny. That great useless lump Geoff came looking for her and now she wants to go back to Nottingham and marry him after all.'

'But surely that's good news.'

'*Good* news, is it? Are you thick or something?

She needs her money back. It's going to leave me right up the creek.'

'Oh, I see. But that doesn't mean you'll lose the business, does it?' Mary asked. 'After all, you were managing before.'

'Only just. It was Jenny who introduced me to Grayson's and she was so good at altering all those seconds. It made a terrific difference to our profits.'

'You can still buy from Grayson's, can't you?'

'Yes, but I can't do what Jenny did. I've never been any good at sewing. My profits will take a nose-dive.' Erica took out a handkerchief and dabbed at her eyes. 'Look, no need to say anything to Mum. You know what she is; she'll start going on and on about it and I can do without that.'

'Of course I won't mention it if you don't want me to, but I do think you should have told us all this before. That's what families are for, sharing problems.'

Erica raised a cynical eyebrow. 'I don't remember you doing much problem sharing.'

'That's different. Look, suppose you . . .'

'See what I mean?' Erica snapped. 'Soon as you confide in people they start telling you what to do.'

'I was only trying to help.'

'Well, *don't*! I can do without it.' Erica blew her nose loudly. 'I'll deal with this my own way.'

'OK, whatever you say.'

'And for a start I'll be moving into the flat as soon as Jenny's moved out. It'll be good to have a room to myself again. I'll save a bit of money that way too.'

'Surely it would be better to let the flat and get rent for it.'

'Oh, what a *good idea*! Do you think I wouldn't do that if I could? I can't let it because the only way in and out is through the shop and I couldn't risk my stock.'

'No. I see. But couldn't you — '

'Oh *shut up*, can't you, Mary? You're just making things worse. Put your own life in order before you start telling me what to do.' Erica barged out of the kitchen, slamming the door behind her, and Mary heard her footsteps pounding up the stairs.

Dora had heard them too and when Mary went back into the living-room she raised an eyebrow. 'Where's Erica?'

'She's got a bit of a headache — gone to lie down.'

'Is she all right? She hasn't been herself for days.'

Mary shrugged. 'She's a bit off-colour but she'll be fine.'

Vivien looked up from the jigsaw she was doing on the floor. 'She's mad cos Jenny is going to get married,' she said.

Dora looked at Mary. 'Is that true?'

'I think so, but Erica's fine with it.'

'But won't it mean Jenny will have to go back to Nottingham? Erica will miss her. She's been such a wonderful help.'

'She'll miss her, yes, but she'll be OK,' Mary said. 'You know Erica, she always bounces back.'

Upstairs Erica lay on her bed, her eyes closed and her brain seething with frustration. Families! Who needed them? Always interfering and thinking they knew best when they hadn't got a clue! There had to be a way she could get through this and keep Erica's, even if she had to cut back on the things she'd been planning. If only she'd known Jenny was going to let her down she wouldn't have had the new window lighting system installed or ordered carpet for the shop. The present carpet was worn threadbare and covered in stains. It gave out all the wrong signals.

She sighed and sat up. If only she could stop it going round and round in her head. It was driving her mad. In an attempt to take her mind off it she reached out to the bedside table and picked up the latest copy of her favourite film magazine. Looking at the contents list on the first page, she saw that there was an interview with someone described as 'a promising newcomer to British films'. She turned to the centre pages, curious to see who it was.

The moment she turned the page her attention was riveted. Smiling up at her was a photograph of Paul Snow, or Paul Summers as he now called himself. One half of the centre-page spread was filled with photographs of him in his Mayfair apartment. Relaxing in his lounge; standing on his balcony overlooking Green Park with his hair tastefully tousled by the wind; selecting a suit from the wardrobe in his luxurious bedroom. Her lip curled. *Smug bastard!*

She began to read the article on the facing page, which made a point of mentioning his war record. *Anyone would think he was Field Marshal flaming Montgomery!*

It seemed he had signed up for two starring roles with Pinewood Studios in the coming months and his agent was presently negotiating terms for a leading part in a West End stage production. Asked if there was a romance in his life he hinted that there was someone special but he wasn't prepared to reveal her name, other than to say that she was also in show business. *He was married for God's sake! How dare he!*

He added that on the other hand he wasn't planning to marry for a very long time. *No, and we know why, don't we!*

Did he get many fan letters, asked the interviewer. Oh yes, a great many, especially after the latest film in which he appeared as the young father of a sick child. He'd replied to them all personally of course, but he'd had to stress that the role was pure acting. 'I haven't the first idea about parenting,' came his smiling reply. *You can bloody well say that again, chum!*

Irritated beyond measure, Erica threw the magazine at the bedroom wall. How did these people get away with it?

When she lay down again and closed her eyes, Paul's annoying smile refused to go away. She opened them again to stare up at the ceiling. Then out of her exasperation a daring and preposterous notion suddenly presented itself.

She chuckled to herself at its audaciousness, but when she thought the idea through it did not seem quite so outrageous after all. Why not? she asked herself. It was dog eat dog in the world of business — survival of the fittest, every man for himself. If you wanted to survive in the world today you had to be ruthless. And, after all, she reminded herself with a smile, it had worked before — hadn't it?

★　★　★

On Boxing Day Vivien wakened so excited that it was all Mary could do to make her sit down and eat her breakfast.

'You must calm down,' she told her. 'At this rate you'll be tired out before the curtain goes up.'

At six o'clock she took Vivien along to the theatre and helped her into her costume. Backstage at the Royal, the atmosphere was electric with excitement. It was so infectious that Mary felt quite nervy herself as she joined her mother and Erica in their front row seats just as the orchestra was filing into the pit.

The musicians tuned up and the conductor raised his baton. As they began to play, the curtain rose on the colourful opening scene. The show had begun.

Tommy the Cat quite stole the show with his antics and even came into the auditorium for a while during the interval to amuse the children. Dora was astonished.

'Look at her! I can't get over her. She's so

convincing,' she said. 'Those little kiddies obviously believe that she's a real cat. Look at them stroking her.'

At the final walk-down, the applause was enthusiastic. Theatre Royal pantomimes were renowned for their success and this one was clearly no exception. But the appearance right at the end of Dick and his bride Alice accompanied by Tommy, complete with white bow, almost brought the roof down. Dick bowed and kissed Alice's hand and Tommy turned several somersaults and sat up to wash his whiskers.

When they came out of the theatre it was raining and Mary insisted that Erica and her mother went home in a taxi. 'I'll go and collect Vivien,' she said. 'There's a party backstage but I'm not letting her stay long. She must be worn out.'

She waved them off and then went round to the stage door. Vivien was in a state of high excitement, dancing around the dressing-room in her cat costume minus the head.

'Did you hear them clapping me, Mummy? I was good, wasn't I? I made them laugh. Was I like a real cat? Did Grandma and Auntie Erica like it?'

'Yes. We all loved it. But the others were very good too. You weren't the only person in the show, you know.'

She unzipped the cat suit and peeled it off, hurriedly helping her daughter into her own clothes. 'I can go to the party, can't I?' Vivien asked.

'Just for a little while.'

'Will you stay too?'

'Of course.'

In the green room, the cast was assembled. Someone offered a tray of sherries and Mary took one, only just stopping Vivien from following suit. 'Orange squash for you, young lady,' she said.

David spotted them and made his way through the crush towards them. 'Congratulations, Vivien,' he said. 'The best little puss-cat in the business.'

Vivien rubbed her head against his arm and purred. He laughed. 'Still in character, I see.'

'She's not staying long,' Mary told him. 'I think she's had enough excitement for one day.'

'I don't blame you. Just tip me the wink when you're ready and I'll take you both home,' he said.

Later, as they drew up outside 27 Gresham Terrace, David touched her arm. 'Will you come and have a quiet drink with me at the Minsmore?' he asked.

She hesitated. 'It's late.'

'Not all that late. I'm sure your mother won't mind. You've been so busy over the past week what with work and Vivien's rehearsals, I've hardly seen you out of working hours. You deserve a break.'

Dora was delighted to hear that she was going out with David. 'Just you go and enjoy yourself,' she said. 'I'll give young Tommy here a saucer of milk and put him to bed, won't I, love?' She bundled a giggling Vivien up the stairs and turned to her daughter. 'Don't look so anxious.

I'll get her calmed down. Just go off and relax for once.'

The Minsmore Country Club was on the outskirts of Ferncliff. Mary settled back in the passenger seat of David's car, realizing for the first time how tired she was. As she stifled a yawn, he turned to her.

'Did you have a good Christmas?'

She sighed. 'Family Christmases are always a bit fraught, aren't they? Erica was upset. Her business partner is pulling out to get married and it threw her into a black mood.' She looked at him. 'What about you?'

'Spent the day with Dad. We had lunch at the Crown. Two lonely bachelors pulling crackers and pretending to be festive. A bit pathetic really.'

She laid a hand on his arm. 'I wish I'd known. You and your father could have come to us.'

He smiled at her. 'Maybe next year will be different.'

The club was quiet after the Christmas rush. They sat in the comfortable lounge by a roaring log fire and enjoyed turkey sandwiches and a bottle of Chardonnay. At midnight David looked at her. 'Come back to the flat with me for coffee?' When she hesitated he added quickly, 'It's just an idea. Say no if you'd rather not.' He smiled. 'We get so little time together, just the two of us, that I don't want to let you go just yet.'

Mary was quiet during the drive back to David's flat. She was tired after the whirl and excitement of the day and the wine had gone to her head a little, but it hadn't stopped her feeling a tenseness about David. Several times she'd caught him looking at her and felt that he was about to say something but when she met his eyes he'd looked away and changed the subject.

David lived in Chandos Court, a rather impersonal block not far from the theatre. He parked the car and they went up together in the lift. Inside, David left her while he went to put the kettle on. The flat was small but she was surprised at how attractive and tastefully decorated it was. Not at all like her idea of a bachelor flat. A large window looked out over the rooftops towards the seafront and she went to look at the view. The moonlit sea looked like rippling black silk and the promenade sparkled with its chains of coloured lights.

'It's so lovely to have the lights back again, isn't it?' she said as he came out of the kitchen. 'I still haven't quite got used to it.'

He didn't reply but took her in his arms and kissed her. 'I've been wanting to do that all evening,' he said with a sigh. 'Mary, look, I meant to lead up to this. I intended to make it a romantic occasion, but I'm not very good at that kind of thing and anyway, I can't wait any longer.' Reaching into his pocket he took out a tiny black leather box and opened it. Inside, a beautiful sapphire and diamond ring nestled against white velvet. She gasped, lost for words, and he went on, 'Will you marry me?' He continued hurriedly, 'I'm not trying to rush you into anything, Mary, but if you could just wear my ring — if we could be engaged, tell people.'

He looked into her eyes. 'I love you so much, darling, and I want everyone to know it. Please say yes.' He took the ring from its box and picked up her left hand, but she pulled it away, her throat tight and her heart beating fast.

'David — don't. I can't.' She turned away. 'I wish you hadn't done this.'

'But why? What's wrong? I'm not asking you to . . .'

'Stop! Please.' She turned to face him. 'David, sit down. There's something I have to tell you. I owe it to you. It's not fair to let this go on any longer.' She took his hand and drew him down on to the settee. 'David . . .' She swallowed hard. This was the hardest thing she had ever faced. 'David, I can't marry you or even be engaged to you because I'm still married to Paul Snow.'

He frowned at her. 'I know you must still *feel* that you are, but . . .'

'No, David, you don't understand. Paul is still alive. He wasn't killed as everyone thinks.'

'He wasn't? Then why . . . ?'

'When he came out of the army he wanted to take up his acting career again. He told me quite frankly that our marriage had been a mistake — that he didn't want me any more — didn't want *us*, Vivien and me. We were . . . in the way. That was the last time I saw him. Which was why I came home.'

He looked shocked. 'My God! That's awful. How could he? I'd have thought..' He stopped and looked at her. 'So why did you tell everyone he was dead?'

'I didn't. Not really. It was all a misunderstanding. When we first arrived Vivien told Mum that her daddy was dead. It seems she'd just assumed that's what I meant when I told her he wasn't coming home any more. I was tired and still in shock about the whole thing at the time so I just let it go at that. Somehow it was easier to let people believe it than to admit I'd been thrown aside like a piece of rubbish. I always meant to put it right, but the longer it went on, the more people who thought Paul was dead, the more difficult it became to confess.'

He stared at her for a moment, then got up and went to the window. 'Have you been in touch with him since?'

'No. He's made a success of his acting career — changed his name and been in one or two films.'

'I take it he knows where you are. I mean, he must be sending you money for Vivien.'

'No. When I left Yorkshire I didn't leave a forwarding address.'

'That was unwise if you don't mind my saying so. It must have been very convenient for him, though.' He got up and walked across to the window. 'I can't see that there's a problem,' he said at last. 'Just write to him and ask for a divorce.'

'It's not as simple as that. I told him at the time that I'd never consider divorce.'

'Why?'

She shrugged. 'I don't know. I was angry and upset at the time — didn't see why he should have it all his own way.'

'But you know that with him being in the public eye it's going to come out sooner or later, don't you? It would be a whole lot better for those close to you if the truth came from you.'

'I suppose so.'

He looked at her. 'Mary, do you love me? Really love me, I mean?'

She went to him and took his hand. 'Oh, David, of course I do. There's nothing I want more than to marry you. This lie I've been living — it's been like a great threatening cloud hanging over me. I've hated deceiving you more than anyone.'

'Well, now that you've told me why not grasp the nettle and get it over with once and for all?'

She was silent for a moment. 'I suppose I only need tell Mum. She's the only other person who matters.'

'I think you're forgetting someone else who matters even more.'

She sighed. 'Vivien, you mean. I know. I'd hoped to keep it from her for a while yet. It isn't easy to know that your own father doesn't want to know you.'

'You think it'll get easier?'

She looked at him. 'I think she'll deal with it better when she's older. But Mum — as you say, better to tell her before she finds out from someone else.'

'I agree. You're going to have to be brave.' He pulled her close. 'Darling, write to him and tell him you've met someone else and you've changed your mind about divorce. Put it all behind you and look forward to the future — our future.'

★ ★ ★

The Sunday after Christmas, Dora received an invitation to go and have tea with John Lorimer. He had tea ready for her when she arrived, laid out on a tea trolley in front of a blazing fire.

'Oh, John, how cosy,' she said as he steered her towards an armchair. 'What kind of Christmas did you have?'

'Very pleasant. Just David and me,' he told her, pouring two cups of tea and handing her a plate of sandwiches. 'I asked you round this afternoon because I have some news for you.' He saw her startled look and held up his hand. 'Nothing earth-shattering, mind, but news.'

Dora took a sandwich. 'Is it about . . . ?'

'Your tramp? Yes. I tried all the night shelters first. They told me that they know this man as Paddy Smith, but they weren't sure that it was his real name. At the Salvation Army shelter they told me they thought he was an ex-serviceman, so from there I went to the British Legion.'

'Oh, John, you've been to so much trouble.'

He shook his head. 'I told you it wouldn't be easy. The Legion were reluctant to give out any information until I told them I might have located family for him.'

Dora leaned forward in her chair. 'So they told you who he is?'

'Not exactly. It seems that this man was picked up by the British Liberation Force in Germany

150

just before the end of the war. They were of the opinion that he'd escaped from a German prison camp. He was in a bad way — obviously been living rough for a long time. He was close to starvation and suffering from bullet wounds, which made them think he was an escaped POW. He was shipped home and spent a very long time in hospital, eventually making a reasonable recovery. But who he was, his name or rank or background, was a complete blank to him.'

'Didn't he have any identification?' Dora asked. 'What do they call them — dog tags?'

'Apparently not. There was nothing to associate him with any of the services, although the feeling is that he probably belonged to one of them. And there were no enquiries about anyone fitting his description.' He shook his head. 'It's not an unusual story by all accounts. When he came out of hospital he apparently took to the road. It seems that's the way he prefers to live.'

'So we're none the wiser.'

'I'm afraid not.' John leaned across to refill her teacup, smiling kindly at her. 'Perhaps it's for the best, my dear.'

'Is he still here, in Ferncliff?' Dora asked.

John shook his head. 'No. The people at the Salvation Army night shelter said they hadn't seen him since the end of the summer.' He looked at her. 'You know there is a way you could find out for yourself'

She looked up. 'How?'

'It shouldn't be too difficult to trace your husband. If he's found, you'll know that 'Paddy' isn't him. You know, after all this time, divorcing

151

him would be a simple matter of desertion.'

'Not to Mike it wouldn't,' she said. 'He was brought up a strict Catholic and he told me dozens of times that he'd never ever let me go. If I tried to divorce him now he'd find out where I was too.'

John frowned. 'You're still afraid of him, after all these years?'

She sighed. 'Let's just say I don't consider it worth the risk.'

'And yet you were keen to know if this vagrant was your husband.'

'Because he looked so down on his luck — so pathetic.'

John smiled to himself. If he lived to be a hundred he'd never understand women. 'So what do you want to do now?' he asked.

'Maybe we'd better just forget about it, but thank you for all you've done, John,' Dora said.

'That's what I hoped you'd say.' He handed her a plate of cakes. 'Now to happier things. Let's talk about that young granddaughter of yours. I've got tickets for the panto for next Saturday, the final night. How about coming with me?'

★　★　★

In the first week of January the weather changed. The light fall of snow that had looked so pretty for New Year turned to slush under the icy rain that fell out of a grey sky.

Going back to school after the Christmas holidays did not go down well with Vivien. All the fun and excitement of being in the panto and the fuss all the grown-ups had made of her was over and the prospect of school routine seemed dull and boring. And if she was expecting an accolade from her schoolmates she was to be sadly disappointed. Katie Roberts, a bigger girl from the next class, approached her in the playground as soon as she arrived on the first morning of term and stood in front of her, hands on hips and eyes glittering with challenge.

'Suppose you think you're *it*, Vivien Snow, just because you were in the pantomime. Well, me and my mum thought you were awful.'

'I *wasn't*. I was very good,' Vivien insisted, her lower lip thrust out. 'Everyone said so. So *there*!'

'Well, we didn't think so. My mum goes to the pictures every week and she knows.'

'Well, Miss Sheppard said I was good and she's the *producer*. She should know better than your mum.'

Katie laughed. 'You looked daft in that silly cat outfit. You didn't even have anything to say anyway.'

'That's 'cos cats can't speak, *stupid*!'

'I'm not stupid — *you* are!' Katie grabbed a handful of Vivien's hair and pulled hard. 'You're the stupid one. Stupid *and* a dunce. You get all your sums wrong.'

'Ow! Let go! I don't get my sums wrong.'

'Yes you do. Your friend Vicky told me — so *there*! She says she hates you! No one likes you, Vivien Snow. No one wants to be *your* friend!'

When she'd reduced Vivien to tears, the other girl skipped off to rejoin a group of her friends who'd been watching. They all turned their backs and ran off to play, leaving Vivien quietly sniffling in a corner till the bell went.

At playtime she asked Vicky if it were true what Katie had said. The other little girl shook her head.

'I never said you got your sums wrong.'

'Why was she so horrid to me? Why doesn't she like me?' Vivien asked.

Vicky shuffled her feet. 'Well . . . I think it's because you show off.'

Vivien stared at her. 'I *don't!*'

'You do — a bit,' Vicky said.

Vivien's lip trembled. 'But you'll still be my friend, though, won't you?'

Vicky considered for a moment. 'If I do, Katie and her friends will be horrid to me too.'

At that moment Katie came over and took Vicky's arm. 'Come and play with us,' she invited, shooting Vivien a spiteful look. 'Don't have nothing to do with the *cat*. She smells.'

Vicky hesitated, biting her lip and looking from one to the other, torn between loyalty and a desire to be popular. Vivien felt her face turning red.

'Go on then!' she shouted at her friend. 'You go and play with them. I don't care!' To her dismay Vicky ran off with Katie, leaving her standing in a corner of the playground with a big lump in her throat and tears trickling down her cheeks.

The bullying went on all week. Every playtime Vivien was reduced to standing alone in the playground feeling abused and abandoned. She said nothing at home, feeling too ashamed and humiliated, but her behaviour became more and more difficult as the days went on. Things came to a head on Sunday evening when she continued to push her food round her plate in spite of being told repeatedly to eat it. Weighed down by her own worries, Mary finally lost her patience with her.

'Vivien! I won't tell you again. Grandma has made you a lovely supper. Now just eat it properly.'

'I told you. I don't want it.' Vivien pushed her plate so hard that it toppled over the edge of the table and landed on the floor. Mary sprang up in exasperation.

'You naughty girl! Now just go and get a cloth and clear up that mess.'

'No!'

'Do as you're told.'

'*Shan't.* I hate you! I hate everybody!' Vivien jumped down from her chair and ran out of the room, sobbing noisily. Mary ran to the door in time to see her daughter disappearing at the top of the stairs.

'*Vivien!* How dare you speak to me like that!' she shouted. 'Come down here this minute!' The bedroom door slammed shut and she was about to follow when Dora laid a restraining hand on her arm.

'Leave her.'

'If you ask me she's getting this from Erica,' Mary said. 'It's a good job she's moved out. If there's one thing I won't have, it's tantrums and spoilt behaviour. She's going to learn to behave properly if it's the last thing I do.'

Dora steered her back into the room. 'Come and finish your supper. Let her cool off a bit.'

'I think all this theatre is going to her head too,' Mary said as she sat down, her appetite quite gone. 'From now on it's going to be school only. I'll make sure of that.'

'I've an idea it's more than that,' Dora said. 'Let me deal with her. I'll go up in a little while and see if I can get to the bottom of it.'

Dora left Mary washing up and went upstairs. She tapped gently on the door and opened it to see Vivien lying on her bed.

'Can I come in?' she asked. Vivien didn't answer but turned over, her face to the wall. Dora sat down on the edge of the bed.

'What's wrong, pet?' she asked softly. 'That little girl who was so rude downstairs wasn't my little Vivien, so where do you think she's gone?'

After a pause Vivien rolled on to her back and turned huge tear-filled brown eyes on her grandmother. 'I *am* me, Grandma.'

'So, are you telling me you've changed into someone else? Because I don't much like the little girl you were just now downstairs.'

'S-sorry.' The tears welled up and began to trickle down her cheeks.

'Would a cuddle bring the other Vivien back, do you think?'

Vivien sat up and threw herself into her grandmother's arms, burying her face against the warmth of her jumper to sob out her frustration.

'There that's better. Now, suppose you tell me

156

what's really wrong?'

'Everyone h-hates me,' Vivien hiccupped. 'No one will play with me at school any more. Even Vicky won't speak to me: at least not while the others are there.'

'What others?'

'Katie Roberts and her friends. Katie said I was awful in the pantomime. She tells everyone not to play with me. She says I *smell*!'

'Have they hurt you?'

Vivien shook her head.

'So it's just words?' She felt Vivien's head nodding against her chest. 'Well, you know what they say — sticks and stones will break my bones but words can never hurt me.'

'But they *do*, Grandma. They do hurt. I *was* good in the pantomime, wasn't I?'

'Of course you were.'

'So why do they say I wasn't?'

'It doesn't matter what they say. You know you did your best and pleased a lot of people and that's all that matters. You had a nice time being in the panto, didn't you?'

'Yes.'

'Well, maybe this Katie and her friends wish they could have been in a pantomime too.' She kissed the top of her granddaughter's head. 'They're jealous, pet, that's all it is. But some day soon they'll get bored and everything will go back to normal again.'

'Will it?'

'Yes. I promise.' Dora took out her handkerchief and dried Vivien's tears. 'Now, I think your mummy was very hurt by what you said to

157

her, so how about coming down and telling her you didn't mean it?'

Vivien looked up, a small tremulous smile lifting the corners of her mouth. 'All right.'

Later, when Vivien was in bed and Mary and her mother sat together in the living-room, Mary said, 'This has made up my mind. No more taking part in any shows. It's not worth being bullied and losing her friends for. I'll cancel the dancing classes too.'

'Oh no!' Dora looked up from her knitting. 'Don't deprive her of something she enjoys so much. She's got a natural talent. Maybe we should be encouraging it. That reminds me, I saw something in the local paper.' She got up to find the paper, riffling through the pages until she found what she was looking for. 'Ah, here it is. This woman is starting a stage school, right here in Ferncliff. She's an ex-professional. Stage and radio, it says here. Look.' She passed the paper to Mary. 'Lena Masters. She's been in several West End shows and all sorts and her terms look quite reasonable.'

Mary read through the advertisement and looked up doubtfully at her mother. 'I don't know. I'm not at all sure that it would be good for Vivien.'

'Of course it would. And she'd love it.' Dora looked at her daughter. 'I know I've said this before but I think she gets her talent from her father. Don't you think he'd have wanted to encourage this flair of hers? It would be a kind of memorial to him.'

Mary's heart began to beat faster. This was the

158

ideal moment. If she didn't do it now, she never would.

'Mum.' She licked her dry lips. 'Look, Mum, there's something I have to tell you. I should have told you ages ago.'

Dora looked up. 'Oh dear, that sounds ominous.'

'It's . . . Paul. He didn't die in the war.'

Dora looked stunned. 'What are you saying, girl?'

'He's still alive — very much so. Making a name for himself in the films. But not my name, or Vivien's. He calls himself Paul Summers.'

'But I don't understand.' Dora shook her head. 'Why . . . ?' What . . . ?'

'He told me he didn't want us any more,' Mary told her. 'On his last leave before the end of the war. He wanted an acting career more than anything else, certainly more than he wanted us — his family.'

'And you accepted that?'

'What else could I do? What kind of a marriage would I have had if I'd tried to stop him?'

Dora shook her head. 'I've never heard of anything like it.' She frowned at Mary. 'And you told Vivien he was dead?'

'No! I told her he wasn't coming home any more and she somehow got the wrong idea. No one was more surprised than me when she came out with that, but at the time it gave me a breathing space. I was too ashamed to tell anyone the truth. But I'm really sorry for deceiving you all this time, Mum.'

'And you've kept it to yourself all this time.'

'I know and I'm sorry. But don't you see, Mum? If that's what a stage career and ambition does to people then I don't want Vivien to have anything to do with it.'

9

Jenny moved out of the flat and back to Nottingham two weeks after Christmas. She was willing to stay longer but Erica made it clear that she wanted the partnership to end as soon as possible. The wedding was planned for Easter and to Erica's annoyance Jenny spent most of her time making her wedding dress. Every time she went up to the flat she found yards of brocade draped over the chairs and stiffened tarlatan petticoats hanging from the picture rails. Jenny had even asked Erica to be a bridesmaid, something she had taken as adding insult to injury.

'I don't think so,' she'd told her friend stiffly. 'With having to run the shop *single-handed* I won't be able to take any time off — not for a very long time.'

Geoff came down to Ferncliff every spare moment he could find. Erica found his presence hard to tolerate.

'I felt like an intruder in my own shop,' she complained to Mary on the day she helped her move into the flat. 'Every time I came up here to the flat for anything, there they were, canoodling. Ugh! Disgusting! Made me feel sick. I can't stand the sight of that man. What she sees in him I can't imagine. I'm glad they're gone so that I can start again.'

Mary suspected that there was more than a

hint of jealousy in her sister's attitude. After the disappointment she had suffered it was understandable. 'Never mind,' she said. 'It'll be nice to have your own place and I'm sure you'll manage the shop fine on your own.'

Erica didn't contradict her but she wasn't at all convinced. She'd had to apply for a bank loan with a high rate of interest in order to pay Jenny her money back and this was the slack time of year. It was going to be a real struggle over the coming months to pay the loan back and she wasn't at all sure whether Erica's would be able to keep afloat. There would certainly be nothing left over for her.

At the back of her mind the idea still niggled. It wouldn't let her rest. Every night, when she was tossing restlessly, all her problems going round and round in her mind, it persistently intruded; the quiet little voice of temptation. When people were so devious, when they lied and cheated their way to success, why shouldn't they pay the price, the voice said. Thinking about it like that made it seem quite a sound, upright thing to do. Surely it was her duty as a woman to balance the scales, avenge her sister.

At last, one night she gave in. Getting out of bed, she went down to the room at the back of the shop and got out the typewriter she used for bills and invoices. After several attempts had been ripped out of the machine and tossed away, she came up with something that satisfied her. Taking it out of the typewriter she read it through.

Dear Mr Summers

I just had to write and tell you how much I enjoyed the article about you in last month's Movie Magic. I am already a fan of yours and have seen all your films so far, even those where you only had a small part. However, there were one or two things in the article that puzzled me.

You say you have no plans to marry — yet you do not mention that you already have a wife. You say you have no experience of parenting, and yet you have a young daughter. *I thought I might write to the magazine and tell them they have their facts wrong. Journalists are so sloppy these days, aren't they? I'm sure they'd be grateful to someone who pointed out these errors. They'd probably also be interested to know that you abandoned your wife and child at the end of the war in favour of your acting career.* That is so romantic, isn't it? *Also that you have never paid one single penny in maintenance for your child.*

I am sure that as an honest man with an outstanding war record you would want these truths out in the open, but if for some reason you do not perhaps we could come to some arrangement. Far be it from me to ruin anyone's career!

Write to me in confidence care of the General Post Office in Nottingham. And by the way, in case you are wondering, I

do not live there.
   Yours sincerely — a truth-seeker.

She smiled to herself. Reading that should wipe the smug smile off his silly face! Well, she'd written it and got it out of her system, she told herself. She didn't actually have to post it. How could she, anyway, when she didn't know his address? Folding the letter, she slipped it into an envelope and put it in her handbag where no one was likely to find it. Then she went back to bed.

★ ★ ★

On Monday morning at the office, Mary told David that she'd put her mother in the picture about Paul.

'How did she take it?' he asked.

'Like she takes most things — in her stride. It all came up because she was suggesting that we send Vivien to this drama school opening in Ferncliff.'

David looked puzzled. 'What did that have to do with it?'

'Mum thinks Vivien gets her talent from Paul. She was saying it would be what he would have wanted, a memorial even. That seemed a good opportunity to tell her the truth.'

'Well, at least you got it over with.'

'Yes. It's a relief.'

'So did you decide to send Vivien to drama school?'

Mary frowned. 'I'm still not happy about it. She's been bullied at school because of the pantomime. It's made her so unhappy.'

'That's just kids' stuff. It'll blow over.'

'I know, but is it all really worth it? But it's not only that. Paul's obsession with his acting career made him such a selfish person. I'd hate Vivien to turn into someone as egocentric and ruthless as him.'

'Maybe he would have been that way anyway. I have a feeling it was more about Paul's nature than the theatre. And remember that Vivien is half your daughter.'

'Maybe you're right.' She looked up at him. 'You think I should let her go to the drama school then, do you?'

'It's up to you, of course, but she certainly has talent. Why don't you go and see the woman who runs it before you make up your mind? Check out what kind of thing would be expected of Vivien and whether you think the pressure on her would be too much. Then, if you're happy, ask Vivien herself. She may not fancy the idea anyway.'

Mary smiled. 'Oh, I think she will.'

He reached across to touch her hand. 'And what about you — us? Now that you've told your mother about Paul, what's the next move?'

She had been dreading the question. 'I don't know.'

'Why not just send a friendly letter in the first instance?' he suggested. 'Find out how the land lies. Surely Paul won't put any obstacles in your way when he knows you want to end the marriage.'

'I suppose not.'

He looked at her. 'You do want to end the marriage, don't you, Mary?'

'Of course I do. It's just . . . ' She shook her head. 'I don't know — having to meet him again. Going to court and all that. Maybe he won't want the publicity.'

He took both her hands and made her meet his eyes. 'And that's all? No other reason?'

'No other reason, I promise. Anything I ever felt for Paul has been dead for a long time. I love *you*, David. I just wish it could all be over and done with.'

'So do I, but it has to be done before we can start a new life together.'

That night after her mother had gone to bed, Mary sat up, a writing pad on her knee, trying to compose the 'friendly letter' that David had suggested. But try as she would she could not find the right approach. Too friendly and it sounded as though she wanted him back. He might even think she wanted to cash in on his success. On the other hand, if she made it too formal it would sound threatening, as though she was thinking of taking him to court for maintenance; something her pride would never allow her to do. In the end she decided that the best approach would be to ask for a divorce outright. That way he could hardly miss the point. But even that she found difficult to phrase and in the end she put the pad away and went up to bed.

★   ★   ★

166

Winter seemed to last an eternity. Snow fell almost daily, collecting in deep drifts and making roads and pavements lethal. Vivien was enrolled at Stage Coach, Lena Masters' new drama school. She attended two afternoons a week, straight after school, and Saturday mornings. Mary found the fees hard to find out of her salary, but Vivien loved it so much that she considered it worth the sacrifice. The school was already in early preparation for a show, planned for early autumn. It was to be a showcase for the school. Vivien could talk of nothing else.

The letter Mary had finally written to Paul was still tucked away at the bottom of her underwear drawer. She could not find the courage to post it. She and David had taken to spending time together at his flat after the theatre closed on Saturday evenings. Sometimes she would cook them a meal, which they would eat on trays in front of the fire. It was the one time of the week when they were able to relax together, but David was growing impatient. Every time he asked if she had received a reply to her letter, Mary had hedged.

'You have *sent* him a letter, haven't you?' he asked one evening.

'I told you I'd written.'

'Written, yes, but did you ever actually send it?'

He'd hit the nail on the head and Mary got up to clear away their empty plates. 'We've just got to be patient,' she said, carrying the plates into the kitchen. She put them into the sink and began to run water on them. David followed her.

'Mary, that's not an answer.' He put his hands on her shoulders and turned her to face him. 'Tell me the truth. I think you owe me that much. Did you send the letter?'

She lowered her eyes. 'I'm sorry, David. I did write it, but somehow I just couldn't bring myself to post it.'

'Why not, for heaven's sake?' He ran a hand through his hair in exasperation. 'What's stopping you?'

'I don't know. I'm sorry, I just can't explain why.'

'It seems to me that there can only be one reason. You still love him.'

'No!'

'Well, you're certainly in no hurry to marry me, are you?'

'You know that's not true.'

'Do *I*!' He left her to walk to the window, staring out into the night. 'I think it's time you examined your true feelings, Mary,' he said, his back to her. 'I thought we had something special, you and I, but now I'm beginning to wonder if it's all on my side.'

She went to him and put her arms around him. 'Oh, David, of course it isn't. I do love you. I *really* do. It's just that it seems so — I don't know — demeaning, begging to be set free from a man who doesn't want me anyway.'

'Do you still *want* him to want you — is that it?'

'No!'

He held her at arm's length. 'Look, I've got an idea. Let's go away for a break together.'

She stared at him. 'Away? Where?'

'Anywhere. The theatre is closing for a week next month for redecoration. We could get right away, just the two of us. Anywhere you like — London, maybe. Even Paris or Rome if you fancy that. The choice is yours. What do you say?'

She shook her head. 'It's mad! I don't know if . . . '

He covered her mouth with his hand. 'No excuses. You know your mother would take good care of Vivien. She's free at the moment. The café doesn't open till May.' He drew her close. 'Mary, a few days alone together should make up your mind for you once and for all. So what do you say?'

She laid her head against his shoulder. 'Oh, it sounds lovely, David. If only we could.'

'Of course we can. What's to stop us?'

She smiled. 'Well, all right. Let's do it.'

★   ★   ★

In the end they chose London, checking into a smart hotel in Knightsbridge on the Monday afternoon. Dora had had reservations about the trip, pointing out unnecessarily to Mary that she was still married to Paul, but in the end she had grudgingly agreed that they deserved a break.

On their first evening they went to see *Oklahoma* at the Theatre Royal Drury Lane and later had dinner at a small intimate restaurant close to the theatre. When they got back to the hotel it was late. Mary was nervous. It was so

169

long since she'd shared her bed with a man. She'd only ever made love with one man — Paul. She felt inexperienced and naïve. She had no doubts about her love for David. They had so much in common — laughed at the same things and enjoyed being together. They were so comfortable together that sometimes they even seemed to read one another's thoughts. But now that they were taking things a step further she was so afraid of letting him down. Suppose she proved to be a disappointment? Would it ruin everything?

He had ordered champagne to be waiting in their room and as she took off her coat he lifted the bottle from its ice bucket and opened it with a loud pop, pouring two glasses and holding his own up in a toast.

'To us — our future.'

She echoed the toast and took a sip, wrinkling her nose as the bubbles tickled. She had never tasted champagne before and she wasn't sure that she liked its sharp, astringent feel on her tongue, but David was trying so hard to create a romantic atmosphere so she smiled and said, 'It's delicious,' feeling more than ever like a schoolgirl, gauche and unsophisticated. David put down his glass.

'Just for these few days there's no one else in the world but us,' he said. 'Just hang on to that thought.' He took her glass from her and drew her into his arms, looking down into her eyes in surprise. 'You're trembling.'

'I know. It's silly but I'm nervous.'

'Don't be.' He kissed her. 'I love you so much,

Mary,' he whispered against her hair. 'If you love me too then nothing can go wrong.'

'Thank you for this evening, darling. I enjoyed the show so much. I'll always remember it.'

He rubbed his cheek against hers. 'I hope there will be something more memorable for us than the show.'

* * *

When she opened her eyes next morning she could not at first remember where she was, then she turned her head on the pillow and saw David, still sleeping beside her, and her heart contracted. He had been so sweet, so gentle, that her nervousness and inhibitions were quickly forgotten. With kisses and caresses he had aroused her to heights she had never experienced before. She remembered crying out his name at the peak of her passion and falling gently asleep in his arms feeling safe, warm and utterly loved. It was as he had said; loving each other as they did, nothing could possibly have been wrong between them, and now they belonged together like two halves of the same whole.

As though sensing her eyes on him, he wakened and she saw the sweet recognition slowly dawn in his eyes. 'Good morning, darling.' He reached up a hand to cup her face. 'Tell me I'm not still dreaming.'

'Well, if you are then so am I.'

'Did you sleep well?'

'Better than I have for a long time.'

He laughed. 'Me too.' He stretched out his

arms and then pulled her down to nestle against his shoulder with a sigh of contentment. 'Isn't it wonderful? We have three more whole days and nights.' He twisted his head to look down at her. 'We won't waste a minute of them, will we?'

★ ★ ★

Erica's spring visit to Grayson's Fashions was the first she had made alone. Her January sale had gone well, mainly because she had let a lot of her unsold stock go at knock-down prices. However, it did mean that she now had money for new stock. Grayson's spring designs were lovely. She looked at the prices and did some hasty sums on the little pad she always carried with her. Without the cheap seconds to subsidise her, she would need to buy more than she had budgeted for if she were to have a good choice for her customers. The shop rent was overdue and she'd had a phone call just a few days ago to say that the new carpet was ready for delivery. She looked through the rails again, trying to pare down her order to the minimum.

She was making her choices when Mr Gerald Grayson, the senior of the two brothers who owned the firm, noticed her and came across.

'Good morning. Jenny not with you today?'

Erica shook her head. 'Jenny and I have parted company. She was married at Easter so I'm on my own now.'

'That's a shame. It must be hard for you, managing on your own.'

'It is. Oh, but don't worry,' she added hastily,

'I won't keep you waiting for your money.'

He laughed. 'I'm not worried. You are one of our best payers.' He looked thoughtful. 'As a matter of fact I've been hoping you'd come in. There's something I'd like to discuss with you. Will you come through to the office?'

Gerald's office was tiny, not much more than a cupboard. A desk filled up most of the space and there were bales of cloth, swatches and catalogues piled up all around it. 'Have a seat.' He pulled out a chair.

When she was seated opposite him, he opened a drawer and took out a sketch pad, passing it across the desk to her. 'Take a look at these.'

As Erica flipped over the pages her eyes opened wider. On each page was a rough sketch of a dress or coat. Wide, calf-length skirts flared out from tiny nipped-in waists. There were stand-up collars, flared peplums that sprang out from the waist to make it look even smaller, coats with stand-up velvet collars and wide sleeves ending in turned-back velvet cuffs. The whole concept was completely fresh and different and she looked up at Gerald with shining eyes.

'These are smashing,' she said. 'The style is the complete opposite to what everyone has been wearing. Women will go mad for it. Where did you get them?'

Gerald took the pad from her. 'I was over in Paris recently with our designer, snooping around to see what I could ferret out. This is the theme of Christian Dior's new collection. He's calling it the New Look.' He winked and tapped

173

the side of his nose. 'Don't ask me how I got it.'

'It's certainly a new look all right.'

'This is what's known as industrial espionage,' he went on. 'So it's all very hush-hush. They could sue me for everything I own and more if it got out. It's practically a hanging offence. But I know I can trust you.' He looked at her, one eyebrow raised.

'Of course. I won't breathe a word.'

'We'll get permission to reproduce once the launch is over, but I want Grayson's to be first in the field. Our designer has been busy and our own versions are already in production, using only our most discreet and trusted staff. Naturally there's no question of releasing them until after Dior's launch in June.'

'Naturally.' She was beginning to wonder where this was leading.

'The thing is, Erica, would you be interested in taking a few samples to try out?'

Her heart leapt. '*Would* I!'

'I'm only offering this to a few valued customers. The only condition is that if they go well you would have to guarantee us a good order.'

Her heart sank. 'What kind of good?'

'A grand's worth — minimum.'

Erica caught her breath. *A thousand pounds' worth!* 'I'm pretty strapped for cash at the moment, Gerald,' she said. 'I had to pay Jenny back what she put into the business. I need to replace the carpet in the shop, the rent is overdue and . . . '

He held up his hand. 'No need to go on. I

know what it's like to run a business. But this is an opportunity you can't really afford to miss. Maybe you could get a loan.' Erica was silent, thinking of the bank loan she had already taken out and the frightening amount of interest it would accrue if she failed to pay it back on time.

'Look,' Gerald said, 'let me send you the samples. You can pay me when you've sold them, and I guarantee your customers will be wanting more.'

'I'm sure they will, but . . . '

'Erica, my dear, if you never take any chances in this business you're dead in the water before you start,' he told her. 'Just think, you'd be one of the first provincial shops in the entire country to offer Dior's New Look.'

The thought was too seductive to resist. Erica closed her mind to all the ruinous things that could happen and made up her mind on the spot. 'OK, Gerald, I'll do it.'

'Fantastic! The samples will be summer frocks, of course. I'll get them sent off to you the minute CD's launch is off the stocks. Later there'll be autumn suits; winter coats with lush velvet trims; jersey dresses. And the evening-wear . . . ' He kissed his fingertips. 'Out of this world! Need I go on?'

★　★　★

Erica sat in the station buffet waiting for the train back to Ferncliff and thought about what she'd done. She took out her bank statement and looked at the balance, unable to see how she could possibly part with a thousand pounds by June, even with the samples Gerald had promised her. But how could she let a chance like this pass her by?

As she tucked the bank statement back in her handbag she saw the envelope containing the letter she had written to Paul lying at the bottom. Should she? Her heart quickened at the thought. She could address it to him at Pinewood Studios — and post it here in Nottingham as she had intended. Who could ever possibly find out?

★　★　★

Dora could see the change in Mary the moment she came home from London. She waited to be told what was going on but when no explanation was forthcoming she decided to speak her mind.

'It's not right, you know,' she said one evening as they washed up together after the evening meal. Mary looked up.

'What's not right?'

'I think you know what I'm talking about,' Dora said. 'When you went away together, you and David, you went as man and wife. I'm right, aren't I?' she challenged.

Mary put down her tea-towel. 'In a way. We love each other, Mum. David has asked me to marry him.'

'Knowing full well that you're already a married woman?' Dora looked scandalized. 'I don't know. I don't, really! Since the war, proper moral behaviour seems to have flown out of the window.'

'I'm asking Paul for a divorce,' Mary told her. 'I've written him a letter. I posted it this morning.'

Dora looked a little placated. 'Well, I'm glad to hear it. Though why you couldn't have waited till you were free before starting up with someone else, I don't know.' She tipped away the washing up water and turned to her daughter. 'And when are you going to tell Vivien, may I ask? It's downright wicked to let that child go on believing her father is dead.'

'I'll tell her soon, I promise. Can't you be pleased for me, Mum? Life hasn't been easy for me all this time. Don't I deserve a little happiness?'

'It's been hard, I grant you,' Dora said. 'But no harder than for a good many others. And we don't all get what we deserve either.'

* * *

The following afternoon, after Mary picked Vivien up from school, she turned the corner of Gresham Terrace to see a strange car parked outside number 27. When they reached the front door she turned to Vivien.

'It looks as though Grandma's got visitors. You'd better go upstairs and wash your face and hands.'

The little girl ran upstairs and Mary opened the living-room door. A man was standing with his back to her and her heart gave a lurch. She knew who it was even before he turned to look at her.

'Hello, Mary.'

'*Paul!*'

He looked well, but different. The suit he wore was well cut and looked expensive, and the weight he'd put on suited him. His hair was longer than he used to wear it and his skin was tinged with a healthy tan that had clearly not been acquired in England.

Dora came through from the kitchen carrying a tray of tea. 'I think you two need to talk,' she said. 'I'll go upstairs. Give me a call when you want me to bring Vivien down,' she added meaningfully. She put down the tray and walked out of the room, shooting Mary a look as she closed the door behind her.

'This is a surprise,' Mary said. 'Do you want some of this tea?'

'What I want is an explanation,' he said.

'About what?'

'About the letter you sent me.'

'Wasn't it self-explanatory?'

'On the contrary, it was ambiguous to the point of obscurity. I can only gather that you want money.'

Mary frowned. 'All I want is a divorce — as I said in the letter.'

'You said you wanted to 'come to an arrangement',' he said. 'And what's all this about replying to the post office in Nottingham? What on earth are you playing at, Mary?'

'I haven't the slightest idea what you're talking

about,' she said. 'I didn't write anything like that. In fact, I only posted my letter to you this morning so you can't even have had it yet.'

He took an envelope out of the inside pocket of his jacket and handed it to her. 'Are you saying you didn't write this?'

She read the letter through and looked at him, her colour rising. 'I certainly did not. How could you imagine that I would write to you anonymously?' she asked. 'It's rubbish, anyway. It sounds like some demented teenage fan.'

'A demented teenage fan who knows I have a wife and child? Who else apart from your family knows?'

'Plenty of people in Yorkshire know you are married. And there are your army friends. Any number of people could have written that, so why accuse me?' She frowned. 'Anyway, how did you know where to find me? I didn't leave a forwarding address.'

'I guessed you'd come back to Ferncliff.'

'And yet you never wrote or tried to get in touch.'

He ignored the question. 'I expect you want some maintenance money for Vivien.' He began to take his wallet from his pocket. 'I admit it was wrong of me not to attend to things properly before. But it can soon be put right.'

Mary held up her hand. 'When you do get my letter you'll see that I ask you for nothing except a divorce.'

'That might be difficult.'

'Why?'

'At this stage of my career I don't really need

179

that kind of publicity. It wouldn't be popular with the studio.'

'I see. So once again your career comes first? What I want doesn't matter. I've met someone else, Paul. I want to remarry and I need a divorce. Surely legal proceedings would be in your real name. No one need know.' She looked at him. 'What made you change your name anyway? Was it so that no one could possibly associate us with you?'

'No. I wanted to make a fresh start. Summers after Snow seemed somehow appropriate.'

'Thank you.'

He shrugged. 'It wouldn't be possible to keep it secret anyway, name change or not. Somehow the press always finds out.' In the stunned silence that followed he said, 'While I'm here I'd like to see Vivien.'

'You'd *what?*' She could feel her heart thudding at his effrontery. 'You come here accusing me of writing you anonymous letters and telling me you can't agree to a divorce because it might harm your public image. And then you calmly ask to see the daughter you haven't the slightest interest in.'

'I never said I wasn't interested in her.'

'For all you knew she and I could have been starving in the gutter.'

He smiled patronizingly. 'Oh, come on, Mary. Don't be melodramatic. I am still Vivien's father remember. I do have certain rights.'

'I'm not so sure about that. Anyway, it's difficult.'

'What do you mean, difficult?'

'When I told Vivien that you weren't coming home again she assumed you'd been killed.'

His eyes widened. 'And you let her believe it? Is that what you're trying to tell me — that she thinks I'm dead?'

'As you made it clear that we wouldn't be seeing you again I thought it best. Would you rather I'd explained that she and I were in the way of your career so you'd dumped us?'

'There are ways of explaining things to a child.'

'Then maybe you should have explained them to her and not left it to me.'

He crossed to the mantelpiece where there was a photograph of Vivien in the butterfly costume she had worn in the previous year's pantomime. 'Is this her?' he asked, picking it up. 'Your mother was telling me how talented she is.'

'Oh, was she?'

He smiled. 'This must be from the pantomime she was in.'

'Yes. Last year's.'

'She's pretty.' He put the photograph back and turned to her. 'You're not really going to refuse to let me see her, are you?'

She knew she had no choice; her mother had made that clear too. Going to the door she opened it and called up the stairs. 'Mum! Will you tell Vivien to come down now, please.'

A moment later Vivien stood in the doorway looking at the man standing by the fireplace. Mary noticed with irritation that Dora had changed her into her best dress. 'Grandma says you're my daddy,' she said. 'I thought you were dead.'

'Well, I'm happy to say that I'm not.' Paul sat down in the armchair and held out his arms. 'Come here and let me look at you. You were a very little girl when I last saw you. Now you're a big girl.'

Vivien smiled and went slowly towards him. 'I'm in the junior class at school now and I'm learning to be an actor-ess. I've been in two pantomimes and I go to Miss Masters' drama classes — and dancing.'

Paul glanced up at Mary. 'That must be expensive.'

'We manage,' she said.

Paul gently drew Vivien on to his knee. 'Did you know that Daddy is an actor in the films?'

'Are you?' Vivien looked at him with shining eyes.

'You'll have to ask Mummy to take you to see my next film,' he said. 'It's called *Haywood Moor*.'

'Are you coming to live with us?' Vivien asked.

Paul shook his head. 'No. I'm afraid that's not possible. But you and I will have to see each other now that I'm back again, eh? One of these days I'll take you to look round the film studios. You'd like that, wouldn't you?'

'Oh, yes, *please*! When?'

'We'll see. Now, will you run upstairs again to Grandma while Mummy and I have a little talk?'

'You will come again soon, won't you?' Vivien asked, sliding reluctantly off his knee.

'Or you can come and visit me in London.'

Vivien clapped her hands. 'Soon?'

'Yes, soon. I promise.'

When she had gone Mary looked at him reprovingly. 'You shouldn't have made promises you have no intention of keeping.'

'But I do intend to keep them,' he said. 'Vivien is a lovely child. She's a credit to you.'

'Thank you.' She didn't add, *No thanks to you*, but her expression said it all.

'She's obviously interested in a stage career,' Paul went on. 'I'd like to pay her drama and dancing class fees.'

'There's no need.'

He sighed. 'Mary, don't be difficult. Obviously you must be finding it hard to make ends meet.'

'You've never lost any sleep over that before!'

He ignored the barbed remark. 'I'll send you regular maintenance money for her from now on, now that I know where you are.'

'I've told you, Paul, there's nothing I want from you except a divorce. Surely there must be a way to keep things out of the papers?'

'I don't know. I'll have to see.' He frowned. 'That isn't my priority at the moment.' He pulled the letter out of his pocket again. 'The mystery of this letter remains. Clearly you didn't write it so who did?' He put the envelope on the mantelpiece. 'I'll leave you to dispose of it. On the whole I think the best thing is to ignore it.'

Mary shrugged. 'It's your problem, Paul. As I told you, nothing to do with me.'

Vivien chattered excitedly about Paul all through supper, so thrilled about the daddy who had returned magically from the dead and turned out to be a film actor. It was like a fairy tale come true. As Mary was tucking her into bed she looked up at her accusingly.

'Why did you tell me my daddy was dead?' she asked.

'I didn't. It was only what you thought.'

'So why didn't you tell me it wasn't true?'

'He said he wasn't coming back any more, Vivien. You were a very little girl at the time. It was hard to explain it to you.'

Vivien looked into her eyes. 'Don't you love Daddy?'

Mary sighed. 'Darling, grown-up people sometimes change. They stop loving one another and then they can't stay together any more. Daddy was away for a long time during the war. It changed him — made him stop wanting to be with us.'

Vivien frowned. 'But he came back today so that must mean he's changed again, mustn't it?'

'I don't know.'

'Perhaps he'll ask us to go and live with him in London,' Vivien said, her eyes dancing. 'Wouldn't that be lovely?'

Mary took both her hands and held them tightly. 'Vivien, listen, darling. Daddy won't ask us to go and live with him. It's not going to happen.'

Vivien's lip trembled. 'He *will*! He might. You don't know, you just said. You told me he was dead and that wasn't true. I want to go and live with my daddy!'

'Just go to sleep now,' Mary said wearily. 'We'll talk about it some other time.' But she knew in her heart that Vivien wasn't going to let it go as easily as that.

That night Mary dreamed about David. They were walking along the cliffs with Vivien skipping beside them. He turned to her, taking her in his arms to kiss her, but when she opened her eyes it was Paul's face that looked mockingly down at her.

He laughed. 'How could you imagine you could keep my daughter from me?' he shouted. Then suddenly he pushed her towards the cliff's edge. The last thing she saw as she fell was Paul walking away with Vivien. They were both laughing.

She wakened with a start, her skin clammy and her heart thudding. She had a bad feeling about today's visit. Whoever had written that anonymous letter to Paul had set something in motion; something she had an ominous feeling that she would be powerless to stop.

10

The letter arrived ten days after Paul's visit. Mary recognized the writing as soon as she saw the letter lying on the mat. Picking it up, she quickly slipped it into her pocket to read later in private. Until she knew its contents she didn't want her mother to question her about it. She didn't get the chance to read it until she came home for lunch. Dora had gone to the beach café and she had the house to herself. In the kitchen she slit open the envelope and found the letter written in Paul's own handwriting on a single sheet of paper.

Dear Mary

As I am between jobs at the moment this would be an ideal opportunity to have Vivien here for a visit. I would like to have her for the weekend but I am sure you will consider this too long for her first visit. Would you agree to a day? I realize that she is too young to travel alone so you will have to come with her, but I'm sure you will appreciate that I would very much like to have some time alone, to get to know her after all this time. If you are in agreement with this perhaps you could telephone me on the number above.

Since we last met I have received the

letter you sent me and I would like to take this opportunity of apologizing for the misunderstanding.

Looking forward to hearing from you
Yours truly, Paul

Yours truly indeed! She flung the letter down in disgust. He expected her to take Vivien up to London and then get herself lost for the rest of the day! What a cheek! In her opinion he had forfeited all his parental rights when he had walked out on them both. She stood thinking for a moment, then picked up the letter again and put it in her handbag, deciding to say nothing until she had thought it through.

After Vivien was in bed that evening she showed the letter to her mother.

'I can't think why he's taking this sudden interest,' she said. 'I can't help feeling that he's just doing it to spite me.'

Dora looked up. 'Well, you can hardly blame him if he is,' she said. 'Letting the child think her father was dead.'

'Mum! He walked out on us, abandoned us without a single qualm and apparently forgot all about us until now.' Mary sighed. 'Anyway, I've explained about that,' she said. 'I never meant Vivien to think he was dead. It just happened. The point is, what do you think I should do?'

'I think you should take her,' Dora said. 'As you say, Paul has neglected you both but maybe he wants to try and make it up to you.'

'He's not proposing to make anything up to *me*,' Mary reminded her. 'He won't even give me

187

a divorce so that I can marry again. I'm only the courier. I'm expected to take Vivien to him in London and then get lost for the rest of the day.'

'Yes, well I admit that's a bit much, but you have to think of Vivien. After all, he is her father and she's so excited to have found him again.' Dora thought for a moment. 'I could always come with you if you like,' she said. 'I take it you'd go on a Sunday?'

Mary shrugged. 'I don't know. I expect Paul will have all the say over that too. Whenever it is it won't be very convenient.'

★ ★ ★

Mary told David about the forthcoming visit next morning. She had already told him about Paul's unexpected visit. So far he had been evasive about it, keeping his opinion to himself. But when Mary told him he had asked her to take Vivien up to London to see him, he was clearly disturbed.

'I don't understand the sudden interest,' he said.

'Well, to be fair I left Yorkshire without leaving a forwarding address.'

'He soon worked out where to find you when he thought you'd written him a threatening letter.'

'I expect he was busy getting his career started,' she said.

'Why are you defending him, Mary?'

'I'm not! I told him, all I want is a divorce.'

'And he refused. Now he's suddenly taken up

the role of father again. Are you going to agree to it?'

'I don't see that I can refuse.'

'And all because of this damned anonymous letter. Have you any idea who sent it?'

'Of course not.' She shook her head. 'Anyway, that's the least of my worries at the moment.'

'Well, you'd better ring him as he says,' David advised. 'Use the office phone in the lunch hour.'

'I'll try to get him to agree to a Sunday.'

'Right, but if that doesn't suit him we'll arrange cover for you so don't worry about it.'

Mary nodded. She was wondering how she and her mother would while away the hours with no shops open on Sunday. Maybe they could visit an art gallery or cinema.

In her lunch hour, she telephoned the number Paul had given her.

'Hello — Paul Summers.'

'Paul, it's Mary. I got your letter. I'll bring Vivien for the day. Have you any particular day in mind?'

'I thought perhaps this coming Saturday.'

'She has her dancing class on Saturday,' Mary said. 'It's a working day for me too.'

'Surely you could get time off just this once,' Paul said. 'And I'm sure missing one dancing class isn't going to be catastrophic for Vivien.'

She sighed. 'I suppose not, though it really isn't very convenient. I'll have to check if I can get the day off. Saturday is our busiest day here at the theatre.'

'I suppose you could always put her on the train in charge of the guard,' he suggested. 'I'd be there to meet her at the other end.'

Mary bristled. 'She's a child, not a parcel! I'm sorry, Paul, but I wouldn't dream of it. Anything could happen to her. And let's face it, you haven't exactly proved reliable in the past, have you? How do I know you wouldn't forget all about her?'

'I suppose I deserved that,' he said. There was a pause and then he said, 'So — do you think you can manage it?'

'It doesn't look as though I have much choice in the matter, does it?' she said. 'Mum was going to come with me if it had been a Sunday, but now it looks as though I'll have to come alone.'

'I'll get you a ticket for a matinée,' he said. 'And I'll arrange lunch for you somewhere nice.'

'Don't put yourself out on my account.'

'Mary, I'm trying to be as reasonable as I can.'

'Yes. I suppose you are.'

'I've looked up the trains. There's one that gets in to Waterloo at 10.15. It leaves Ferncliff at nine o'clock. Would that be all right for you?'

'It will have to be, won't it?'

'I'll meet you at the station.'

'I'm sure Vivien will look forward to it. Goodbye, Paul.'

She told David when he came back from lunch. He shrugged. 'Well, at least the office is closed on Saturdays and I'm sure Jessie and Rose will cope in the bar for once.'

She looked at him. He hadn't said much but the tightness around his mouth spoke volumes about what he was thinking. 'This isn't easy for me, David,' she said. 'But I didn't really feel I could refuse. Paul is Vivien's father, after all.'

He didn't return her look. 'It's none of my business, Mary. You must do as you think best.'

'David.' She went to him. 'Please don't be like this. It isn't at all what I want. You must realize that, but if I antagonize Paul he might never agree to the divorce.' She put her hands on his shoulders. 'Nothing can change the way I feel about you. You know that, don't you?'

'Do I? I'm not so sure.' He took both her hands and held them tightly, his eyes troubled as they looked into hers. 'You know what I'm afraid of, don't you? Seeing him again — being with him is going to be a testing time for you.'

She shook her head. 'If you think I have any feelings left for Paul . . . '

'You might think you haven't, but you were married a long time, Mary. You have a child together. I can't help wondering if his interest in Vivien is simply a way back into your heart, especially as he's refusing to consider a divorce.'

'You're wrong,' Mary told him. 'We hardly had any married life at all. We weren't much more than kids when we married and he was away for so much of the war. When it was over, after all he'd come through, he'd changed. I suppose we both had. We were like strangers. All that romantic puppy love had gone.'

'And now he's changed again. He's a film actor with all the glamour that goes with it.'

'Do you really think I'm as shallow as that?'

He kissed her lightly. 'No. It's me. I'm just so afraid of losing you, Mary. The thought tears me apart.' He sighed. 'Of course Paul has the right to see his daughter. I daresay she's excited at the thought too.'

'She doesn't know about it yet.' Mary smiled. 'A visit to London will be a big adventure for her let alone anything else.'

She was right. When she picked Vivien up at the school gates that afternoon and told her that they were to go to London on Saturday, the little girl's face lit up.

'To see my daddy, you mean? Like he said. Will he take me to the film studios?'

'I don't know what he has planned for you. You'll have to wait and see.'

'Are you coming too?' Vivien's face was slightly anxious as she looked up at her mother.

Mary shook her head. 'As far as London, on the train. Daddy wants to have you to himself for the day.'

Vivien was quiet as she digested this. 'I won't be able to go to dancing,' she said.

'I'll ring and explain,' Mary told her. 'One Saturday won't matter.'

'Wait till I tell Vicky. How long will it take to get there? What shall I wear?' Vivien skipped ahead. 'Can I have a new dress?'

★ ★ ★

Erica hadn't been home for several weeks. Not since her visit to Grayson's, in fact. Disappointingly, she had received no reply to her letter to Paul and her sales had not picked up sufficiently to risk an order of the size Gerald Grayson had specified. Things were looking

192

decidedly black for Erica's.

The day before, Gerald had rung to ask if she still wanted the samples he had offered and she had decided that there was nothing for it but to lay her cards on the table.

'Look, Gerald, to tell you the truth I couldn't guarantee you the kind of order you mentioned,' she said. 'Since Jenny asked me to buy her out I've had a real struggle making ends meet and I don't want to get into debt over my head.'

He paused. 'Look, Erica, how about this? I'll send you an advertisement for your local press and you put it in at your own expense then I'll send you the samples on sale or return,' he suggested. 'See how the line goes with your customers and we'll talk about an order after that. If they don't sell, no problem, you can send them back and all you'll have lost will be the advertisement money.' He chuckled. 'Except that it won't happen. Yes, I've got that much faith in this new line.'

Erica's heart leapt. 'Gerald, are you sure?'

'Told you, I've got enough faith in this to risk a little gamble,' he told her. 'And I hate to see a valued customer going through a bad patch. So, what do you say? The samples will be ready in about a fortnight. Do I send them?'

'Well, that would be marvellous!' Erica said. 'It'll be just in time for the summer season.'

'Right then, it's a deal. 'Bye, Erica, and good luck!'

She put the telephone down with a lighter heart. She'd been feeling quite despondent lately. Panicking in the long, sleepless hours of the night, she had toyed with the idea of cutting her losses and putting the business up for sale. This could be a lifeline — just the chance she needed. Her only regret was sending that letter to Paul. His silence was ominous. What had he done with it? Did he show it to the police? Suppose they were able to trace it to her?

She looked up as the shop doorbell rang and was surprised to see her sister walking in. 'Mary! This is a surprise.'

'It must be. I wonder you still recognize me,' Mary said dryly. 'Mum was only saying yesterday that we'd have to pay you a visit if we wanted to see you.'

'I've had a few problems,' Erica admitted. 'Business hasn't been too good. But it looks as if everything's going to get better after all.'

'Oh, how's that?'

Erica gave a mischievous grin. 'Can't tell you at the moment, but just you wait and see. Erica's is about to hit the big time!'

'I'm glad to hear it.' Mary held up a paper bag. 'I've brought some sandwiches. I thought we could share our lunch hour. I've got some news.'

'That sounds exciting. Come through to the back,' Erica said. 'I can hear the shop bell from there.'

As she put the kettle on and took plates from the cupboard Erica chattered about the shop, complaining for the hundredth time about Jenny and how she had practically wrecked the business.

'But as I said, things may be about to start

194

looking up,' she said as she seated herself opposite her sister. She raised an eyebrow. 'So — what's this news of yours?'

'I had a visit from Paul.'

'From Paul!' Erica paused, a sandwich halfway to her mouth. 'What did he want?'

'He'd had an anonymous letter. Someone threatened to tell the public at large that he was married with a child. He thought it came from me.'

'*You?*' Erica swallowed hard.

'I know. I was so insulted. How could he even imagine I'd do a despicable thing like that?'

Erica took a deep breath. 'I suppose it's one of the problems of being famous. There must always be jealous people who want to bring you down.'

'As it happened I had written to him,' Mary went on. 'To ask him for a divorce. David has asked me to marry him.'

'Oh! Congratulations.'

'So when he started talking about a letter I thought at first he meant the one I'd sent. Anyhow, to cut a long story short, he met Vivien and they got along like a house on fire. Now he wants me to take her up to London next Saturday to see him. He's even talking of having her up there for the weekend.'

Erica gave a rueful smile. 'And the divorce?'

Mary sighed. 'He refuses — says his studio wouldn't like it.'

'Any mention of all the money he owes you?'

'I told him, I don't want money, just a divorce.'

'Huh! More fool you. He must be earning a fortune now he's in the films.'

'I don't care about that. I'm just hoping that by letting him have access to Vivien I can change his mind.'

Erica averted her eyes, very carefully selecting a sandwich 'So — did he find out who sent this anonymous letter?' she asked casually.

'No. He said he was going to ignore it. He gave it to me and asked me to dispose of it.' Mary looked at her sister. 'You can't pay heed to every lunatic who tries to blackmail you, can you?'

'No, of course not.' Erica paused, chewing a mouthful of sandwich. 'So, did you? Dispose of it, I mean?'

'No. I found it fascinating, to tell you the truth. I've never seen an anonymous letter before.'

'Oh. So where is it now? Have you got it with you?'

'No, it's in my dressing table at home. I suppose I should throw it away really, but you never know.'

Erica coloured slightly. 'What do you mean, you never know?'

'Oh, I'm not sure. It's typewritten but something about it might strike a chord; a word or a phrase. After all, it must have been written by someone who knows us.'

'I'd throw it out if I were you,' Erica said. 'It's not healthy, having a thing like that hanging around.'

Mary laughed. 'Not like you to be superstitious.'

'I'm not. It's just — I don't know — morbid.'

Mary shrugged and looked at her watch. 'I'd better go. I promised Mum I'd have a go at the ironing before I fetch Vivien from school. She asked me to invite you for Sunday dinner, by the way. Will you come?'

'Yes, I'd like that.'

Mary stood up and brushed the crumbs from her skirt. 'Good. No doubt Vivien will be itching to tell you all about her day in London.'

★ ★ ★

Vivien could hardly contain herself on the journey to London, asking Mary every few minutes if they were nearly there. Much to her disappointment the new dress she had begged for had not materialized. She was wearing her best dress and her school blazer along with the new white sandals her grandmother had bought her as consolation.

True to his word Paul was waiting for them at Waterloo station. He stood at the barrier looking handsome in grey slacks and a blazer, a navy and red cravat tucked into the neck of his white shirt. He greeted them with a smile.

'It's good to see you.' The greeting was clearly for Vivien and Mary stood to one side.

'Would you like me to leave now?' she asked. 'Shall we meet here at six o'clock? There's a train for Ferncliff at a quarter past.'

Paul frowned. 'No need for that. Come back to the flat for coffee first.'

'I'd rather not if you don't mind,' Mary told him.

'Oh, well in that case . . . ' He took out his wallet and handed her an envelope. 'There's a ticket in there for the new show at the Adelphi,' he said. 'It's a revue. I hope you enjoy it. There's also a reservation for lunch at Luigi's. It's a little Italian restaurant not far from the theatre. I have an account there. Just charge it to me.'

'I think I can run to my own lunch, but thanks anyway.' Mary took the envelope and put it in her handbag.

'Right then. See you back here at six.'

Mary watched as Vivien tucked her hand trustingly into Paul's and walked away from her without a backward glance, chatting animatedly to her father as though they had never been apart. Her heart twisted inside her. Whoever had written Paul that anonymous letter had something to answer for. Little could they have known what they were setting in motion.

Perversely, she had decided not to use the theatre ticket or the restaurant reservation, determined not to be beholden to Paul for anything. But after she had wandered round the Oxford Street shops for two hours, her feet were aching and six o'clock seemed a long way off. She took the Underground to Covent Garden and wandered down to the Strand just to see where the restaurant was. Outside Luigi's an appetizing aroma of Italian food wafted out every time the door opened and finally she gave in and went inside.

As she ate at her solitary table, she thought

longingly of the weekend she and David had spent in London. They had been so happy. At the time she'd had no inkling of what was round the corner for her. She only hoped that allowing Paul to see Vivien would change his mind about the divorce. If it did then it would all have been worthwhile. If David could see her now, eating alone and counting the hours until she could collect Vivien and go home, he would realize that he had nothing to worry about. She was the last person Paul wanted to spend time with.

She sat through the revue, without much interest. The humour seemed banal and the music dull and tuneless. When she came out of the theatre it was still only five o'clock. She went into a café and drank tea she had no thirst for, then caught the Tube for Waterloo, grateful that the day was almost over.

She saw Vivien waving to her from the other side of the concourse. She was wearing a different coat and carried a massive teddy bear.

'Look what I've got, Mummy! Daddy bought him for me. I'm going to call him Bruno. And I've got a new coat and a new dress, look.' She undid two buttons of the impractical cream coat to reveal a pale blue dress with an intricately smocked bodice. 'We got them all at Harrups,' she concluded.

Paul was smiling. 'Harrods, actually,' he corrected, holding up the familiar olive green bag. 'Her old clothes are in here.'

Mary bridled. *Old clothes*, indeed. She took the bag from him, resisting the temptation to snatch it. 'Harrods is rather out of our everyday reach,' she said. 'But we do try not let our clothes get too *old.*'

His smile was maddeningly calm. 'You know perfectly well what I meant. Look, the train isn't in yet, what about a cup of tea?'

'I've already had one, thanks.'

'Well, let me reimburse you for the train fare.'

'That won't be necessary.'

Paul bent and pressed some coins into Vivien's hand. 'Look, why don't you run across to that kiosk and buy a comic to read on the train?' As she ran off he turned to Mary. 'Look, we have to talk. I've been thinking about your request for a divorce and I have a suggestion to make.'

'I see.' She tried hard not to let him see how pleased and hopeful she was.

'If you don't mind me saying so, this obstructive attitude of yours doesn't help.'

'I'm sorry.'

'I understand that you feel resentful, but I think we should try to put the past behind us for Vivien's sake. Can we meet?'

'I suppose so. When and where? I can't promise to keep coming up to London like this.'

'I could drive down to Ferncliff if you like. A week tomorrow — Sunday?'

'That would be better.'

'Best if Vivien doesn't know about it for now. I'll meet you in the town centre, outside the town hall, and we'll drive out and have lunch somewhere. Can you manage that?'

'I think so.'

Vivien came running up with her comic and at that moment their train steamed in. Standing on tiptoe, she reached up her arms to kiss her father.

'Bye-bye, Daddy, and thank you for all the lovely things you bought me.'

He hugged her. 'That's all right, darling. See you again soon. Be good.' He looked at Mary over the child's head and mouthed the word *Sunday*. She nodded and took Vivien's hand, hurrying her along the platform.

Vivien chattered all the way back to Ferncliff about her day with Paul. It appeared that they had not gone shopping to Harrods alone. Paul's new girlfriend had accompanied them. It seemed her name was Serena and she had helped Vivien choose her new clothes.

'She's an actor-ess like I'm going to be,' Vivien said. 'She's ever so pretty. She was in a film with Daddy but she didn't have to speak.' She frowned, searching for the right words. 'It was a walk-on part, but next time she'll have words — *lines* to say as well. She's got lovely blonde hair, all short and curly.' Vivien held a lock of her own hair out to look at it. 'I wish I had blonde hair like Serena's.' She looked at Mary. 'We went back to Daddy's flat after and Serena made us tea and we had cakes and ice cream. It was lovely.' She leaned against Mary's side, hugging the gigantic bear closer. Her eyelids were beginning to droop. 'Wouldn't it be lovely if we could go and live in London?'

Mary watched as the big brown eyes began to close. 'Yes,' she muttered. 'Lovely.'

★ ★ ★

Erica arrived at half past eleven the following day, sniffing appreciatively in the hall as she took off her coat. 'Yum! Mum's roast beef. Has she made an apple pie for afters?'

Mary nodded. 'No expense spared for the prodigal daughter.'

'Oh, come on, it's not that long since I was home,' Erica said.

'Anyway, it's not Mum's apple pie and roast beef. It's mine,' Mary pointed out. 'If you remember Mum has to be at the beach café Sundays as well as in the week. She's coming home for lunch especially but she'll have to go back.'

Erica grinned mischievously. 'Better and better. So I'm the prodigal sister!'

Mary laughed in spite of herself. 'You're incorrigible, Erica Flynn.'

'Ah, but you love me just the same.' Erica opened her bag and produced a bottle of sherry. 'Especially when I bring the booze. Come on, get the glasses.'

Vivien came running down the stairs. 'Auntie Erica! I haven't seen you for ages. I've got a lot to tell you. I went to London yesterday to see my daddy.'

Erica hugged her niece and gave her sister a meaningful look over the child's head. 'Did you now? Well, I shall want to hear all about that.'

In the kitchen Mary poured two glasses of sherry for herself and Erica and a fizzy lemonade for Vivien.

'We went on the train,' Vivien began. 'And Daddy met us at the station. We went to his flat first . . . ' The words tumbled over each other as Vivien unfolded the story of her exciting day. When she had finished, Erica laughed.

'Well, *what* an adventure! Aren't you a lucky girl?'

'I wanted to wear my new dress today, but Mummy wouldn't let me.' Vivien pouted.

'No? Well, wouldn't do to get it dirty just for Auntie Erica, eh? Suppose you go and get it to show me?' Erica suggested.

When Vivien had put down her lemonade and gone upstairs to fetch the dress, Erica raised an eyebrow at her sister. 'Well, well, he's obviously wasted no time worming his way into her affection,' she said. 'How do you feel about that?'

Mary was stirring the gravy. 'Just as long as I get the divorce it'll be worth it.'

'Not if it means she's going to get discontented with her life here with you!'

Mary turned to look at her sister. 'That won't happen. Vivien and I are very close. She adores Mum too. Then there's school and her dancing classes — all her friends.'

Erica tossed back the last of her sherry and reached for the bottle. 'Kids are mercenary little devils,' she said. 'I wouldn't mind betting that if he wanted to woo her away from you he wouldn't find it too hard.'

'That's rubbish,' Mary said dismissively. 'Look, Mum will be back any minute. Not a word to her about what you've just said. I don't want to worry her unnecessarily.'

Erica shrugged. 'Just as you say.'

The meal was a success and the little family

sat round the table together for the first time in many weeks. Vivien still couldn't help bringing up her visit to London at every opportunity and Erica couldn't resist hinting at the prospect of a change in her fortunes, whilst maintaining an air of mystery.

'All I'm prepared to say at the moment is that it's a new line,' she said. 'Super new designs. You'll see soon enough.'

'You're looking thinner,' Dora said. 'Are you eating properly? I hope you're not cutting down on food.'

Erica laughed. 'Mum! Of course I eat properly, and if I'm thinner that's fine by me. Going to need a tiny waist for these new fashions.'

Dora shook her head. 'I don't know,' she said. 'You modern girls!'

After lunch Vivien asked if they could walk back to the beach café with Dora.

'A walk would be nice after that lunch and it's a lovely day,' Mary said, looking at her sister. 'What do you say?'

Erica shook her head. 'I don't think I could move,' she announced. 'Tell you what, you three go and I'll wash up. Afterwards I might get a deckchair out and sit in the back yard — get some sun. I've nowhere to sit out at the flat. It'll be a treat.'

Mary and her mother went off with Vivien skipping ahead of them. Once again Dora expressed her concern for Erica's thinness.

'She looks worn out,' she said. 'I just hope this new business thing she's pinned so much hope on works out. She's put everything she's got into that shop.'

Mary said nothing, wondering to herself if her sister was plotting something devious yet again.

Vivien stopped suddenly and came skipping back to them. 'I haven't got my skipping rope,' she said. 'Can I go back and get it?'

Mary frowned. 'Not now. You can play skipping when we get home.'

Vivien pouted. 'I want it now. I want to show Grandma how I can do the bumps. Vicky showed me. I can go and get it on my own and catch you up.'

Mary sighed. 'No, you'd have to cross the road. I'll go. You go on with Grandma and I'll pick you up at the café.'

'Come on, let Mummy get it for you,' Dora said. 'I might find you an ice cream cornet when we get to the café.'

'Oh, all right then.' Vivien slipped her hand into Dora's and they went off together.

The front door had been left on the latch and Mary let herself in and went straight upstairs to get the skipping rope from the toy box on the landing. Her own bedroom door was open and to her surprise she saw that Erica was inside. She had her back to Mary, obviously unaware that she had come in. She was sitting at the dressing table and seemed to be searching for something in one of the drawers.

'Erica! What are you doing?'

The other girl spun round. 'Oh my *God*! You scared the living daylights out of me,' she said. 'Fancy creeping up on people like that!'

'I came back for Vivien's skipping rope.' Mary walked into the room and looked down at the jumble of underwear that Erica had created. 'What are you doing in here anyway?'

Erica coloured. 'I — I was looking for a clean handkerchief,' she said. 'I came out without one.'

Mary pointed to the hankies, once in a neat pile at one side of the drawer but now strewn about. 'A particular one that you wanted, was it?' she asked pointedly.

Erica hurriedly began to straighten the mess. 'No. Oh, there they are. I didn't notice them.'

Suddenly a suspicion began to form in Mary's mind. She opened her mouth to say something then changed her mind.

'Shall we go down then?' she asked, pushing the drawer shut.

Erica stood up and turned away. 'Yes, all right.'

Mary handed her a clean handkerchief. 'Here, you're forgetting what you came for.'

Shamefaced, Erica took the hanky and went out on to the landing. When she had started to descend the stairs, Mary quickly opened one of the small drawers that flanked the dressing-table mirror and took out an envelope. Tucking it into her pocket, she closed the bedroom door and followed her sister downstairs.

★　★　★

When David heard about Vivien's day in London he said nothing, but when Mary told him that Paul was driving down to Ferncliff to meet her next Sunday he looked upset.

'It's clear to me that he wants you back, Mary.'

'No! It's to talk about the divorce. He said so. He's had second thoughts.'

But he shook his head. 'I wonder.' He looked at her. 'We've spent hardly any time together lately, Mary. Since all this started you've been — I don't know — distant.'

'No! Preoccupied perhaps but not distant.' She went to him. 'David, it's a worry to me. I want it all sorted out and settled. If you only knew how much I missed you when I was in London last week.' She reached up and put her arms around his neck. 'I couldn't stop thinking about our weekend there and how happy we were.' She looked into his eyes. 'Why can't you believe me when I say I love you?'

His arms went round her and held her close. 'I want so much to believe that everything will be all right,' he said. 'It's just that I have this ominous feeling.' He looked down at her. 'Will you do something for me?'

'Of course. Anything.'

'Will you wear the ring I bought you?'

She hesitated. 'I'll wear it — but on the other hand.'

'No.' He turned away. 'That won't do.'

'It's an engagement ring,' he insisted, 'not a wedding ring. It symbolizes a promise. A commitment. Won't you even give me that much?'

'Of course I'm committed and I've already promised to marry you as soon as I'm free,' she told him. 'I don't need to wear a ring to prove that to you, do I? Can't you see, David, keeping on the right side of Paul is the only way to get what we want.'

He sighed. 'I only hope you're right, but it really couldn't have come at a worse time.'

'Why?'

He took her hands. 'Mary, I may have to go away for a few days soon.'

'Go away? Where?'

'On a theatre management course. Thorne Theatres have made a bid for the Royal and it has been accepted. You know the owner is elderly and so is the board of directors. It'll be a real shot in the arm for the theatre, and for Ferncliff itself. 'But they'll want me to retrain.'

'I see.' Mary could see that it was a good business deal, but all she could think of at that moment was Vivien and how to hang on to her. Now, just when she needed David's support, he was going to be preoccupied with this take-over.

★　★　★

When she arrived at the town hall the following Sunday, Paul was there, waiting in his car.

'Good morning.' He leaned across and opened the passenger door for her and she climbed in.

'Hello. I hope I'm not late.'

'Not at all.'

Mary had taken trouble over her appearance this morning. She wore her favourite blue cotton dress, crisply starched and pressed, and a new pair of white sandals with a matching bag. The day was warm and sunny and Paul had the car's soft top down. As they drove, the breeze caught her hair, lifting it away from her face and whisking the colour into her cheeks. He turned to look at her.

'You're looking very nice.'

'Thank you.'

'I thought we'd find somewhere quiet for lunch. Do you have any preferences?'

She shook her head. 'I can't afford to eat out very often so I wouldn't know.' She looked at him. 'Perhaps a country pub?'

'We'll drive until we see a likely place, shall we?'

They found a quiet pub with a restaurant sign outside about ten miles inland and Paul pulled over on to the forecourt. Inside it was dim and quiet. A pleasant woman showed them through to the restaurant and handed them a menu, recommending the Sunday roast, which they duly ordered. When she had withdrawn, he looked at her.

'I suppose we may as well get straight to the point,' he said.

Mary's heart began to beat faster. 'The divorce?'

'First things first.' He paused. 'Vivien is a delight,' he said. 'I enjoyed her company last week more than I could ever have imagined.' He smiled wryly. 'I couldn't believe what I'd been missing. She was so entertaining and so talented. She danced for us and sang one of the songs from this show the drama class is putting on. She's so bright and obviously gifted. She's worth encouraging.'

'We do encourage her,' Mary told him.

'Of course you do. You've done a wonderful job of bringing her up.' He reached across the table to touch her hand. 'The thing is, Mary, I could do so much more for her.'

She could feel her stomach tightening with apprehension. 'I told you, Paul. I don't want your money.'

'And I'm not offering it to you. If Vivien lived in London she could attend one of the excellent children's drama schools. Later she could go to RADA.'

'But she doesn't live in London. And I have no intention of moving.'

Paul sighed. 'Mary, you're not getting it. What I'm suggesting is that you let her come and live with me.'

She stared at him. 'You're joking!'

'Far from it.' He shook his head. 'In return I'm happy to allow you to go ahead with divorce proceedings as long as we keep the whole thing under wraps.'

She was speechless for a moment, hardly able to believe her ears. 'You're asking me to choose between my child and my future?' she said at last.

'It's for Vivien's benefit,' he said. 'Surely you can see that. You want her to have the best, don't you? Well I think I can provide it.' He paused, trying to assess her frame of mind. 'And what's more,' he added, pressing his point home, 'if you were to ask her I think she'd jump at the chance.'

11

It was at that moment that their food was served. Mary looked down at her plate and her stomach churned with nausea. She knew she would not be able to swallow a mouthful. What Paul was suggesting was preposterous. How could he expect her to give up her child? Surely even David would not allow her to make such a sacrifice. She put a forkful of beef into her mouth and tried in vain to chew it. Paul was tucking into his with obvious enjoyment. He looked up at her.

'What's wrong — beef tough? Mine is excellent.'

She put down her knife and fork, her cheeks burning. 'How do you expect me to eat after the bombshell you've just dropped on me? How can you be so insensitive, Paul?'

'I'm sorry you see offering our daughter the best education I can as insensitive.'

'Anyway, how would you care for a little girl — a man alone in a London flat? Who would look after her while you worked?'

'Serena,' he said calmly. 'She lives in the flat below mine. She and Vivien got along like a house on fire last week. She adores children and she's more than willing to help.'

'But she's an actress. She'll be working too, won't she?'

Paul smiled. 'Serena's a lovely girl but she's no

211

Sybil Thorndike. I'm prepared to bet that she'd give it up tomorrow for the chance of a family.'

'Her *own* family perhaps,' Mary said. 'But you and she aren't even married.'

'An adjustment I hope to make once our divorce is through.'

Inside Mary was seething. 'An *adjustment*? Does she see herself as an adjustment, Paul? A means to an end?'

'Perhaps she's not as uncompromising as you, Mary,' he said. 'She's in love with me and she's willing to accept my daughter as her own.'

'And when she has a child of her own? Or when one or the other of you gets bored with the arrangement?'

'That won't happen.' Paul ate the last of his food and pushed his plate away with a sigh of satisfaction. 'That was delicious.' He looked across at her barely touched plate. 'If you're not going to eat that what about some dessert? I seem to remember there was sherry trifle on the menu.'

She didn't reply, but got up from the table. 'I'll see you in the car park,' she said.

In the ladies' cloakroom she locked herself into one of the cubicles and gave way to the tears of frustration and despair that she had been fighting back. It was a total disaster, but she would not let Paul see that he had upset her. He would see it as a sign of victory. There had to be an answer to this. But what? And where did she go to find it?

When she went out to the car park, he was waiting for her in the car, drumming his fingers impatiently on the steering wheel. As she climbed in beside him he glanced at her. 'Are you all right?'

'Of course.' She looked at him. 'You're not going to get away with this, Paul. You think you can walk out, abandon us, even saying you don't care, then walk back into our lives two years later and demand to have custody of a daughter you hardly know? Well, it's not going to happen. I'll apply for a divorce on the grounds of desertion.'

'You'll need to wait three more years yet for that to be grounds,' he told her.

'All right then, adultery. I wonder how this Serena of yours would like being named as the co-respondent.'

Paul's face darkened. 'Don't bring Serena into this.'

'You're not leaving me much choice, are you? Then there are all the years I've struggled without a penny from you. How would a judge view that?'

'Positively when I show that I'm willing to make up for it a thousandfold by giving our daughter the best education and the best life I can. Any judge worth his salt would throw your plea out. After all, what can you offer her?'

'A mother's love. Vivien and I are very close. Anyway, mothers always get preference when it comes to custody.'

'Not when I can prove your adultery.'

She stared at him, the breath stopping in her throat. '*What*? What are you talking about?'

'You and this David Lorimer. Vivien told me that you and *Uncle* David had spent a weekend in London together. She even told me that you went to see *Oklahoma* and that you stayed at the Royal Talbot Hotel. I've already obtained proof that you shared the same room.'

Mary's heart was thudding with fury. 'You pumped a seven-year-old child for information like that?'

'I didn't have to. She's very forthcoming, our daughter.'

'You're *despicable*, Paul!'

He smiled. 'So it's true. Listen, Mary, this can be as easy or as difficult as you like. The choice is yours. But one way or another I'm going to get custody of Vivien. I can afford the best lawyers there are. So you might as well get used to the idea.'

They drove on in silence for the next few miles, Mary's head spinning as she tried to think of a way out of this nightmare dilemma. Finally she turned to him.

'I could always go to the press,' she said. 'How would your adoring public feel about a man who abandoned his wife and child and then came back after two years' silence to steal the child from her mother? Doesn't sound very romantic, does it?'

He drove on, his eyes on the road ahead. 'Do you really want your name — and more important, Vivien's — dragged through the mud like that?' He shot her a triumphant glance. 'I warn you, Mary, if you as much as breathe a word about me to the press you can say goodbye to a divorce. I'll make sure you're never free to marry anyone.'

Back in Ferncliff he dropped Mary off at the town hall where he had picked her up. She got out of the car without a word and began to walk away. He leaned out and called to her,

'I'll wait to hear from you then, Mary. You've got the number. And don't leave it too long, will you?'

Vivien was spending the day with Erica and Mary made her way slowly through the streets to the shop, feeling as though she had been to hell and back. As she rang the bell she hurriedly composed a fictional description of her day out.

Erica came through the shop and raised the door blind to let her in. 'Vivien's upstairs with her colouring book,' she said, drawing Mary into the little back room. 'I've just been doing some paperwork and typing some letters to save time tomorrow. How did you get on?'

Mary shook her head. 'It was a disaster. I'll tell you later. You haven't said anything to Vivien about me meeting Paul?'

'No, of course not.'

'Is she all right?'

'She's fine. We've been on the beach most of the day. Took a packed lunch. She loved it. She's getting to be a really good little swimmer.'

'Good.' Mary looked vaguely at the half-typed letter still in the typewriter. 'Your ribbon needs replacing,' she said.

'I know. I'll buy a new one tomorrow. It's a job I tend to put off. It makes such a mess of my fingers.'

Upstairs in the flat Vivien was full of her day at the beach and luckily didn't ask too many

215

questions about her mother's day. Erica invited them both to stay for tea, but Mary refused, saying that she was going to prepare supper for Dora's return from the café.

As they walked home to Gresham Terrace, Vivien chattered happily about the beach and how far she could swim. Mary looked down at her daughter and wondered despairingly how much longer she would have to enjoy her company.

When Vivien had gone to bed, Mary busied herself in the kitchen preparing supper. Dora arrived home tired and pleased that the meal was ready and the table laid. As they ate Mary told her mother what Paul had suggested. As she had expected, Dora was outraged.

'We can't let it happen,' she said. 'Surely he'd never get custody of the child after all this time?'

Mary shook her head. 'He seems to have thought it all out very carefully,' she said. 'He even thinks he can prove my adultery.'

Dora's mouth dropped open in astonishment. 'How on earth can he do that?'

'When Vivien was with him last week she let slip that David and I had spent a weekend in London. She even remembered the name of the show we saw and the hotel where we stayed.'

'That child has ears like a bat!' Dora said. 'Who would have thought she'd remember details like that?' She shook her head at Mary. 'Didn't I tell you at the time that no good would come out of it?'

'How could we have imagined this kind of trouble, though?'

'So what are you going to do? What will you tell David?'

'I haven't the vaguest idea,' Mary said wearily. 'I'm exhausted just thinking about it. All I want to do is have a long hot bath and go to bed.'

She lay in the bath until the water was almost cold, her eyes closed and her head still spinning with all that had happened. She couldn't risk David being named as co-respondent and she couldn't prove Paul's adultery with Serena. Paul was right when he assumed that she wouldn't relish having her name and Vivien's blazoned all over the pages of the gutter press. The only way to get a quiet divorce was to agree to let Vivien go. Would she want to go to live with Paul in London? No one could make her go if she didn't want to — could they? Would the prospect of life in London, visits to the film studios and an education at a top children's drama school be too tempting for her? Was she a selfish mother to want to deny her all these things? The questions chased through her mind until she was dizzy. She raised her eyes to the ceiling. If only she could find all the answers written there for her to read. *Read!* Suddenly she remembered the anonymous letter, still burning a hole in the pocket of the floral dirndl skirt she had worn on the day she had found Erica in her bedroom. She must have read it a hundred times, trying to see some clue as to its sender. Now something clicked into place. This afternoon, at Erica's — the half-written letter in her typewriter. The fact that the ribbon was worn wasn't the only thing she had noticed.

It could be the fault of the fading ribbon or the fact that the machine was old and worn, but something about that letter had stirred something deeply buried in her subconscious. She had read the anonymous letter so many times that she almost knew it by heart. *I thought I might write to the magazine and tell them they have their facts wrong.* Why did that particular line have such significance?

She got out of the bath and dried herself hurriedly, then she went into her room and took the dirndl skirt from the wardrobe. The crumpled letter was still in the pocket. She smoothed the notepaper out and looked at it. There were eight h's in the sentence. All of them had their tops missing just like the h's in the half-finished letter. Not only that but the type was so pale that it looked grey. *My God — Erica!*

★ ★ ★

Dora opened up the café as usual at half past nine, putting the Wall's ice-cream advertisement board and the day's menu outside. She glanced across the promenade. Yes, he was there again, just as he had been since the day they first opened for the summer season, leaning against the side of one of the glass-covered shelters. He was still unshaven and wore the same tattered army greatcoat and down-at-heel shoes. Not for the first time she found herself wondering if the shelter was where he had spent the night. He looked up and caught her eye.

'Top o' the mornin' to you, missus,' he called,

waving a grimy hand. 'Would you be after sparin' a bite to eat for an auld feller?'

It was the same every day. She held up her hand and went inside to make the usual doorstep bacon butty. She added a generous dollop of brown sauce then, folding it into a paper napkin, she handed it to Vera, one of the new waitresses. 'Take this across to the tramp,' she said, trying not to meet the look of reproach in the woman's eyes. 'I know I shouldn't encourage him but he looks so pathetic. He'll go when he's eaten it.'

'He wants to try doing an honest day's work if you ask me,' Vera said. 'Still, you're the boss.'

Dora watched from the window as Vera crossed the promenade and gave the man the sandwich. She saw him touch his forehead in salute. He looked up towards the window where he knew she would be watching and his lips framed the words, 'God bless you, missus.' It was what he always said. Dora swallowed hard as she watched Vera turn away with a disapproving shrug and make her way back to the café.

★　★　★

'I'll ask you again — did you write this letter to Paul?' Mary waved the letter under her sister's nose. She'd made a special trip round to the shop at closing time after dropping off Vivien at her drama class.

'Whatever makes you think that?' Erica tried to look innocent.

'Because it was definitely typed on your machine. Look — a faded ribbon and a damaged

H. Bit of a coincidence, don't you think?'

'It could have been any machine,' Erica said. 'Why blame me?'

'Because it's just the kind of devious thing you would do. Look, don't keep lying about it, Erica. Everything points to your guilt. You needed money. You've got a hate thing about men — especially successful men. And this was written on your typewriter. I even caught you looking through my underwear drawer for it, no doubt hoping to destroy it! If I took it to the police, they'd have ways of proving it.'

Erica blanched. 'The police! That's a bit drastic, isn't it? Anyway he ignored it, you said so. You also said he must get hundreds of letters like that.'

'No, *you* said that!' Mary threw the letter on to the floor. 'And all the time you knew it was you. Do you have any idea of the trouble you've stirred up? Do you realize that I'm about to lose Vivien over this?'

'Lose Vivien! What do you mean?' Erica took a step back. She'd never seen her normally placid sister incandescent with rage.

'He wants custody of her. He's making it a condition of the divorce. I'm going to lose my daughter, and it's all your fault. If you hadn't written that stupid letter none of this would have happened.'

Erica watched helplessly as her sister burst into a torrent of tears. The sight made her stomach quake. 'Surely it won't come to that,' she said. 'He's bluffing.'

'No, he *isn't*. He can afford the best lawyers in

London to plead his case. I won't have a leg to stand on. And if I don't agree he'll divorce me, naming poor David, and get custody of Vivien anyway.'

'How can he do that?'

'Because he knows David and I spent a weekend together in London.'

Erica shrugged. 'Well, you wanted a divorce, didn't you? There's always a price to pay. And he'd have to give you access to her.'

'Access? Don't you understand? I'm about to lose Vivien! My child. The one person who means everything in the world to me! *Oh, how could you!*' Beside herself with anger, Mary lashed out at her sister, striking her a resounding slap across the cheek. Shocked, Erica staggered back against the wall, her hand to her face. The sisters stared at each other for a moment, then Erica burst into tears.

'Oh God, Mary, I'm really sorry. I never meant any of this to happen. I was so worried about the business. You wouldn't ask him for any money and there he was swanning around, rolling in it, showing off and getting away with everything scot-free. I just thought it would serve him right.'

Mary was in tears now too. She reached out her hand to touch her sister's reddening cheek. 'I shouldn't have hit you. I'm sorry, it's just that I'm at my wits' end and when I found out it was you that wrote that anonymous letter — my own sister . . . '

'I know. I know. I'd have felt the same.' Erica took out her handkerchief and dabbed at

Mary's face. 'Don't cry, love. Look, I think we both need a cuppa. Let me put the kettle on and we'll think what to do,' she said. 'Two heads are better than one, as they say.' The corners of her mouth lifted in a rueful grin, the old Erica surfacing again. 'Even if they're only sheep's heads!'

They sat opposite each other at the table, sipping their tea. 'I got up and wrote the letter one night when I couldn't sleep,' Erica explained. 'It was just to get things off my chest. I really never meant to post it. Then, the next time I went up to Grayson's, Gerald Grayson told me about this exciting new fashion that's coming out. He said I could be one of the first shops in the country to stock it. The trouble was that he wanted me to guarantee a thousand quid order.' She looked at Mary. 'It was like my big chance was there — just out of reach. On the way home I found the letter in my bag.'

'And you posted it,' Mary finished for her.

Erica nodded. 'Much good it did me anyway. I still can't afford that order.'

'Much good it did any of us.' They sat silently for a moment then Erica asked, 'What does David think about it?'

Mary sighed. 'He doesn't know yet. He's away on a theatre management course. The Royal has been bought out by a big company a bit like Moss Empires. That's another thing. I don't even know if I'll still have a job once the take-over goes through.'

Erica shook her head. 'What a mess.'

Mary smiled wryly. 'That's putting it mildly.

He'll be back tomorrow and I'm dreading telling him.'

★ ★ ★

As it happened, Mary was to face David sooner than she thought. She had just put Vivien to bed that evening when there was a knock at the door. Dora answered it and came into the living-room a moment later followed by David. He was smiling.

'I got back earlier than I'd expected,' he told her. 'They let us go soon after lunch so I thought I'd surprise you.'

Mary's heart was beating fast. 'That's nice. It's good to see you.'

'I thought you might like to have a run out,' he suggested. 'A drink, perhaps. I've such a lot to tell you.'

Mary glanced at her mother. 'Will that be all right?'

'Of course. You go. I'll be here for Vivien.'

In the car Mary was silent and David glanced at her several times before saying, 'Is anything wrong, darling? You look upset. I thought you'd be pleased to see me.'

'I am! It's not that.' She bit her lip. 'Oh, David, I've got something to tell you. It's not very good news, I'm afraid.'

He pulled over and stopped the car, turning to look into her tear-filled eyes. 'Darling! What on earth's happened? I think you'd better tell me now.' He took her hand and looked into her eyes. 'It's something to do with Paul, isn't it?' She nodded. 'What, then? He won't give you a divorce?'

Mary took a deep breath. 'He will, but on one condition. He wants Vivien.'

He stared at her. 'That's ridiculous. No court would award him custody.'

'He seems to think they would.' She sighed. 'There's worse. He knows that you and I spent that weekend together in London. He says he has proof that we shared a room and if I don't agree he says he'll plead adultery on my part and get Vivien anyway.' David looked stunned and she went on. 'Don't worry, David. I won't let that happen. None of this is your fault and I won't see your name dragged into it.'

'Never mind that. What do you intend to do?'

'What can I do? I'm at my wits' end. Paul can afford the best lawyers and I can't. If he goes ahead he'll probably win.'

'What about Vivien? Has anyone thought of what she wants?'

'How can I ask her, David? She's a child — a little girl. What's more she's a star-struck little girl. The offer of a glamorous life in London would be a dream come true for her.'

'Then maybe you should let her go.'

'*What?*' She stared at him. 'Do you know what you're saying?'

'He'd have to give you access. She could come home to you at weekends.'

'*No!*'

He shook her gently. 'Mary! It means we could be married.'

Her eyes filled with tears. 'I can't give Vivien

up just like that. It would feel like a betrayal.'

'Look, if he's going to get her anyway, wouldn't it be better to let it happen amicably?'

Mary frowned and shook her head. 'I can't believe you're saying this,' she said. 'Everyone except me is talking about Vivien as though she's some kind of possession — a piece of furniture!'

David turned away and for several minutes they were silent, then he said, 'Of course, this could be his way of getting you both back.'

'That's rubbish. He doesn't want me. He already has a new girlfriend. She's an actress but she's so besotted with him that she's prepared to give up her career to care for his child.'

'You sound bitter.'

'Well, wouldn't you?' she flung at him.

He started the car again and they drove for a while in silence. Mary glanced at him, regretting her impatience. The last thing she wanted to do was quarrel with David. 'You haven't told me how the course went,' she said.

He didn't look at her. 'Are you really interested or are you just being polite?'

She laid a hand on his arm. 'I'm sorry I was snappy, David. It's just that I'm almost at my wits' end. I haven't slept since all this started. I really am interested in the course, though.'

He glanced at her. 'As a matter of fact it was really interesting. This take-over is going to make a huge difference to the Royal.'

'Not too much difference, I hope. I'm not about to lose my job, am I? That's all I need.'

'Of course you're not. In fact you'll probably

get a rise in salary. It means more money will be available for better shows. A whole new look for the place too. Lavish refurbishment, which isn't before time.'

'It all sounds really exciting.' Mary tried hard to sound enthusiastic.

'It will be. We may even be getting some prior to West End try-outs. There's to be a big advertisement campaign — lots to do.'

They had a quiet drink in the little pub that was their favourite and Mary tried her hardest to relax, but it was no use. She couldn't force herself to share David's enthusiasm for the new venture, exciting though it sounded. In the end the conversation lagged so much that David looked at his watch.

'I think I'd better get you home,' he said. 'You look tired out.'

As he drew the car up in Gresham Terrace he turned to her. 'I'm afraid you're going to have to make a decision over Vivien soon, darling,' he said. 'He's a swine to put you through this and I can't begin to imagine what you must be going through. But looking at it from a practical point of view, until it's sorted out you're not going to be able to think of anything else.'

She shook her head. 'I'm sorry, David. I'm really sorry.'

He drew her close and kissed her. 'Don't be. It must be hell for you, but I have a feeling that if you don't make up your mind soon the decision might well be taken out of your hands.'

'The possibility that I might lose my child is horrifying,' she said. 'It's like living in my worst nightmare.'

'And I feel completely helpless, which is hell for me too.' He kissed her again. 'I love you, Mary, and I really want to help you through this, but it seems that all I can offer you is to be here when and if you want me.'

She swallowed the lump in her throat. 'I know, and believe me it means a lot.' She reached up to kiss his cheek. 'See you in the morning.' She got out of the car and watched as he drove away. He clearly didn't really understand how she felt. How could he when he'd never had a child of his own? Never in her life had she felt so alone as at that moment.

The next morning's post brought another letter from Paul, pressing her for a decision and asking her to ring him. When David had gone out for his lunch break she dialled Paul's number.

'Paul, you'll have to stop badgering me,' she said. 'I can't make a life-changing decision for myself and my child in five minutes.'

'Of course. I realize that.' He sounded quite reasonable. 'Look, why don't you let her come and stay for a weekend? Maybe she could spend part of her school holidays up here, just to see how she likes it. After all, it has to be as much her decision as yours.' There was a pause then he asked, 'Have you mentioned it to her yet?'

'No.'

'Then I suggest you do.'

'And if she says she doesn't want to come and

stay with you again?'

'Then I won't press her.'

He sounded so cool and confident that her heart turned to ice. Paul was already convinced that he had won.

12

Paul collected Vivien in his car on Friday afternoon, promising to bring her back safely on Sunday. David, knowing that Mary had reservations about the visit suggested that they go out for the day on Sunday, hoping to take her mind off her misgivings.

They drove along the coast to Kenstone Bay and had lunch in a quaint little quayside restaurant where the speciality was freshly caught fish. It was a glorious day and the food was delicious. David had been determined to make the day special and tried his hardest all day to lighten Mary's mood, but he couldn't get past her preoccupation. All day her mind was elsewhere as she wondered what Vivien was doing and hoped she was missing her. As the afternoon drew on, David suggested going back to his flat where he hoped she would be more relaxed but she shook her head.

'I've had a lovely day, David,' she said. 'But Paul has promised to have Vivien back by teatime and I don't want to be out when she arrives.' She was too busy looking at her watch to notice his mouth tightening with frustration and disappointment. As he dropped her off, she leaned across to kiss him.

'I'm sorry to cut our day short, darling. I've enjoyed it so much and I know you understand.'

To her relief Vivien hadn't arrived when she

got in, but as the time went by and they failed to show up she grew more and more annoyed. The hours ticked by as she stood in the front-room window, waiting and worrying. Six o'clock became eight, then half past, and her annoyance became anxiety which developed into panic. Suppose there'd been a crash? Suppose it was a police car that turned up instead of Paul's sports car? She was sure he drove too fast anyway. Should she go out to the phone box on the corner and begin ringing round the hospitals?

It was after nine when Paul's car drew up outside and Mary rushed to open the front door, relief and anger almost overwhelming her as she greeted them sharply.

'Where on earth have you *been*? I've been worried sick. You said teatime! I've been imagining all kinds of things.'

'Well, we're here now.' Paul was maddeningly unrepentant as he stood smiling mildly on the doorstep. 'If you were on the phone I would have rung, of course, but as you're not . . . '

'Well, don't just stand there, you'd better come in now that you are here,' Mary snapped. 'It's a school day for Vivien tomorrow. She's going to be good for nothing. I'd better get her straight upstairs to bed. Mum will make you some tea if you like,' she added over her shoulder as she hurried Vivien towards the stairs.

He shrugged. 'I don't want to put anyone out. I'll get a drink on the way back.'

'Well, if you're sure.' As she reached the landing she heard the front door slam and looked out of the window. To her annoyance she saw that there was a young woman with blonde hair in the passenger seat. As though he felt her eyes on him, Paul looked up at the window and waved. She turned away angrily and minutes later she heard the purr of the engine as he drove off.

Vivien looked up at her reproachfully. 'Why were you so horrid to Daddy?' she asked. 'I've had a lovely time and you didn't even let me say thank you for having me.'

'It was wrong of Daddy to bring you home so late.' Mary relented a little at the disappointed look on her daughter's face. 'Are you hungry? Do you want something to eat?'

'No. We had dinner on the way home.'

'*Dinner!*'

'Yes. At a posh hotel. The waiter brought me a cushion to make my chair higher and I had roast chicken and . . . ' Vivien frowned with the effort of remembering the right words. 'Chocolate *grattoo* for pudding.'

'Chocolate gateau?' Mary shook her head. How typical of Paul to fill the child up with rich food at bedtime. How old did he think she was?

Mary bundled her into her pyjamas. 'Well, you'd better get to sleep now or you'll never wake up for school in the morning.' She tucked the bedclothes in and bent to kiss her. Vivien smiled sleepily.

'We went to the zoo *and* the film studios to watch them filming. Daddy introduced me to the director, Mr Slater,' she said. 'He said I could call him Max. Serena came too. She's ever so lovely, Mummy. Daddy says I can go and stay with them again soon if you say so.' She gazed up appealingly into Mary's eyes. 'I can go, can't I?'

Mary turned away to draw the curtains. 'I suppose so,' she said resignedly.

Downstairs she complained to Dora. 'He thinks he can have custody of Vivien just like that, and he hasn't got the faintest idea how to care for a child.'

Dora looked up from her knitting. 'He'll learn,' she said blandly. 'Vivien will soon teach him.'

'Filling her up with all that rich food. And no doubt they were stuffing her with ice cream and all sorts of other rubbish all afternoon. I wouldn't be surprised if she was up all night being sick.'

'That's what I mean.' Dora smiled. 'A few nights mopping up after her should get the message through to him.'

Mary stared at her mother. 'This is all a joke to you, isn't it?' she exclaimed. 'Don't you realize what it means to me? Do you really want to see me lose her?'

'Of course I don't,' Dora said. 'And I'm not worried because I don't believe for one minute that it will come to that.'

'Well, I just hope you're right.'

⋆ ⋆ ⋆

To Mary's chagrin Vivien wasn't sick that night. She slept like a log and was up bright and early for school next morning, chattering to her

232

mother all the way to the school gates about her wonderful weekend and how much she had enjoyed herself.

The moment her mother had gone she ran off to find her friend Vicky. 'You'll never guess where I went at the weekend,' she said. 'I went to London to stay with my daddy again. He's a famous film actor and he took me to the film studios to see them making a film. We went to the zoo as well and on the way home last night we had dinner in a posh hotel. I had chicken and . . . '

'Is the *cat* telling lies again?' It was Katie Roberts, who had been standing behind Vivien, listening to all she said. 'You don't want to believe a word she says, Vicky.' She laughed and Vivien's face turned bright pink.

'It's *not* lies!' she shouted. 'It's true. My daddy's name is Paul Summers and he's been in *hundreds* of films. I might be going to stay with him for the whole of the summer holidays — so there!'

'Liar, liar, pants on fire!' Katie jeered. 'Anyway, if he was your real dad his name would be the same as yours — so *there*!'

'He *is* my daddy. Summers is his stage name — so yah boo to you. You don't know *anything*!' She gave Katie a push, sending her staggering backwards. Regaining her balance, the other child leapt forward, red-faced, and yanked Vivien's hair, bringing a wail of pain from her.

'Ooow! You're a *pig*, Katie Roberts!' Vivien kicked out, catching Katie on the shin. Immediately the two girls were slapping and kicking each other, their flailing blows punctuated by squeals of fury that quickly drew a crowd of other children.

'Children, *children*! Stop that at once.' The teacher on playground duty had seen the fight break out and hurried across to part the squabbling girls. 'Stop it this minute, do you hear?' She grabbed each of them, one in each hand, and held them apart, giving them both a reproachful look. 'Nice little girls don't fight. Now, what's it all about?'

'She said I tell lies!' Vivien said, tears coursing down her cheeks.

'And she *does*!' Katie broke in. 'She's always boasting. Now she says her dad is a film star and that she's going to be one too. She's a rotten little swank! It's not true, is it, miss? That means she's a liar.'

'You don't know that it's not true, Katie, and calling someone a liar is very nasty anyway.' The teacher held on tightly to Vivien's hand. 'I think you'd better come inside with me, Vivien,' she said. She turned to the others. 'Off you go and play now,' she said. 'Only another ten minutes until the bell so make the most of it.'

In the classroom, Miss Jones sat a sniffling Vivien down and drew up a chair beside her. 'Have you got a clean hanky?' Vivien nodded and fished inside the pocket of her dress. 'Right, dry your eyes and wipe your nose, there's a good girl.'

Vivien did as she was told and took a deep shuddering breath.

'That's better. Now, do you want to tell me about it?'

'My daddy *is* an actor in the films,' Vivien told her. 'You can ask Mummy if you don't believe me.'

'I haven't said I don't believe you,' Miss Jones said gently. 'But some things are best kept to yourself. You have to remember that not everyone is as lucky as you. Katie would probably like to have the chances you have. Like taking part in the pantomime, for instance. Maybe you should try to remember that and not rub in your good luck.'

'She shouldn't have called me a liar, though,' Vivien sniffed. 'Anyway, I wasn't even talking to her.'

'I'm sure you know that a lot of children haven't got their daddies any more because of the war.' Miss Jones paused, searching for a tactful way of getting to the truth. 'I thought you and your mummy were alone too.'

'We were,' Vivien told her earnestly. 'We thought Daddy was dead but he isn't. He came back to life and now he's in the films. And he wants me to go and stay with him and he's got a lovely girlfriend called Serena.'

Miss Jones listened to the tumbling words and resolved to have a word with the child's mother. Vivien had always had a vivid imagination and fantasizing was very common at this age. If the poor child had lost her father in the war it was understandable that she should want to romanticize him. She smiled.

'It all sounds very nice, Vivien,' she said. 'But

if I were you I'd keep it to myself for now. Suppose we let it be our secret, eh? Just between you and me.'

Vivien looked at her pityingly. Clearly Miss Jones didn't believe her either. Well, they could just wait and see. She'd show them. Maybe she wouldn't be staying at this school much longer anyway.

Later that afternoon, when Vivien and her friend Vicky were alone in their favourite corner of the playground, she leaned forward conspiratorially.

'If you promise you won't tell anyone I'll tell you a big secret,' she said.

Vicky looked at her with big round eyes. 'I won't tell,' she promised. 'Go on.'

Vivien took a deep breath and looked around to make quite sure no one was listening 'Well, Daddy says that if I go and live with him I can go to this special school where children learn to be actors. It costs ever so much money but he'll pay because he says I've got . . . ' She frowned. 'I've got tamlent.'

'What's tamlent?'

Vivien shook her head. 'I'm not sure but I think it's something good to do with acting. He even took me to see the school. It's not very far from where he lives.'

Vicky looked at her with round eyes. 'Do you really want to leave here?' she asked. 'What about your mummy and your grandma? Won't you miss them?'

'Oh, I'd still see them,' Vivien told her nonchalantly. 'And you too. Daddy says I could come home quite often. I hate this school anyway,' she added with a toss of her head. 'I can't wait to get away from Katie Roberts. She's a nasty jealous pig.' She glanced ruefully at her friend and reached out to take her hand. 'I wish you could come too, though, Vicky.' Suddenly she was tired of secrets. Grabbing up her skipping rope she said, 'Come on, let's go and practise the bumps. I can do three without stopping. Can you?'

★ ★ ★

At the office next morning Mary poured out all her exasperation to David. She found herself going back over all that had happened the previous evening again and again.

'He obviously didn't give a damn about how worried I'd be. *Four hours* late, they were. And fancy stopping off to feed her a huge meal at bedtime.'

He sighed and looked at her. 'Mary, could we get on with next month's invoicing, please?'

'Sorry.' She flushed, half with shame and half with resentment. 'Sorry to bother you with my problems.'

He got up from his desk and came across to her. 'Mary, of course your problems concern me,' he said patiently. 'You know that. After all, my future as well as yours depends on what happens. But with this take-over coming up we have to concentrate on what's happening at the theatre during working hours.'

'I know.' She couldn't meet his eyes.

'Your mind just isn't on your work. Would you like some time off?'

'No!' She looked up at him, her eyes full of tears. 'I've said I'm sorry. I'll work this afternoon to make up, but can't you try and understand what losing my child means to me? Every time she comes back from Paul's I can feel her slipping a bit further away from me.'

He drew her gently to her feet and kissed her. 'You'll never really lose Vivien,' he said. 'She's your child. She's been with you since the moment she was conceived. You can divorce Paul but you can never divorce Vivien.'

'Of course I can't, but don't you understand, David — she'll forget me. Paul keeps bringing this girl — this Serena — along. Vivien is so taken with her.'

'It's all a novelty. She's a child!'

'He even brought her along last night. I saw her in the car.'

He sighed and turned away. 'That's what's really bothering you, isn't it, Mary? That Paul has someone else.'

'If she's trying to take my place with Vivien, yes!'

'Just with Vivien?'

'Of course just with Vivien. Oh, David, can't you get it into your head that Paul means nothing to me any more. How could he after what he did to us?'

He shook his head. 'Love is a powerful emotion, Mary. It isn't easily killed.' He turned away. 'I know that to my cost. Don't you see — each time Vivien visits Paul I can feel you slipping away from me too.'

She got up and went to him, turning him round to face her. 'There's no reason for you to doubt me, David. I love you. I never thought I'd love anyone the way I loved Paul, but I do — even more so. Please believe me.'

He pulled her into his arms and held her close. 'I love you too — so much.' He kissed her. 'But loving for the second time is fraught with anxiety. The thought of losing you is heartbreaking. You would tell me if there was any danger you might change your mind, wouldn't you?'

'There isn't. I don't know what I'd do without you.' She kissed him and pushed him gently away. 'Now we'd better get on with some work. Tell you what, I'll slip out for some sandwiches and work through my lunch break.'

★ ★ ★

Erica was on top of the world. The samples from Grayson's Fashions had arrived by special courier a week earlier. Unpacking them excitedly in the stockroom, she'd gasped with excitement. They were exquisite. Something completely different that she knew her customers were going to love. Standing in front of the mirror, she tried on one of the summer dresses. It was a lovely shade of jade green, made of a silky material that slipped sensuously over her body as she slid into it. It had tiny cap sleeves and a nipped-in waistline from which a flared peplum sprang, accentuating her slender waist and the curve of her hips. The panelled skirt flowed to mid-calf

239

length and as she moved the soft material swirled around her legs making her feel really special. She could hardly wait to see the reaction of her customers. Out of the carefully packed box came five more dresses, each slightly different but every bit as gorgeous as the first. Erica put them on hangers and got out the iron to press them. This New Look was going to be the shop's salvation. She was sure of it. She couldn't wait to clear and redress the window with them.

Gerald had sent her the advertisement last week and she had put it in the local paper. Several customers had asked her what the mysterious New Look was like but she had told them to wait and see. Now their curiosity was about to be satisfied.

All six dresses had sold before the week was out. By the time Grayson's version of the latest fashion was released for sale, her delighted customers had already seen the launch of Dior's New Look in the fashion magazines and national papers, but they had expected it to be months before it reached the provincial high-street shops. Erica telephoned Gerald excitedly a week later with news of the sell-out, asking if she could have a few more.

'I can't give you that big order yet,' she said. 'But I'm sure it won't be long at this rate. The New Look is a roaring success here in Ferncliff.'

There was a pause at the other end of the line and for a moment Erica was afraid he was going to turn down her request. 'I promise I'll give you an order as soon as I can, Gerald,' she assured him.

'Mmm. Yours is one of the few shops I had picked out to have the first batch of my new styles,' he said. 'We need to strike while the iron is hot. I really need you to follow up seriously if this is going to work, Erica.'

Her heart plummeted. She'd die if he turned her down now. Customers kept coming in and asking when the new stock would be in. They were going to be so disappointed if it never arrived. 'Just a few more months and I'll be set up,' she pleaded. 'Can't you trust me for a little while longer, Gerald? I promise you the money will be safe. My customers are almost fighting over the dresses. They keep on asking when I'll have more.'

'Yeah? Well, that's good, of course.' There was another pause and then he said, 'Look, how about I come down there so we can talk about it? I've never seen your shop and a little trip to the seaside might be very pleasant. I'm sure we can work out some kind of compromise.'

'Down here — to Ferncliff? Well, OK.' Erica was slightly taken aback. When he saw it would he think her little shop was too small and humble? Maybe he wouldn't want her to take part in his launch after all. She'd have to try to smarten the place up even more if he was coming. 'When were you thinking of coming?' she asked.

'How about next Sunday?'

'Next Sunday?' She began to panic. 'Well — all right. You're welcome, of course, but I'd have thought weekends were precious to

241

someone who works as hard as you do. Won't your wife mind?'

'She's got her own interests,' he said. 'She won't even notice. Anyway, this is strictly business. Are we on for Sunday then?'

'Yes, fine.'

'Right. I'll drive down. It should take me a couple of hours so if I start out early I could be with you by mid-morning. That all right?' He chuckled. 'Or do you like to spend your Sunday mornings in bed?'

'Not a bit. I usually do my paperwork on Sundays.'

'A girl after my own heart.' He chuckled again. 'Maybe you know of somewhere quiet where we could have lunch. See you Sunday then.'

As she replaced the receiver, Erica looked round the shop. She could do a special display in the space at the bottom of the stairs, with flowers and one of her evening dresses. She'd redo the window too — make it look really classy with a swathe of velvet and the little gilt chair she'd bought recently at an auction sale, some of that diamanté stuff from Woolworths. It looked really sparkly under the spotlight. It wasn't really the season for evening dresses but they always caught the eye.

She worked hard each evening after closing time, vacuuming every corner, pleased that she had splashed out on the new carpet. All the woodwork and mirrors in the shop were polished to within an inch of their lives and the new displays looked elegant and classy. She even managed to find time to have her hair done and

242

on Sunday morning she was up bright and early tidying the flat. She'd obviously have to invite him upstairs at some stage to freshen up after his long drive.

Gerald arrived a good half hour early on Sunday morning. Luckily Erica was dressed and ready. She'd had trouble sleeping and had risen early to make up her face carefully and put on the green New Look dress, which she hadn't been able to resist keeping for herself.

When she heard the bell she went to the window and saw Gerald's car parked below in the street. Hurrying downstairs, she opened the door.

'Gerald! You're earl — I mean, you've made good time.'

He chuckled. 'Not *too* early, I hope.'

'No! Not at all. Come in.' He looked different this morning and she quickly realized that it was because she had never seen him in casual clothes before. She had only ever seen him at the factory where he always wore a dark business suit, shirt and tie. This morning he wore grey slacks, a pale blue open-necked shirt and blazer. His hair was different too; not so slicked back, almost tousled, in fact. The effect was to make him look much younger — almost good-looking, Erica mused — for his forty-odd years.

'The flat is through the shop,' she said, leading the way. 'I'd have liked to have a separate entrance made but it would have meant losing some space in the shop and I . . . ' She checked herself, aware that nervousness was making her talk too much. 'I'll make you . . . er . . . I mean,

243

would you like some coffee?'

'Yeah, thanks. That'd be great.' He was standing in the shop, looking around him. 'Well, well, so this is Erica's. Very nice, I must say. It's a good position too, right in the middle of this shopping parade. Do you get any trade from the summer visitors?'

'Oh yes, lots. But I've a good clientele among the residents as well. They're busy during the summer months but they certainly make up for it in the off-season. That's when they do all their socializing. There are lots of classy dinners and dances so the evening-wear goes well. They like their glitz and glitter, do the landladies of Ferncliff.'

'Excellent! You've obviously got the situation well sized up.' He looked at her. 'It hasn't escaped my notice either that you're wearing a Grayson's dress.'

'Oh.' She bit her lip. 'I hope you don't mind, Gerald. I couldn't resist it. It was such a perfect fit. Might have been made for me.'

'I agree. Don't apologize.' His eyes swept appreciatively over her figure. 'You're looking very lovely today. As for minding, who could be a better walking advertisement for Grayson's Fashions?'

Upstairs in her living-room, he looked out of the window. 'What a nice view. You can actually see the sea from here. I think you've done very well.'

Erica put the tray of coffee down and looked up at him hopefully. 'Well enough for you to take a risk on me, Gerald?'

He smiled. 'We'll talk about that later. Now, did you think of somewhere we could eat?'

'The Minsmore Country Club is nice. A bit off the beaten track. Quite exclusive so the summer visitors don't crowd the place out.'

'Sounds just the ticket. Drink your coffee and we'll get going then, shall we?'

The Minsmore was quiet and Gerald obviously approved. They had a drink in the bar and then the waiter showed them to a secluded corner table. Gerald seemed relaxed over the meal, chatting about trivial things, and before long Erica began to grow fidgety and impatient. When was he going to start talking business?

At last, as they retired to a quiet corner of the lounge and Gerald seated himself beside her on the plush banquette, and as the waiter set down their coffee tray, he leaned back and slid his arm along the back of the seat.

'So tell me, what's your financial position, Erica?' he asked.

She flushed. He had a perfect right to ask, of course. After all, she had been direct with him. She took a deep breath. 'Well, as you know, paying Jenny back what she'd put into the business made a bit of a hole in my bank balance. Up till then we'd been doing really well. I had to take out a bank loan to keep afloat and I'm still paying that off.'

He nodded. 'Mmm. Getting into loans is a tricky business. It always amazes me, the amount of interest they charge. Criminal, if you ask me.'

'I know. So that's why I need you to help by cutting me some slack, Gerald.' She held her breath. She hadn't meant to be quite so blunt, but she was getting desperate. She glanced at him and saw that he looked faintly amused.

'You haven't considered taking on another partner?'

'No!' She shook her head. 'Once bitten, twice shy!'

He nodded. 'I know what you mean, but what about a *sleeping* partner?'

'Sleeping? How do you mean?'

He laughed. 'Well, someone older maybe, with what they call a disposable income. Someone who wouldn't want to run off and get married. Someone who'd be happy to let you have a free hand with the running of the place?'

Erica looked doubtful. 'Where would I find someone like that?'

'There are people out there with cash to spare who'd rather take an interesting gamble than stick with the boring banks. You could advertise in one of the financial papers.' He looked at her. 'Or maybe you already know of someone.'

'No. Not really.' Erica sighed. This wasn't going the way she had hoped and disappointment was beginning to tug at the corners of her mouth. 'The business wouldn't feel like mine any more,' she said. 'I don't want to be beholden to anyone or have to ask every time I get a new idea.'

He smiled. 'Well, maybe that's wise.' His arm dropped around her shoulders, his hand cupping her shoulder, and he gave her a little squeeze. 'You know, Erica, you're a girl after my own heart — strong and independent. I like that in a woman. I've always admired you.' His face was very close to hers and when she turned his eyes looked deeply into hers. 'But I'm sure you're aware of that, eh?' He pressed his thigh gently but insistently against hers.

'Well, I don't know about that.' She moistened her lips. 'But thank you anyway, Gerald.'

For a moment his eyes smouldered into hers then suddenly he looked at his watch. 'Good heavens! Is that the time? I think we should go. I've a hell of a long drive ahead of me.'

'Yes, of course. I'll see you in the car park,' Erica said. 'I need to powder my nose before we go.'

In the Ladies, she stared at herself in the mirror. If she was reading this situation correctly, Gerald was hinting at something more intimate than cash when he mentioned a 'sleeping partner'. The warm pressure of his thigh against hers and the look in his eyes said it all. He was making a pass at her and she had the distinct impression that the ball was now in her court. If she played her cards right this could go her way.

She combed her hair and applied fresh lipstick, then she straightened her stocking seams and her shoulders and walked out to the car park, determined to meet this fresh challenge head on.

⋆   ⋆   ⋆

It was soon after dawn next morning when Gerald Grayson slipped out of the shop door and into his car. Looking up towards the

247

window, he waved before putting the car into gear and driving away.

Looking down at him, Erica returned the wave and folded her dressing gown around her in a triumphant little self-hug. It had been a long time since she'd had a man in her life, let alone her bed, and she had to admit that she'd enjoyed Gerald's eager, hot-blooded love-making more than she'd have thought possible. Clearly his wife wasn't very interested in that side of their marriage and that was a big plus as far as she was concerned. Appreciative of her enthusiastic response, Gerald had generously promised that a large selection of New Look outfits would be on its way to her within the week, hinting that there would be more to come if she kept him as happy as he'd been when he left this morning.

Erica looked sleepily at the clock. It was ten past five. She could have another of couple of hours' sleep if she went back to bed now. She'd need it if she was to face tomorrow without last night's energetic excesses showing in her face. She chuckled to herself as she made her way back to the bedroom. *Sleeping partner indeed!*

13

When Vera tapped on the door of the beach café's little office and told Dora she had a visitor, she looked up in surprise. She wasn't expecting anyone.

'Who is it?' she asked.

Vera shook her head. 'Some man. He says it's important. Shall I bring him in here?'

'No.' Dora's heart jumped into her mouth. She hadn't seen the tramp for over a week now. Could his memory have returned? Had he come to tell her he knew who she was? She stood up, shocked to find that her knees were trembling.

'No, it's all right, Vera. I'll come through.' She followed the girl back into the café where to her relief she saw John Lorimer sitting at a table by the window.

'John! What a nice surprise. It's not often I see you down here.'

He rose to meet her, taking her hand warmly. 'To tell you the truth I give the prom a wide berth in the season,' he said. 'I hate crowds.'

'What can I do for you?' Dora asked. 'A coffee or something to eat?'

He shook his head. 'I'm not here as a customer. Can we go somewhere private?'

'Of course. Come through to the office.' Dora wondered what he could have to say to her as she ushered him through to her office. As she opened the door she smiled apologetically. 'Sorry about the lack of space. Not much more than a cupboard, but there's room enough for me and a filing cabinet.' She found him a chair. 'Sit down. Let me order you some coffee at least.'

'No, thank you, Dora.' He sat down. 'My dear, I thought you might like to know that the man you enquired about — the tramp who has been hanging around for so long — had an accident last week.'

Dora's heart gave a lurch. 'An accident! What kind of accident?'

John shook his head. 'I'm afraid he was hit by a bus. He was crossing the town square and it seems he was rather the worse for drink — lurched out from behind a parked car. The driver didn't stand a chance of avoiding him.'

'Oh dear.' Dora swallowed. 'I thought I hadn't seen him around for a while. Is he badly hurt?'

'I'm afraid so. A broken leg and a very bad head injury which is causing some concern. He was in a coma for a couple of days and now apparently he slips in and out of consciousness.' He paused. 'The police got in touch with me because of the enquiries I made about him recently at the British Legion and the Salvation Army.'

'I see. How bad is he, John?'

'The doctors don't hold out much hope of recovery, I'm afraid. Malnutrition and alcohol plus his old war wounds have taken their toll of his constitution.'

Dora bit her lip in an effort not to let John see that she was upset by the news. 'Where is he?' she asked. 'I mean, the General Hospital, naturally, but what ward?'

'Not the General.' John looked uncomfortable. 'He's in St Cuthbert's.'

'St Cuthbert's? But that's the old workhouse.'

'I know, but as they couldn't locate any next of kin and there's no money . . . ' He looked at her. 'You're not planning to go and see him? Dora, are you sure you want to?'

'Oh yes. I feel I must. I — I need to,' she added inadequately.

'Well, it's Cowell Ward, but I don't think you should go alone.' He touched her hand. 'Do you want me to come with you?'

'No. Thank you all the same, John, but I'd rather go on my own.' A thought occurred to her. 'Will they let me see him?'

He shrugged. 'There doesn't seem to be anyone else so I'm sure they will. 'When will you go?'

'This afternoon,' she said. 'I'll leave Vera in charge. She's a good girl.'

'Will you come and see me afterwards?' John asked. 'I'll be at home, or if you prefer I'll meet you somewhere.'

'No, I'll come to you,' she said. 'Thanks for letting me know, John.' She reached for his hand. 'You're a good friend.'

He held her hand warmly in both of his. 'I'm always here if you need me. I'm sure you know that.'

Dora found Cowell Ward with difficulty, trawling the warren-like corridors of the old Victorian building till she located it, and when she enquired of the sister in charge she was asked if she was a relation of 'Mr Smith'.

Dora shook her head. 'I manage the beach café. He used to come every morning for his breakfast.'

The sister nodded. 'Well, it's good of you to come. I doubt if he'll recognize you, though,' she said. 'When he's conscious he's not making a lot of sense, but it's sad to be alone in the world when you're as ill as he is, so thank you for coming anyway.' She pointed down the ward. 'You'll find him in the end bed.'

Dora was shocked by the man's appearance. He looked so frail, smaller than she remembered him. She'd been expecting him to look ill, but the fact that they'd shaved off his beard and most of his hair so as to bandage his head made him almost unrecognizable. He lay on his back with his eyes closed. She bent close and whispered, 'Mr Smith — Paddy.' When there was no response she whispered, 'Can you hear me?' Still the man in the bed made no move. She drew up a chair and sat down. Touching one of the gnarled hands that lay on the covers, she began to talk to him. He seemed to be deeply asleep or even unconscious. She'd heard it said that the hearing was the last sense to remain alert so if it was Mike perhaps he would hear and make sense of it. If not, nothing she said would matter now whoever this man was.

'I never wanted to leave you, Mike,' she whispered. 'It was the drinking and your violence that drove me away. I never wanted you to miss seeing your children grow up. They're fine girls, Mike. Erica has her own business and Mary has

252

a lovely little girl called Vivien. You're a grandfather, Mike. You would have loved that — if only you'd . . . ' She stopped speaking as the eyelids fluttered and opened. The green eyes that looked up at her were so like Erica's that she caught her breath. At that moment she was almost sure that this was the man she had married. She leaned towards him.

'Mike, is it really you?' she said. 'Did you hear what I said? Do you know me? Did you know who I was when you came to the café? If you did, why didn't you say something?'

But there was no expression in the glazed eyes that looked up at her and a moment later they closed again. She sat with him a while longer, but he did not open his eyes again. Eventually she rose and stood looking down at him. 'God rest you,' she whispered. 'Sleep tight.' On a sudden impulse she bent and brushed his forehead with her lips, her throat tight with tears as she walked away down the ward.

She had almost reached the door when the man in the bed opened his eyes again. Turning his head he looked towards the figure disappearing through the swing doors and his lips silently framed one word. '*Dora*.'

★ ★ ★

John opened the door quickly to her ring at the bell. He had been waiting for her but he had not been prepared for her tears. In his living-room with the French windows open to the garden, he sat her down and made tea for her.

'You shouldn't have gone,' he said. 'If I'd thought you'd be as upset as this I wouldn't have come to you with the news this morning.'

'I'm glad you did,' she said. 'Mike was a terrible man when he was in drink, but he didn't deserve an end like this. If it really was him.'

'You're still not sure then?'

'Not completely. He woke up for a minute while I was there. I'd been talking to him as though he was Mike, but he obviously didn't know who I was.' She sighed. 'It made me feel I should have done more to save my marriage — helped Mike to change his ways.'

'You were very young,' John said. 'A task like that is almost impossible and you had the girls to think of. You really mustn't feel guilty.'

'But I made vows,' she said. 'Marriage vows are made to be kept.'

'He made vows too,' John said. 'To love and to cherish. Doesn't sound as though he did much of that. Mike let you down, Dora. All these years you've struggled on alone to bring up his children. He could have found you if he'd tried hard enough.' He sighed. 'And I'm afraid there's something else I have to tell you. They rang me just before you arrived. Paddy Smith died just after you left. The end was very peaceful, they said.'

'Oh, John. Now I'll never know, will I?'

He drew her close and held her while she wept. 'I'm sorry, my dear. But it's over. You did your best.'

★ ★ ★

'I can't wait to show you what's just come in!'

Erica sounded excited when she telephoned Mary at the theatre. It was half-day closing and she suggested that Mary join her at the shop for a bite to eat at lunchtime.

'I've got a surprise for you. Just wait till you see it!'

When Mary arrived, Erica was just pulling down the door blind. She let her sister in and led her upstairs to the stockroom, throwing the door open with a flourish.

'There! What do you think of that?'

In the doorway Mary gasped. 'Wow! Where did all these come from?'

'Grayson's. It's called the New Look.'

'I know. I've seen it in the papers.'

'The order only arrived this morning so I haven't had time to unpack it all. Come on, you can help me with the rest.'

As they drew garment after garment out of the tissue paper they were packed in, there were gasps and exclamations from them both. There were dresses, suits and two-piece outfits, skirts and jackets. Erica was almost beside herself with excitement.

'These are going to be the making of Erica's,' she said. 'I hope they've all been saving their clothing coupons! I'm going to press them all and re-do the window a bit later on, but first of all I want you to choose something for yourself.'

Mary stared at her. 'Me?'

Erica laughed. 'Yes, you! You deserve it. I want to make it up to you for the mess I've caused.'

Mary sighed. 'There's nothing you can do

about that. Vivien's besotted with Paul now. He's pressing me to let her spend most of the summer holidays with him and this Serena person.' She looked at her sister. 'Anyway, you can't afford to give your stock away.'

'You can leave that to me,' Erica said. 'I know what I can afford. I want Mum to have a dress too.'

'You're mad!' Mary laughed, holding a blue and white creation in front of her at the mirror. 'This one's gorgeous. But what's happened? Have you won the pools or something?'

'Better than that.' Erica smiled enigmatically. 'Much better! But this is about you, not me. Look, why don't you let Vivien go to Paul's for a few weeks? It would give you and David some time together, to get to know one another better.' She winked. 'That's if you still need to!'

Mary looked doubtful. 'Oh — well, I don't know about that.'

'What's to stop you? Didn't you tell me that the theatre is closing for refurbishment?'

'Yes, for three weeks in August.'

'There you are then. You and he could swan off for a holiday somewhere romantic together. I'm sure he wouldn't say no.'

But Mary was looking at her sister's radiant face. 'What's got into you, Erica? I haven't seen you this pleased with yourself for ages. Not since . . . ' She broke off. 'Have you met someone? A new man?'

'Not exactly.'

Mary looked around at the newly arrived stock

doubtfully. 'You haven't taken out another loan, have you?'

'No.' Erica burst out laughing. 'Oh God, your face! OK, I suppose I'll have to put you out of your misery.'

'Have you been up to your old tricks again?'

'Depends what you mean by old tricks.' Erica laughed. 'All's fair in love and the fashion business! Gerald — Gerald Grayson, that is, came down to spend the day with me last Sunday and he and I have come to an amicable agreement.' She giggled. 'A very amicable agreement!'

'In what way?'

'What way do you think? He took me out for a slap-up lunch and during the course of conversation he made it clear that he finds me attractive.'

'Yes?'

'He also hinted that I could occupy a corner of his life that his wife isn't interested in — in return for some stock.'

'*Erica!*' Mary's mouth dropped open. 'Tell me you're joking. Please!'

The smile vanished from Erica's face. 'Don't look at me like that. Listen, Mary, I went out on a limb to get the money for this place. I was jilted in front of all my friends and family, but I didn't lie down and give up. I made it work for me. Then Jenny let me down for some bloke and I almost went under. I was on the point of bankruptcy. If I can get the business on its feet again by letting a man help me do it, then I reckon it's what you might call poetic justice.'

'*Letting* a man? Don't you mean *using* a man?'

'Don't be so bloody sanctimonious,' Erica snapped. 'It's a fair exchange. We both win. Like I said, it's a bargain — between two adults.' She shook her head. 'I'm surprised that you of all people can't understand the way I feel. Paul let you down; walked out on you and left you with a kid to bring up. Now he wants to take her away from you.'

'And whose fault is that?'

'OK, it's because of what I did. But you're just letting it happen. You might as well lie down and let him walk all over you. Where's all your get up and go, Mary? Why don't you fight for what's right?'

'What's *right*! You wouldn't know what's right if it jumped up and bit you!' Mary picked up her coat. 'I can't accept your offer, Erica. Not under the circumstances.'

'OK, *be* like that then!' Erica watched as her sister walked out of the shop. Then she went into the back room, slammed the door and burst into tears.

★   ★   ★

Vivien had arrived home a couple of days before with a letter for her mother in her school bag. It contained a request for Mary to visit Mrs Hapgood, the headmistress, at her earliest convenience. She had telephoned from the office that morning and made an appointment for this afternoon, but as she walked towards Cable

258

Road Elementary School her mind was full of her sister's deviousness. In her opinion Erica was playing with fire. Sleeping with someone else's husband to get what she wanted was sure to backfire on her and she didn't want to be a party to it.

It wasn't until she actually arrived at the school gates that she began to feel apprehensive about the coming meeting with Mrs Hapgood. She had never been summoned to the school about Vivien before. Had she been naughty? Normally she was a good girl in school, enjoying her lessons, getting on well with the other children and liking the teachers. She hoped that the visits to Paul were not starting to disrupt that pattern.

As she waited in the corridor outside the head's office, the familiar sounds and smells of school brought back memories of her own schooldays. Sitting here it seemed that little had changed, yet so much had happened during the intervening years. At last the bell went for playtime. Classroom doors opened and children burst out, full of noise and energy, eagerly making for the playground. After a moment or two Mrs Hapgood's rotund figure emerged from a door at the end of the corridor and she came towards her, smiling.

'Mary, my dear. Thank you for coming so promptly. Do come in. Would you care for a cup of tea?'

'Thank you.'

In the office the headmistress indicated a chair. 'Please sit down.'

A junior teacher arrived with a tray of tea and Mrs Hapgood busied herself pouring. She handed Mary a cup.

'Help yourself to milk and sugar.' She leaned back in her chair and took an appreciative sip. 'Is your mother well?'

'Very well, thank you.' Mary was finding it hard not to enquire why she had been summoned. Instead she sipped her own tea and waited. At last Mrs Hapgood put down her cup and drew her chair up closer to the desk. Leaning forward, she put her fingertips together in the way that Mary remembered so well. It was usually an ominous sign.

'Mary, I've asked you here today to ask if all is well at home.'

'At home?' Mary was slightly startled by the enquiry. 'Yes, everything is fine — thank you.'

'It's just that Vivien's teacher has been finding her a little difficult lately. Her concentration isn't what it was and her work is suffering. I wondered whether . . . '

'I'll speak to her,' Mary put in. 'As far as I know she still enjoys school, but if there's . . . '

Mrs Hapgood held up her hand 'I'm afraid that's not all. I'm sorry to say that last week Miss Jones found her . . . er . . . fighting with another child in the playground. When she reported the matter to me I thought it was high time we had a little chat about it.'

'*Fighting*!' Mary was appalled. 'You mean, physically?'

'Yes. And quite viciously apparently. Kicking and scratching; very unpleasant.'

260

'But what was it about? I mean, there must have been a reason.'

'Exactly. The other child said that Vivien had been telling lies — boasting.'

'Boasting about what?'

'Miss Jones tells me that Vivien insists that her father has come back to life and is a famous film star. She has been telling the other children that he is going to send her to a private school in London.'

Mrs Hapgood stopped, dismayed to see tears welling up in Mary's eyes.

'My dear, I didn't mean to distress you but I felt you should know. It's not unusual for children of Vivien's age to romance about the way they would like life to be, but with Vivien being in the pantomime at the Theatre Royal and now this, some of the other children are beginning to dislike and resent her. She was such a delightful little girl when she first arrived, which is why I wondered if anything had happened to upset her.'

Mary reached for her handkerchief, blew her nose and swallowed hard in an effort to compose herself. Crying in front of her old headmistress was unthinkable. She decided reluctantly that there was nothing for it but to tell her the truth.

'Vivien's father left us at the end of the war,' she said. 'He had been a student actor when the war broke out and he wanted to go back to it without — without the encumbrances of a wife and child. At the time I told Vivien that her father wouldn't be coming home any more. She assumed that he was dead.'

'And you didn't put her right?'

'It was hard to explain to a five-year-old. When he became successful he found us again and began to take an interest in Vivien.'

'I see. So it's true then?'

'It's true that she's been to London to stay with him,' Mary said. 'I think he would like to have custody of her.'

'Custody?' Mrs Hapgood's eyebrows shot up. 'So there's no hope of a reconciliation?'

'I'm afraid not.'

'I'm so sorry to hear that,' Mrs Hapgood said. 'And I do hope that you manage to come to a satisfactory arrangement. Please don't think I'm interfering when I say that for Vivien's sake you should try to resolve things soon. The present situation is clearly affecting her badly.'

'I realize that.' Mary swallowed her resentment. 'Thank you for alerting me. I shall speak to Vivien about it tonight.' She stood up. 'And thank you for the tea. Good afternoon, Mrs Hapgood.'

As she walked home Mary was seething with humiliation and annoyance; with Erica whose questionable morals had let her in for all this; with Mrs Hapgood for obliging her to disclose the private details of her failed marriage; but most of all with Paul for wanting and getting the best of all worlds and leaving her to pick up the pieces. As for Vivien, who was about to get the telling off of her young life, none of it was her fault. It was all so unfair. Life was so unfair. When would it ever get better?

She had stopped telling David about her

problems, feeling that it wasn't really fair to burden him with them. All he wanted was for her to be divorced so that they could be married. She wanted it too. It all seemed so easy. If only it was.

When the theatre closed that evening he asked her if she would like to go for a quiet meal with him at the country club and although she wasn't really in the mood she agreed. In the car she was silent, still upset about the trouble she'd had with Vivien earlier.

When she had taken her aside after school and told her about her interview with Mrs Hapgood and what had been said about her, the child burst into tears.

'They all hate me,' she sobbed. 'Even Vicky. She doesn't want to be my friend any more because if she plays with me the others won't speak to her either.'

'If you didn't show off so much they wouldn't get angry with you,' Mary pointed out. 'We had all this after the pantomime. No one likes a show-off.'

'They're jealous, that's all. I *hate* them. I don't want to go to that school any more. I want to go and live with Daddy.'

Mary's heart lurched but she forced herself to remain calm. 'That's another thing,' she said. 'It was wrong of you to say that Daddy was going to send you to a private school. You exaggerated. That's nearly as bad as telling lies.'

'It's *not* eggs-agretting,' Vivien said, struggling with the word. 'It's *true*! Daddy said that when I go and live with him he's going to send me to a proper stage school. He even took me to see it. I wish I was there now instead of here. I bet no one there would call me a liar!'

'Where did you get the idea that you were going to live with Daddy anyway?' Mary asked, cut to the quick by Vivien's apparent indifference.

'He told me. He said that if I go and live with him, you and Uncle David can get married, and that's what you want.'

Mary shook her head. 'That isn't quite true, Vivien. I only want to do what's right for you — what you want.'

'Well, I want to go and live with Daddy.'

'Are you sure about that?'

'*Yes!* I don't like it here any more. Everyone's so horrid! They're all nasty to me at school and now you're blaming me for it.' She stamped her foot. 'It's not fair!'

'I think you'd better go to bed now,' Mary said, swallowing hard at the lump in her throat.

Vivien stared at her, her eyes round and filling with angry tears. 'Bed? But I haven't had any supper.'

Mary hardened her heart. 'Do you think you deserve any supper after what you've just said?'

Vivien's face crumpled. 'I want my daddy!' she wailed as she stomped up the stairs. '*I hate you!*'

Mary knew it was just a childish tantrum but the echo of the words had been ringing in her head all evening as she worked. Was this what it had come to? Had her own child really come to hate her? Maybe she would be happier with her father who could give her so much. Perhaps she was selfish, wanting to hang on to her. Suddenly she realized that David was speaking to her. She turned to look at him.

'Sorry. What did you say?'

'I said, a penny for them.'

She shook her head. 'Not worth it. I had a bit of a run-in with Vivien earlier. She's getting quite defiant — rude even.'

He grinned. 'It happens. I expect we all went through that phase at her age.'

She glanced at him. He really didn't have a clue and suddenly she resented him for it. 'Her headmistress sent for me. I went along this afternoon,' she told him. 'I was hauled over the coals because Vivien has been showing off and fighting.'

'Fighting? Vivien? Oh dear.' She could see that he was trying hard not to laugh.

'It's not funny, David.'

'Don't you think you're overreacting, darling? All kids go through a rebellious stage. At least it shows she's standing up for herself.'

Mary gave an explosive little snort. 'Oh really, David! You don't even try to understand how serious this is. Paul is using Vivien to get at me. He's trying to force my hand by promising her all kinds of luxuries. He's got the poor child so that she doesn't know whether she's coming or going. I can't understand his sudden fascination for her after all this time. All I can think is that he just wants to punish me for something. Now, all Vivien can think of is getting away from me and Mum and Ferncliff and going to live with her precious father.'

David pulled the car over and switched off the engine. 'Darling, I'm sorry. You're wrong, you know. I do try to understand when you confide in me.'

Mary shook her head. 'I don't talk to you about it any more because I can see that you're getting fed up with it all. How can I expect you to understand anyway when you've never had a child of your own?' Ashamed of the spiteful jibe and of the tears that were beginning to trickle down her cheeks, she dashed them away with the back of her hand. 'I'm sorry. That wasn't fair. I'm not fit company for anyone tonight. It's been a horrible day. Will you take me home now, please?'

He paused. 'Actually, I did have something I wanted to talk to you about.'

'Not tonight, David. Can it wait till tomorrow?'

'Of course it can.' He started the engine and pulled the car back on to the road. They drove back to Ferncliff in silence and when David stopped outside the house she turned to him. 'You won't mind if I don't ask you in, will you?'

He shook his head. 'You have a nice hot bath and get some sleep.' He cupped her chin and kissed her. 'I'm always here if you want me, Mary. Don't shut me out.'

'No. I'm sorry to be such a pain.'

'I love you,' he whispered, kissing her forehead.

She touched his cheek briefly then got out of the car. Watching him drive away she reflected that she didn't deserve his love.

Dora met her in the hallway, her face concerned. 'You're late. I was beginning to wonder where you'd got to,' she said. 'Vivien was broken-hearted because you sent her to bed without her supper this evening.'

Mary sighed. 'Oh, don't start, Mum. I've had enough for one day.' She glanced up the stairs. 'Is she still awake?'

'No, cried herself to sleep about an hour ago. What on earth is wrong, Mary?' Dora looked at her daughter's stricken face and relented. 'You look all in. Come and sit down. I'll make you some cocoa.'

As Mary sipped the hot drink she told her about her meeting with Mrs Hapgood and her subsequent scene with Vivien. Dora shook her head.

'I know it's difficult for you but I can't help feeling that you're not handling this as well as you could. Vivien was so upset after you'd left. She told me what's been happening at school and about the row you had. She was sorry she said that she hated you. She's just a child, Mary. You know she didn't mean it.'

Mary nodded. 'Of course I know. And I know she didn't mean to be rude. It was just a tantrum, but I'm so worried about what all this business with Paul is doing to her. I'm so afraid of losing her, Mum.'

Dora shook her head. 'Perhaps you're holding on too tight,' she said. 'And what about David? You don't spend much time with him these days, do you?'

Mary sighed. 'To be honest, Mum, I can't

think about anything but Vivien at the moment.'

'If you're not careful you'll be losing him too.' Dora was silent for a moment then she looked up at her daughter. 'Maybe it's time I told you something about your own father.'

Mary looked surprised. 'You've never spoken about him before.'

'No. You and Erica were babies when I left him. I had to leave, Mary. It wasn't as I led you to believe. I loved him so much when we married, but I soon found out to my cost that he was a violent man. He drank too much and when he lost his job it got worse and worse. In the end I couldn't stand the beatings any longer.'

'Oh, Mum!' Mary reached out a hand to her mother. 'I had no idea. You never said anything.'

'I wanted to put it behind me,' Dora told her. 'I tried hard to remember him as he was when we first met and I didn't want you and Erica to think badly of a father you'd never even known. He was never anything but gentle with you. He loved his little girls and I believe he would always have loved you.'

'Mum, why are you telling me all this now?'

'Recently something has happened to make me feel I was wrong to let you lose touch with him.' Dora paused to look at her daughter. 'A man kept coming to the café, a tramp, asking for food. He was so like Mike — your father — that I asked John Lorimer to see if he could find out who he was.'

'And did he?'

'No. This man was someone who'd been picked up at the end of the war. He'd been wounded and was in a bad way. He'd lost all memory of who he was or what had happened to him. They thought he may have been an escaped prisoner of war.'

'And you thought he might be . . . Mike?'

Dora shook her head. 'I don't know. He was unkempt and dishevelled, but there was just something about him — his eyes.' She looked up. 'I'll never know now, Mary. He was badly injured in an accident last week and this afternoon he died.'

'Oh, Mum, how sad.'

'John heard and he told me. I went to see him in the hospital. I thought there might be some recognition — some spark of memory.'

'But there wasn't?'

Dora shook her head. 'No, but it made me think — about you and Paul and Vivien. Maybe you should let her spend time with him, Mary. If you don't you might regret it later as I do. Sometimes love means letting go just as I was forced to let you go when you married Paul. But I didn't lose you, did I, love? Just as you'll never really lose Vivien. You'll always be her mother and there's a really strong bond between you. If you hold on to her too tightly you might break that bond and if that happened you'd never forgive yourself. Think about it, Mary. Now, before it's too late.'

14

At the office next morning David was solicitous, asking Mary if she was feeling better and if she and Vivien were on better terms. She assured him that everything was now fine. It wasn't quite true.

Vivien had been subdued this morning. For the first time she seemed reluctant to go to school and she looked pale and red-eyed from lack of sleep. Mary was racked with guilt.

'When you come out of school this afternoon would you like to go out to tea?' she asked. 'We could go to Molly's Café in the High Street and have those little egg and cress sandwiches you like. You could have an ice cream too.'

But Vivien had shaken her head. 'No, thank you.'

'What's wrong, darling? Don't you feel very well?'

'I've got tummy ache.'

Mary looked at her mother, who reached out to feel Vivien's forehead. 'I'll give you a peppermint drink,' she said. 'That'll soon make it better and you'll forget about it once you get to school.'

On the way to Cable Road, Vivien was still unusually quiet. When they reached the gate Mary looked down at her. 'I know that Daddy wants you to go and spend the summer holidays with him,' she said. 'Are you quite sure you want to go?'

For the first time that morning Vivien seemed to cheer up. 'Oh, yes please.'

Mary nodded. 'All right then. I'll ring him this morning and tell him you're going,' she said. She watched as Vivien went in through the school gates, her heart wrenching as she saw a group of other children turn their backs and walk away from her. Poor little scrap. It wasn't her fault that life was so confusing. Perhaps a break right away from Ferncliff would do her good.

She had meant to ring Paul in her lunch break but before she could do so he rang her. When the telephone rang, David was out of the office escorting the decorator who had been hired to do the refurbishment round the theatre.

'Good morning, Theatre Royal.'

'Mary. It's Paul. I thought you'd have been back to me by now about Vivien's next visit.'

'As a matter of fact I was going to ring you later this morning,' Mary said.

'Well, what's happening?' he asked. 'I need to know if I'm to make plans.'

'She'd like to come,' Mary told him. 'So I suppose she'd better.'

'I'm glad to hear you're letting her come with such a good grace,' Paul said, his voice heavy with sarcasm.

'You know it's against my better judgement,' she said. 'In my opinion you overindulge her.'

'Oh come on, Mary, why can't you admit that I can do more for her than you? Can you really be this selfish? It's our daughter's future we're talking about.'

His tone made her heart pound with anger. 'It's a pity you didn't think of her future before,' she snapped. 'And while we're speaking, what do you mean by filling her head with nonsense about private stage schools? The child is totally confused. You're not being fair to her.'

'I want her to know that there's a better life.'

'It's only your opinion that it's a better life. And stop manipulating us, Paul. Playing us off against each other won't work. It's devious and downright evil in my opinion.'

'Manipulating? I've no idea what you're talking about. Anyway, I'll drive down and collect her if you let me know which day.'

'Paul, let's get this straight,' she said. 'I'll agree to her spending time with you but as to your having custody . . . '

'No divorce if you don't agree,' he reminded her. 'Or do you want that boyfriend of yours to be named in the divorce?'

'You didn't want a divorce in the first place and now you're using it as some kind of incentive. Well, you might be interested to know that I don't intend to press for a divorce any more.'

'Oh dear, what's happened? You and *Uncle David* fallen out?' He sounded faintly amused.

'Vivien breaks up next Friday,' she said, ignoring his goad. 'You can pick her up on Sunday if you like.' And she hung up before he could reply.

David came into the office as she was

272

replacing the receiver. He looked at her flushed face.

'Sorry. I didn't mean to interrupt your call.'

'It's all right, I'd finished.'

'I take it you were speaking to Paul.'

'Yes. He wanted to arrange Vivien's visit.'

He put his hands on her shoulders. 'Relax, darling. You're so tense. You shouldn't let him upset you like this.' He tipped up her chin to look into her eyes. 'It's only a visit. Maybe Vivien and you will benefit from a break.'

She took a deep breath and made herself smile. 'You're right. How did you get on with the decorator?'

'Fine. He's ready to start work as soon as we close the week after next. Mary, there's something we need to talk about. Shall we have our coffee break now?'

'All right, I'll slip through and make it.' As she waited for the kettle to boil she had a feeling that whatever he had to say would present her with more problems. She was right. As soon as they were seated opposite each other with their coffee he began.

'Mary, a few days ago the managing director of Thorne Theatres rang me with an offer.'

'What kind of offer?'

'They've offered me the job of managing the Opera House at Cheltenham.'

Mary's heart sank. 'Oh! So you'll be leaving Ferncliff?'

'Not without you, I hope.' He reached for her hand. 'It's a beautiful theatre, Mary. Much bigger than the Royal and Cheltenham is a lovely town, right in the middle of the Cotswolds. You'd love it. I thought we could move there together. There'll be a job for you too if you want it. It would be a new start.'

She couldn't meet his eyes. 'I . . . don't know.'

'Look, Mary, I wasn't going to mention it but I couldn't help overhearing your last words to Paul just now.'

'Last words?'

'You told him you weren't pressing for a divorce any more. Were you serious about that?'

'I said it partly on impulse. He makes me so angry, holding it over my head like some kind of weapon.' She swallowed hard. 'He's so determined to get custody of Vivien. I thought that if I gave him plenty of access he might be satisfied.'

He looked puzzled. 'But what about us? You do still want to marry me, don't you?'

'Yes.' She shook her head. 'Oh, David, I don't know what I want at the moment, except that I can't bear the thought of losing Vivien.'

For a long moment he looked at her then he drew up a chair and sat down opposite her. 'You know that there's nothing I want more than for us to be together. You and me and Vivien too. Because she's part of you and I know how important she is to you. And this bargain Paul has forced on you — custody of Vivien or no divorce — I can see it puts you in a terrible position. So why don't you call his bluff? Let him do his worst and name me as co-respondent. I don't care. All I ask is that you make up your mind and choose.'

She shook her head. 'I couldn't have your

274

name dragged through the courts. It wouldn't be fair. It might even affect your position with Thorne Theatres.'

He took both her hands and made her look at him. 'Or is it that you're not truly sure?' When she didn't reply he stood up. 'Why don't you go home now? There's nothing much more to do here.'

'But it's only half past eleven.'

'Doesn't matter. Go out and have a walk to clear your head. I'll see you this evening.'

As Mary walked home her heart was heavy. Deep inside she felt that she was in danger of losing David. He must be tired of her inability to make up her mind. It was all so easy to him, she told herself. Whatever happened she would always be Vivien's mother and as such she would always share her with Paul. David hadn't said as much but she could tell that was what he was thinking. But in reality she knew that it wasn't that simple. Whatever her mother said, if Vivien went to Paul she would turn into a different child. They would occupy different worlds. They'd spend less and less time together until in the end they'd be like strangers. She couldn't bear it.

When she picked Vivien up from school she took her out to tea as she had promised. She told her that she had arranged the summer holiday visit with Paul and that she was to be picked up by him next Sunday. The look of excited anticipation on the child's face pierced her heart like a dagger, but she forced a smile. 'Have you had enough to eat?' she asked. Vivien nodded.

'Yes, thanks. Can we go home now and start packing?' she asked eagerly.

* * *

Vivien was up bright and early on Sunday morning. Her case was packed and stood ready by the front door and she had chosen to wear the dress Paul had bought her and her new white sandals. Dora made her favourite breakfast of bacon and tomatoes while Mary sat at the table unable to eat and trying her hardest to smile and appear relaxed. David had suggested that they go out for the day. He was to call for her at midday and planned to drive along the coast and lunch somewhere quiet and peaceful. Neither of them had mentioned Mary's telephone conversation with Paul again and she guessed that he was waiting for her to bring the subject up. Something she dreaded.

Paul arrived just before eleven. As he stepped through the front door Vivien ran down the stairs and launched herself at him.

'Daddy!'

He laughed as he caught her in his arms. 'Steady! I thought we'd stop off somewhere for lunch before we head back.' He disentangled her arms from around his neck. 'Maybe we could go to that hotel you liked where we had dinner the other week.'

'Oh, yes *please*!'

Paul looked up at Mary, who stood at the foot of the stairs. 'Why don't you come too?' he suggested.

She shook her head. 'I'd have no way of getting back and anyway I'm going out later.'

'It's not far from here. I'd drive you back,' he offered.

Vivien looked at her eagerly. 'Oh, do come too, Mummy — please.'

Dora had come into the hall now. 'What a good idea,' she put in. 'Why don't you go?'

Mary frowned. 'David . . . ' she muttered.

'I'll explain to him,' Dora said. 'He'll understand. Vera's standing in for me at the café today so he can have his lunch with me. You'll be back soon after, won't you?'

'Have you back by half past two at the latest,' Paul said. 'The place I have in mind is only half an hour's drive away.'

Vivien hopped up and down, looking from one to the other. 'Please come, Mummy — please!'

Mary looked at the child's eager face and gave in, flattered and pleased that she was still wanted in spite of the treats in store. 'All right then,' she said, reaching for her coat.

Lunch was not a success. Mary felt left out as Paul and Vivien chatted about the film studios and people Mary did not know, including Serena who had recently landed a small part in a West End musical, which was why she was not with Paul today.

'She's busy learning her lines,' Paul explained with a smile. 'Both of them!' He and Vivien laughed heartily, sharing the joke.

In spite of his promise to have her back in Ferncliff by half past two it was after four by the time he drew up outside number twenty-seven.

Mary had been on tenterhooks, wondering whether David would still be waiting for her. She felt so guilty about letting him down, especially as the lunch had been such a fiasco. She kissed Vivien.

'Be a good girl. I'll telephone you every week,' she said. She glanced at Paul, who was tapping his fingers on the steering wheel. 'Take good care of her, won't you?'

'Naturally — what else?'

'And thanks for lunch'

He revved the car noisily. 'Bye, Mary.'

She stood on the pavement and watched as he drove away, her heart full of doom-ridden thoughts about car accidents and deadly diseases.

Inside, the house was ominously quiet. Dora was sitting on a deckchair in the back yard with her knitting. She looked up with a smile.

'This is the life,' she said. 'It seems ages since I had a Sunday off with nothing to do. Get another chair and join me. You can tell me all about — '

'Where's David?' Mary interrupted.

Dora's face dropped. 'He wouldn't stay and have his lunch with me,' she said.

'So where did he go?'

'He didn't say — said he'd see you at the office in the morning.'

Mary's heart sank. He was upset. She shouldn't have accepted Paul's invitation.

All that night she tossed and turned, wondering if Vivien would really be happy parted from her family for so long. Part of her wanted her to have a lovely time, but another — a dark, secret part that she was deeply ashamed of — hoped that she'd be just a little bit homesick. Had they arrived safely? she wondered. Was David angry with her for standing him up? Now that she thought about it, she was sure that Paul had invited her merely to show how close he and Vivien had become and to mess up her day. The lunch was specifically designed to make her feel like an outsider. She was so annoyed with herself for being taken in.

Next morning she arrived at the office looking hollow-eyed and weary. David was late and when he arrived he seemed preoccupied and went off almost at once to telephone the theatrical designers who were to move in and begin work the following week.

When he came out of his office, Mary looked at him. 'David, I can't begin to apologize for yesterday,' she began.

He stopped her with a wave of his hand. 'Please, Mary, don't apologize. Your mother explained that you'd had an invitation from Paul.'

'No! It wasn't just that. Vivien begged me to go with them. I thought I'd be back soon after lunch but . . . '

'You don't have to make excuses to me. You don't owe me anything.'

'*David!*' She got to her feet. 'You don't understand. I was looking forward so much to our day together.'

He shook his head dismissively. 'Of course you were!'

'But you see . . . '

'Mary.' He reached out and put his hands on her shoulders. 'Look, forget yesterday. We have to talk. I've got something to tell you. Please — sit down.' She did as he asked, sinking on to the chair with a feeling of foreboding heavy in the pit of her stomach.

'What — what is it?'

'I've decided to accept Thorne's offer. It's clear to me now that you're totally confused. I know it's not your fault and I don't want you to think I've done this out of pique because of what happened yesterday. Believe me, I thought long and hard about it all last night. I can see how impossible it is for you, being dragged in every direction — everyone giving you conflicting advice. That's partly my reason for going. You need at least one of the people who are pulling your emotions apart to get out of the picture.'

'But not you, David! Not *you*.'

'Yes, me! It seems to me, my darling, that I'm the one dispensable person in your life at the moment so the decision is down to me.' There was a cold feeling inside her as she looked up at him. The expression in his eyes left her in no doubt that he had made up his mind and that there would be no changing it.

'Can't we at least talk about it?'

'No. It's all arranged. I called them from home this morning. I've given my notice at the flat and I'm going up to Cheltenham at the weekend; starting my new job on Monday.'

'So soon?' she breathed.

He nodded. 'There's something else. I've

280

recommended you for my replacement here. You know the job and I'm confident you can do it. You'll have to get someone else in to manage the bar, but that shouldn't be too difficult.'

'*Me!*' She stared at him. 'And they agreed?'

'Of course. Naturally you'll have to work a three-month probationary period. I know I should have consulted you first but there wasn't time. They asked me to recommend someone, you see; someone who could take over immediately.' He looked away. 'I thought it might be good for you to have the extra responsibility — take your mind off other things.'

'I see. You seem to have thought of everything,' she said, her throat tight.

'I've tried to. I had plenty of time last night.' He picked up his briefcase. 'I'm going up to London now — catching the midday train to finalize the details with Thorne's. You can manage here?'

She nodded. 'When will you be back?'

'Tomorrow. I'll come into the office to make sure you're up to date with everything. You'll have three weeks to go through the books and familiarize yourself with the finer points of the job while the theatre is closed. I daresay someone from Thorne's will be down to talk to you. After that it'll be over to you.' He reached out a hand to touch her cheek. 'I'll let you have my address as soon as I know where I'll be staying. And you know I'll always be there for you at the end of a telephone if you need me. Promise me you'll remember that, won't you?'

'Of course.'

She stared at the door for a long time after it closed behind him, then she laid her head down on the desk and gave in to the tears; tears of regret, bitterness and sheer unhappiness.

★ ★ ★

Dora was worried about her daughters — both of them. She was concerned about Erica. The shop which she had admitted had been in trouble over the past months was suddenly and for no apparent reason flourishing. And Erica seemed unnaturally cheerful. There was a flushed, bright-eyed tension about her, as though she was living on the edge, waiting for something to happen. Dora worried in case she was taking some kind of risk — getting herself into debt — or involved in some other kind of trouble. Erica could be so impetuous.

As for Mary, she was so clearly unhappy and fretful. Hollow-eyed from lack of sleep. When questioned she said it was because of the new job that had been thrust upon her but Dora knew better than that. Mary was distraught, both at being parted from her child and at losing David. Dora had been afraid it might happen. He had been so patient, but no man happily shared the woman he loved and Mary had been so distant and preoccupied these past weeks. It seemed there was nothing she could do to change her mood and at last in desperation she telephoned her dearest friend John Lorimer one afternoon from the café. John had never made judgments or betrayed her confidence. He had always been there to listen and give an unbiased opinion over the years and his words of wisdom never failed to help.

'John, there's something I'd like to talk to you about,' she said. 'Could we meet?'

'My dear, of course. When?'

'Would later this afternoon be possible?'

'More than possible. I'll pick you up from the café when you close at six,' he suggested. 'We can go somewhere for a quiet drink and maybe a bite to eat if you like.'

'That would be lovely. Thank you, John.'

He arrived as the café was closing and drove her to a quiet little pub on the outskirts of town. They chose a table in the cool bar with the evening sunshine slanting through the window and as John came back from the bar with the drinks he looked at her enquiringly.

'So, what's worrying you?'

She sighed. 'Need you ask? It's the girls, but Mary mainly.'

John shook his head. 'I can imagine. She's going through a difficult time. How will it end, do you think?'

'I can't imagine. All I know is that until it's resolved she can't move on with her life. I really thought that she and David might make a go of it. I know she loves him. But Paul is asking such a high price for a divorce. He's making things impossible.'

'The man must be completely heartless if he can't see what he's putting her through,' John said. 'And I can tell you now that although he's hiding it well, David is utterly miserable. He's so

283

much in love with Mary that he couldn't bear to see her being torn apart any longer. He felt that if he distanced himself it might benefit her.'

Dora shook her head. 'I'm not sure she'd agree. I know that having his support has meant a lot to her. He's been patience itself, but there's only so much any man can put up with.'

John sighed. 'Between ourselves, I think he feels she'd still like to have Paul back.'

Dora looked up in surprise. 'I can promise you that's not true.' She sighed. 'There's not much we can do, though, is there? Except hope that it will all come right in the end.'

John looked at her. 'What about you? Have you got over your sadness yet?'

'Sadness?'

'About the death of your — of Paddy?'

Dora nodded. 'It's terrible to die like that, alone in the world. What saddens me more than anything is that I'll never know now who he really was, will I?'

John was thoughtful for a moment, then he looked at her. 'You do realize that you're free now to remarry, don't you?' John said.

'Only if Paddy was really Mike.'

'Whether he was or not, enough years have gone by for your marriage to be declared null and void.'

'I suppose that's right.' She laughed. 'Not that it matters, seeing that no one wants to marry me.'

'Nonsense. I do for a start.'

She almost choked on her drink. Putting her glass down, she stared at him, then she laughed.

'John! You old tease.'

'I'm serious,' he told her, reaching out to cover her hand with his. 'You must know by now how fond of you I am?'

'Of course I do. You're my oldest friend and we've grown close over the years.'

'Yes. And?'

'And I value your friendship more than anything.'

'Is that all? You don't think you could . . . love me? Just a little bit?'

She blushed. 'Aren't we a bit long in the tooth for that kind of thing?'

'Speak for yourself. I'm not!' He raised an eyebrow at her. 'I feel exactly the same as I did in my twenties.'

'Oh, John.'

'So, are you going to answer my question?'

She blushed. 'Of course I do, John.'

'Do what?'

'Well . . . ' She lowered her eyes. 'Love you, of course. I suppose I have for ages.'

'Wonderful! I can't tell you how much I've dreamed of hearing you say that. So, as we both feel the same way, why don't we make it official?'

Her eyes sparkled as she looked at him. 'John! You're not actually proposing to me, are you?'

'Well, you're not exactly making it easy but I'm trying damned hard to. I wish I was the romantic type but I'm afraid if I went down on one knee I wouldn't be able to get up again.' He chuckled. 'I think that might spoil the effect somewhat, don't you?' Dora laughed at the image. 'Well, come on, woman, what's it to be?'

John demanded. He glanced around him. 'I don't know if you realize it but you've got the whole pub on pins now. Are you going to say yes or aren't you?'

'All right then — yes.' A sudden burst of applause made Dora look up, blushing with confusion. John hadn't been joking. The room had gone quiet as the other customers had waited to hear her answer. A moment later a smiling landlord made his way across to their table with two sparkling glasses.

'I think this calls for a celebration,' he said, putting the drinks down on the table. Dora cringed with embarrassment as the assembled customers raised their glasses and drank their health. John smiled at her over the rim of his own glass.

'Here's to you, the future Mrs Lorimer!' he said, just loud enough for her to hear.

15

Vivien had been in London for almost three weeks; the longest three weeks that Mary had ever experienced. She had telephoned her twice each week from the call box at the end of Gresham Terrace, though sometimes there had been no reply from the flat. The last time they had spoken Vivien had been buzzing with excitement over some news that Mary found rather disconcerting.

'I'm going to be in a film with Daddy,' she said. 'I'm going to play the part of this little girl who sees a murder. Daddy is playing the murderer and he has to kidnap me to stop me from telling.'

Mary was taken aback. Vivien was only supposed to be spending four weeks with Paul and she'd already had three. How long did it take to make a film? Even she knew it took longer than a week. 'That sounds exciting, darling,' she said. 'Can I speak to Daddy?'

Paul came on the line. 'Hello, Mary. What can I do for you?'

'This film, Paul, is it quite suitable for Vivien? It sounds rather lurid.'

'She knows it's only acting,' he said dismissively. 'Don't worry about her. She can't wait to start filming.'

'That's another thing. How long is it going to take?'

'Is that all you're worried about?' He chuckled. 'Vivien's scenes can all be filmed in one go, quite quickly. It should all be in the can within a month at the most.'

'Another month! The arrangement was for you to have her for four weeks and three of those are almost up.'

'You can't be quibbling over an extra couple of weeks! Have you any idea how much she'll be earning? It'll be a nice little nest egg for her future.'

'That wasn't the arrangement, Paul. We agreed on four weeks.'

'OK, so are you going to be the one to tell her she can't be in the film?'

She bit her lip. Once again he'd pushed her into a corner. Vivien had sounded so excited. How could she disappoint her? 'I need you to give me your assurance that she'll be back in time for the beginning of the new term at school,' she said.

'When's that?'

'September the ninth. But I'll need to get her some new clothes so I'll want her back before that.'

'That should be all right — probably.'

'Well, it had better be, Paul. Can I speak to her again please?'

Vivien's voice came on, bubbling over with enthusiasm. 'Just wait till you see me in the film, Mummy. I've got some nice dresses to wear.'

'Vivien, darling, are you all right? Eating up your greens and behaving properly?'

'Yes.'

'And you're going to bed at the proper time?'

'Ye-es. Sometimes Daddy lets me stay up a bit later if I'm good.'

'And you're feeling all right? No more tummy aches?'

'I did have tummy ache again the other day but Daddy got me some medicine to make it better.'

'Grandma and I miss you.'

'I miss you too, Mummy.'

'Vivien, you do know you can come home whenever you want to, don't you? You don't *have* to be in this film just because Daddy says so.'

'But I *want* to be in the film,' Vivien protested. 'It's going to be lovely.'

Paul's voice came on the line again. 'Stop trying to put her off, Mary. She's absolutely thrilled at the idea of being in a film. Why do you always want to spoil her fun?'

'I don't. I — '

'I can't believe how selfish you've become,' he interrupted. 'Selfish and possessive. She's going to be in the film and she's looking forward to it. But of course that's what's really upsetting you, isn't it?'

'No! I — '

'And she'll be home whenever filming is finished. *All right?*'

Before she could reply he rang off abruptly. She replaced the receiver slowly, her heart heavy as she came out of the phone box. Of course she didn't want to spoil things for Vivien. She wished Paul hadn't said those things in the child's hearing, putting the thought into her head that her mother wanted to spoil her fun. But the idea of being parted from Vivien for another four weeks felt like looking into a big black hole.

At home she went back to her study of the Royal's books. When David had told her she was to become front-of-house manager at the Theatre Royal she'd been taken aback and more than a little apprehensive, but she was determined not to betray his confidence in her. Since he'd left she had worked her way systematically through the business of running the theatre and she was beginning to feel confident that she could do the job. Mr Henderson, the man who had come down from Thorne's to interview and advise her, had been kind and helpful. He had seemed satisfied with the fact that she had advertised for a new bar manager and approved of her choice, a young man who'd had experience at one of the town's largest hotels. Luckily, as Thorne's were paying better salaries, she was able to engage a more professional person.

She missed David even more than she'd expected. She'd had only one brief letter from him since he left. In it he said he was enjoying the new job and liked the theatre and the town very much. He added that he was thinking of buying a small house on the outskirts of Cheltenham. It looked very much as though he was preparing to settle there and Mary's heart ached at the increasing possibility that she had lost him. It was as though Paul was gradually eroding everything that made her life worth living. It was so unfair. She had written back to

David, wishing him well in his new life and light-heartedly drawing his attention to the fact that they would soon be related. When Dora had returned home and told her that she and John Lorimer were to be married she had been surprised. It had never occurred to her that the relationship between John and her mother was anything but platonic. Her first thought after the news had sunk in had been number 27 Gresham Terrace.

'You'll be moving in with John, I suppose,' she said. 'It's a lovely house.'

'And you'll stay here with Vivien,' Dora said. 'I've already notified the landlord and he's quite happy for you to take on the tenancy. Now that you'll be earning a better salary, you'll easily afford it.'

Mary agreed, carefully hiding her apprehension at the speed at which things seemed to be changing. It felt like driving an out-of-control express train. Vivien was to be in a film, Erica's business was booming. Her mother was blooming and looked ten years younger since her engagement to John, and she herself was about to begin the kind of job she had never thought herself capable of. She told herself she should be feeling good about it all. But deep inside, her heart ached for David. She missed him so much that she would have given anything to have him back but she couldn't dispel the feeling that she might have lost him.

Mary hadn't spoken to her sister since Erica had confided to her the doubtful deal she had made with Gerald Grayson, but she was planning to give a party for her mother and John and Erica would obviously be involved. It seemed a good opportunity to bury the hatchet between them but as she made her way round to the shop late on Friday afternoon she was apprehensive. She hated rows and being out of sorts with people, especially members of her own family.

She stood outside for several minutes before pressing the bell for the flat above the shop. Perhaps Erica wasn't alone. Or maybe she'd watched her arrival from the upstairs window and would refuse to answer the door.

She needn't have worried. A few moments later she heard footsteps from inside and the door blind was raised. She and Erica looked at each other through the glass and Erica's eyes widened in surprise as she opened the door.

'Hello — stranger.'

'Can I come in?'

'Not if you've come to preach at me again.'

'Of course I haven't. And I'm sorry if that's what you think I did. I just wanted to talk to you about something.'

'OK. Come upstairs.'

In the flat Erica poured two large gin and tonics and handed one to her sister. 'I reckon we both need these,' she said.

Mary took her glass. 'Thanks.'

'How's Vivien?'

Mary shook her head. 'She's with Paul. It seems she's going to be in a film with him.'

'That's super. She must be thrilled.'

Mary sighed. 'Yes. She is.'

'But by the look on your face you don't approve.'

'Would you?'

'I hope that if I ever have a kid I won't stand in the way of what he or she wants. I hope I wouldn't be that selfish.'

'Thanks! But if you don't mind me saying so, Erica, you don't know what you're talking about. Vivien is hardly more than a baby.'

'OK, whatever you say.' Erica shrugged. 'So is that what you wanted to talk about?'

'No. It's Mum's engagement to John.'

'Don't tell me you disapprove of that too!'

'Of course I don't. I think it's great news.'

Erica grinned as she sipped her drink. 'I have to admit that I was a bit shocked. I mean, they're a bit long in the tooth for romance, aren't they? The mind boggles!'

Mary bit her lip. 'She showed me the dress you gave her.'

'Well, I offered you one too. Do you want to change your mind?'

'Not under the circumstances.'

'Suit yourself. So what's the problem?'

'No problem. I just thought it might be nice to give them a little party to celebrate; just a few friends. We could have it at Gresham Terrace.'

Erica brightened. 'That's lovely idea. But better still, why don't we have it here? Downstairs in the shop. There'd be more room.'

Mary smiled. 'That's a lovely idea. And we could get things ready without involving Mum at all.'

'OK, that's settled then. When shall we have it?'

'Well, would a week on Sunday be too soon?' Mary bit her lip. 'I thought the morning — say eleven till one.' She bit her lip as a thought occurred to her. 'Oh. What about Gerald Grayson, though? Will he be here? I don't think it would be quite appropriate, do you?'

'That's OK. I'll put him off for once. He'll understand.'

Mary looked at her sister. 'It's still on then?'

Erica shrugged. 'It is for now.' She glanced at her watch. 'I'm expecting him quite soon.' She looked at Mary. 'Just between ourselves, I can't see it lasting much longer.'

'Really? Why's that?'

Erica sighed. 'Too long and boring to go into now. Let's just say it's in danger of getting tedious. You know me. I like to paddle my own canoe.'

It was clear that Erica didn't want to discuss the matter further so Mary didn't press it. Instead she suggested they make a list of what to buy and agreed to meet on Monday evening to make a list of guests. It was half past six when Mary left — just half an hour before Gerald arrived.

★   ★   ★

Dawn was breaking as Erica bade Gerald farewell on Monday morning. Watching from the window as he got into his car and drove off, she heaved a sigh of relief. The novelty of having him exactly where she wanted him was beginning to pall, as she had hinted to Mary. Thanks to their bargain the business was now on its feet again and well into profit. Sales were so good that she had managed to pay back her bank loan and the future was starting to look promising. The only snag was Gerald's standpoint on their relationship.

What had started as a fling and a bit of fun was rapidly spiralling out of control. To Gerald the weekend visits seemed to be turning into a serious and full-blown affair. He had become possessive and controlling. He'd even been sceptical when she told him that she couldn't see him next weekend as she and her sister would be hosting her mother's engagement party. Clearly he suspected her of seeing another man.

He had begun to talk alarmingly about divorcing his wife and, even more daunting, had begun making enquiries to see if the shops adjoining Erica's were likely to become vacant so that they could expand the business. The words *us* and *we* that peppered his conversation were making Erica distinctly uneasy. She had even begun to look for alternative suppliers ready for the day when she would have to give Gerald and therefore Grayson's Fashions the elbow — a move which she was beginning to hope she could arrange soon.

She turned away from the window and pulled her dressing-gown around her, shivering a little. They were almost into September now and the mornings were beginning to feel chilly and autumnal. Going through to the kitchen, she filled the kettle and lit the gas under it. Gerald's regular weekend visits were making her feel trapped — that she was no longer in control of her life. She hated the feeling.

The weekends had even stopped being fun. Gerald never took her out these days, his excuse being that he was afraid they might be seen, though she couldn't imagine who could possibly know him in this part of the world. She suspected that he was too mean to buy her a meal, always expecting her to cook for him. And he was so physically demanding! Monday mornings saw her heavy-eyed and half dead on her feet. She couldn't put up with it for much longer. Something had to be done, she decided. But what? And how was she to do it without a scene, not to mention repercussions? She knew by now that Gerald could be vindictive if thwarted. It was a problem that was beginning to occupy her mind night and day. But little did she know that it was about to be resolved in the most unexpected way.

★ ★ ★

It was late afternoon when Erica looked at her watch, happy to see that it was almost closing time. She'd be happy to lock up and go upstairs for a quiet meal and an early night. She was just opening the till ready to cash up when the doorbell tinkled, heralding a customer. She looked up to see a well-dressed middle-aged woman standing in the shop, looking around her with interest.

'Can I help you or are you just browsing?'

The woman turned and eyed her up and down with a look that put Erica on her guard. Clearly this woman was no ordinary customer. Not only that, she looked as though she had something on her mind.

'Miss Flynn?'

'That's right.'

'What time do you close, Miss Flynn?'

'In about half an hour.'

'Well, I suggest that you make it early for once,' the woman said. 'You and I have something to discuss.'

Erica pulled herself up to her full height. 'I'm sorry but you have the advantage,' she said. 'You obviously know who I am but to my knowledge we've never met.'

'No? Well, you'll find that I'm about to put that right.' The woman gave her a frosty smile. 'I think you are better acquainted with my husband. I am Rachel — Gerald's wife.'

For a moment Erica's heart stood still, but she kept her head. 'Really? Well, it's nice to meet you, Mrs Grayson, but I fail to see what we have to discuss.'

'Do you?' The woman turned, flipping over the closed sign on the door. Erica's hackles rose.

'Just a minute. What do you think you're — '

'Is there somewhere we can go?' The woman turned to her with a look that froze the words on her lips. 'It would be best if we speak in private.'

Erica led her into the little room at the back of the shop, closed the door and turned to her. 'Right. What is it you have to say?' she asked, though by now she was in no doubt.

'You have been having an affair with my husband,' Rachel said.

'That's a serious accusation.'

Rachel's look could have melted stone. 'Congratulations, Miss Flynn. You're quick, I'll give you that. Yes, it is a serious accusation. One that I wouldn't make without being very sure of the facts. My husband has been spending every weekend with you here for some time.' She held up her hand. 'No, don't bother to deny it. I've had him followed and I know he has stayed two nights a week on these premises with you. I can give you actual times and dates if you want.'

Unable to deny it, Erica decided to brazen it out. '*So?*' she challenged, thrusting out her chin.

'So — I am here to inform you that it will stop — as from now,' Rachel told her. 'In addition you will receive no more goods from Grayson's Fashions. Not even, I might add, if you were to offer to pay for them with *money* instead of your questionable favours.'

The barbed words stung painfully, but Erica wasn't ready to capitulate yet. 'Surely that is up to Gerald,' she said. 'As managing director of Grayson's Fash — '

'*Hah!*' Rachel's hoarse shout of laughter drowned the words. '*Managing director!* Is that what he told you?' She took a step towards Erica. 'It might interest you to know that Grayson's Fashions was started and built up by my father, who left me the business when he died,' she said. 'Gerald's name isn't Grayson at all, but Kay. The business is *mine*, Miss Flynn. I am

298

owner *and* managing director. Gerald is merely an employee. If I dismiss him, as he *richly* deserves, he will be homeless and penniless. Will you have any use for him then, I wonder?'

Thoroughly taken aback, Erica shook her head. 'I — I had no idea.'

'Clearly! If it wasn't for the fact that you are just one in a long line of gullible young women that Gerald has taken advantage of at my expense, I'd almost feel sorry for you. As it is I feel nothing but contempt.' She opened her handbag and took out an envelope which she threw on to the table. 'You will find your account inside,' she explained. 'I believe you have been receiving stock ever since we brought out our new line. I shall expect prompt payment.' She snapped her bag shut and turned towards the door. 'And I strongly advise you to inform Gerald immediately that your sordid little *arrangement* with him is over.'

Seized with a sudden surge of rebellion, Erica said, 'And if I don't choose to do that?'

Rachel turned to glare at her with piercing black eyes. 'If you don't then I shall sue you,' she returned. 'Not only for alienation of affection but for bare-faced theft. Good day, Miss Flynn.'

'Just a minute!' Erica's positive tone brought Rachel to a halt halfway to the door. 'While we're speaking of legal action, perhaps you should know that I am aware that you stole the new season's designs from the Dior collection in Paris so that you could be first on the market with the New Look.'

The colour left Rachel's face. 'That is a very

serious accusation. I hope you can prove it.'

'Oh, I think I can,' Erica said with a smile. 'I have copies of the sketches your designer made. They are actually dated.' She held her breath as the other woman hesitated. It was a lie, of course. She had no proof at all to back up her accusation, but she was damned if she was going to settle Grayson's bill after putting up with Gerald all these weeks. She reckoned she'd more than earned that stock.

Rachel's shrewd eyes had taken on a wary look. 'Do you really want to go to court over this?' she asked. 'Is it really worth risking your business for?' She sneered. 'Not to mention your reputation? It would make the kind of story the Sunday papers thrive on.'

'I don't care,' Erica said. 'I wouldn't have much to lose. It might even boost my sales. How about you — and *your reputation*?'

The two women stood staring at each other for a long moment and Erica knew in that moment that she'd won. Rachel shook her head. 'All right, Miss Flynn. Have it your way, but don't come back to Grayson's again — ever!'

'Don't worry. I won't.' Erica stepped forward, picked up the envelope from the table and held it out to the fuming woman. 'Don't forget this, Mrs Grayson — Oh, sorry, Mrs *Kay*. I think we're quits, don't you? Oh and by the way, don't get any ideas about boycotting me to other suppliers. You wouldn't want them knowing you'd tried to steal a march on them, would you? In return I'll tell Gerald to get lost. Oh and by the way, you're more than welcome to him.

Do we have a deal?'

Rachel glared at her, her eyes glinting with fury as she snatched the envelope without a word.

Erica walked through to the shop door and opened it. As Rachel walked past her she said, 'Have a safe journey back to Nottingham, Mrs Kay. Nice to have met you.'

Closing the door, she pulled down the blind and leant against it for a moment, waiting for her heartbeat to slow down.

'Bloody hell, that was a near thing,' she told herself as laughter of relief and triumph began to bubble up in her throat. 'Who'd have thought I'd get off so lightly? *And* kill two birds with one stone! You're a card, Erica Flynn,' she told herself. 'They've got to hand it to you. You're a right card.'

16

Mary arrived at the shop promptly at seven o'clock on Monday evening to draw up a guest list. As it was short notice they decided to telephone them from the shop. They'd kept the list down to Dora and John's closest friends and happily most of them accepted.

'Right, so that's that,' Mary said with satisfaction. 'Now we'd better decide what we're going to give them to eat and drink and draw up a shopping list.'

'Yes — I suppose . . . '

Mary looked at her sister. 'You seem a bit down. Are you all right?'

Erica smiled. 'I'm still reeling from shock about something that happened earlier, if you must know.' She related the conversation she'd had with Rachel Kay that afternoon, leaving Mary open-mouthed with astonishment.

'You've got some nerve, I'll give you that,' she said.

Erica grinned. 'More front than Ferncliff, that's me. I've always been good at thinking on my feet, and to be honest it couldn't have come at a better time. I was getting really choked off with Gerald.'

'Yes, but to face up to her like that. And to get away with all that free stock too!'

'*Free*?' Erica snorted. 'You've got to be joking! The thought of actually having to pay Rachel for sleeping with her lying little swine of a husband was enough to make me fight like a flippin' tiger!'

Mary laughed in spite of herself. 'Well, let's just hope that Mum never finds out where her glamorous New Look dress came from,' she said. 'She'd have forty fits.' She looked at her sister. 'And, Erica, promise me you'll never do anything as risky as this again.'

'OK, I promise,' Erica said, crossing her fingers behind her back.

By ten o'clock the arrangements for the party were complete, all except for David's invitation, which Mary had decided to deliver herself over the telephone from the theatre next morning. They said goodnight and arranged to meet at the shop on Saturday evening to clear a space and lay everything out ready.

* * *

When Mary arrived at the office and sat down at her desk the next morning, she found that she was really nervous about ringing David. She took several deep breaths. It was ridiculous — almost as though they were strangers. Suppose he didn't want to talk to her? How would she feel about that?

She dialled the number with trembling fingers and listened to the ringing-out tone at the other end. Just as she was beginning to think that he wasn't in the office, there was a click at the other end.

'Good morning. Cheltenham Opera House.

David Lorimer speaking.'

Her heart leapt at the sound of his voice. 'David, it's me, Mary.'

'Mary!' He sounded pleased. That was an encouraging start. 'What is it? Is something wrong?'

'No, far from it. It's just that we — Erica and I — are giving a little party for Mum and your dad, to celebrate their engagement. It's on Sunday morning. I know it's short notice but we — I — we'd all love you to come — if you want to.'

'A party? That sounds good. What a nice thing for the two of you to do. Of course I want to come. Wouldn't miss it for the world.'

'Really? Oh, I'm so pleased. It's to be from eleven o'clock till one at Erica's shop and I thought that the five of us might go out somewhere for a meal afterwards — if you're free of course.'

'Sounds great. I'll be there.' There was a pause, then, 'How are you, Mary?'

'I'm fine.'

'Enjoying the job?'

'Yes — so far.'

'I miss you.'

'I miss you too.'

'I hope being apart like this has given you a breathing space.'

'Yes — yes, I'm fine.'

'You don't sound fine.'

'Vivien is with Paul,' she told him. 'He's got her a part in a film, so goodness knows when she'll be back.'

'Oh, I see. Well, I daresay she's excited
— about the film, I mean.'

'Yes — yes, it's a wonderful opportunity for
her.'

'Well, I'll see you on Sunday then.'

'Yes.'

'Bye till then.'

'Bye, David.'

As she replaced the receiver she winced with
exasperation. He'd given her the perfect
opportunity to tell him how much she loved and
missed him but instead she'd gone on about
Vivien and this damned film. Why could she
never learn?

The girls had decided not to keep the party as
a surprise, knowing that Dora would be furious
if she was denied her opportunity to dress up for
the occasion. Sunday morning saw her bustling
around at Gresham Terrace. Mary was dressed
and ready to leave at half past nine.

'Now, are you sure there's nothing I can do to
help?' Dora asked.

'Certainly not! You and John are the guests of
honour. All you have to do is turn up. Leave the
rest to Erica and me.'

At the shop everything had already been
pushed back to make space. A trestle table was
set up against one wall covered with a white
cloth for the buffet. During the hour that
followed, the girls worked hard, setting out food
and putting the wine to chill.

At half past eleven, Erica went up to the flat to
change leaving Mary folding paper napkins.
Suddenly the shop door bell tinkled and she

turned to see David walking in. Her heart gave a lurch. He looked so handsome and well groomed in his immaculate dark grey suit. His face lit up when he saw her.

'Hope I'm not too early.' He held out his hands to her. 'You're looking wonderful. I can't tell you how much I've been looking forward to seeing you,' he said.

'It's good to see you, David.'

'I only hope that my going away was the right thing for you,' he said, drawing her towards him. 'For me it's been . . . '

Erica cleared her throat loudly behind them. 'Ahem! Don't mind me, but the guests will be arriving at any minute.'

'Erica.' David dropped Mary's hands and turned to her with a smile. 'How are you?'

'I'm fine, thanks.' She grinned, looking at Mary's flushed cheeks. 'Come on then, David, now that you're here you can make yourself useful. The champers is on ice so you can be chief cork popper.'

Dora and John arrived a few minutes later. Dora looked elegant in her New Look outfit of navy and white with its calf-length flared skirt and flattering little peplum that sprang out over her hips. She and John looked so happy that it brought a lump to Mary's throat. The guests began to arrive soon after and before long the party was in full swing. When everyone was there, Mary suggested that David should open the champagne and propose a toast.

Erica filled glasses and circulated with a tray while David tapped his glass with a spoon to get everyone's attention. 'I'd like us all to drink a toast,' he said. 'To John, my father, and his lovely fiancée, Dora. May you have a long and happy marriage.'

Soon after one o'clock the guests began to drift away. John had booked lunch for the five of them at the Grand Hotel on the Cliff Walk. When it was over, Mary looked at Erica.

'We'd better go back to the shop and clear up,' she said.

David reached for her hand under the table. 'I don't have long,' he said. 'I'll have to set out for Cheltenham soon. There's a directors' meeting at the theatre at eight o'clock.'

'You can leave the clearing up to me,' Erica said quickly. 'Go on, Mary, spend a little time with David. Anyway . . . ' She lowered her voice, leaning close to Mary. 'I owe you a favour. Go on.'

Dora looked at them across the table. 'John and I thought we'd go for a drive,' she said. 'So why don't you take David home for a little while?'

'Well . . . ' Mary looked from one to the other. 'If you're really sure.'

On the hotel steps they said their goodbyes and went their separate ways, John offering to drop Erica off at the shop. On the drive back to Gresham Terrace Mary and David were quiet but as she closed the door behind them he pulled her into his arms and kissed her deeply; a kiss that said everything about the way he felt; a kiss that left them both trembling.

'You have no idea how much I've longed for

that,' he said, his lips against her hair. He looked down at her. 'It didn't work, did it — being apart? Not for me anyway.'

'Nor for me,' she confessed. 'Except to make me see how blinkered and selfish I've been — thinking only of myself.'

He held her close. 'Don't say that. You have Vivien to consider. She means everything to you. Do you think I don't understand that?' He looked down at her. 'Has there been any move from Paul about a divorce?'

She sighed. 'He wants Vivien. And it looks as though he's got her. She's even working with him now in this film they're making. She won't want to come back to Ferncliff after that. Everything here — the school, me, her friends — she sees us all as being in the way of what she really wants.'

David shook his head. 'She's just a child, Mary. Paul has dazzled her with all this glamour. When it comes down to it she's going to be homesick and she's certainly going to want her mother.'

Mary sighed. 'I don't know, David. I wish I could believe that, I really do.' She shook her head. 'But here we go again, talking about my problems. You don't have long and this time was meant to be for you. Tell me about the Opera House and your job — the house you're buying.'

'There's not much to tell. It's nothing without you,' he said quietly. 'The town is great and the job is challenging and absorbing. The Cotswold countryside is beautiful and the little house I've found is perfect. But not for a man on his own;

especially not *this* man. None of it is any good without you, Mary. I thought that once I was away from you, once I didn't see you every day, I'd settle down, get over wanting you so much but I should have known it wouldn't work. It's no use. I think about you all the time, waking and sleeping. All I want is for you to be with me; to share it all with me.'

Tears were trickling down her cheeks now and she hid her face against his chest. 'It's the same for me. It's what I want too. I've been so unhappy, sure I'd lost you. But giving up Vivien is such a high price to pay for the divorce. I'm being torn apart, David, and I don't think I can stand much more.'

He held her close. 'You know I want Vivien too and I agree that you should fight for her. There has to be a way round this, Mary. We'll get the advice of a good solicitor. Let Paul name me if he wants to but we'll win through somehow, I promise you. We have to.' Reluctantly he looked at his watch. 'Darling, I'm going to have to leave soon. The drive back takes me over two hours and — ' A sudden ring at the doorbell made them look at each other.

'That sounds urgent,' David said. 'Are you expecting anyone?'

'No. I'd better see who it is.' Mary opened the front door to find a telegram boy standing outside. He handed her the familiar orange envelope and waited as she tore it open with a feeling of foreboding. Throughout the war telegrams had meant bad news and the feeling persisted. The brief message read:

Please telephone Paul immediately. Serena.

Mary's heart quickened as she looked at the boy. 'Thank you. No reply,' she said. She turned to see David standing behind her.

'What is it? You're as white as a ghost.'

She handed him the telegram. 'It has to be Vivien,' she said. 'Oh God, David, what can have happened? And why is Serena wiring me and not Paul?'

'There's only one way to find out. Where's the nearest telephone box?'

'At — at the corner of the street.' She was shaking and he took her hands and held them firmly.

'Look, it could be nothing. Come on, we'll soon know.'

As they hurried along the street, all kinds of horrors chased through Mary's mind. Vivien and Paul had been involved in a car crash. They were both dead — or horribly injured. Paul had fled the country with Vivien — taken her far away, somewhere where she would never see her again!

Inside the phone booth, she was shaking so much she couldn't dial the number. David put his arms round her. 'Darling, calm down. Take some deep breaths. What's the number? I'll dial it for you.'

His eyes were on her white face as the number rang out at the other end. When a woman's voice answered, he handed the receiver to her. She swallowed hard.

'Serena. It's Mary. I've just got your telegram. What's wrong?'

'Mary — look, don't get upset, but Vivien is in hospital.'

'*Hospital!*' Mary's knees threatened to buckle under her and David put a supporting arm around her. 'Which hospital? What's happened?'

'She'd been complaining of tummy ache. Yesterday she seemed really poorly so we got a doctor to her. He diagnosed appendicitis. Don't worry, Mary,' she added quickly. 'She's in good hands at St Bridget's Hospital and they'll be operating first thing in the morning. It's a small hospital quite near here and . . . '

'Where's Paul?' Mary demanded. 'Why didn't *he* contact me?'

'He's busy filming,' Serena told her.

'*Filming?* You mean he's left her in the hospital all on her own?'

'Not entirely. I've been sitting with her. It's not really his fault. They're on a tight schedule and they had to get another child and shoot Vivien's scenes again. Paul said there was no need to worry you until after the operation but I felt you really should know.' There was a pause. 'She's been asking for you. I've been with her all day but it's you she wants.'

'I'll come at once,' Mary said. 'I don't know when the next train is but I'll be on it. Tell her Mummy is on her way.'

She didn't have to tell David what had happened. He had heard the conversation for himself and now he took charge.

'Right. Never mind the trains, I'll drive you,' he said. 'Go home now and pack a few things — write a note for your mother. I'll make a

311

couple of phone calls to explain where I am and then we'll be off.'

She looked at him. 'But your meeting — your job?'

'To hell with that. Don't look so worried, they'll understand. If they don't then it's just too bad. You need me and that's all that matters.' He took her hand. 'Come on. We don't have any time to waste.'

Although the roads were quiet the drive to London seemed to Mary to take for ever. They finally arrived at St Bridget's Hospital at nine o'clock and Vivien was asleep, but the ward sister let Mary in to see her.

'You can sit with her for a few minutes,' she whispered as she drew the curtain aside. 'She's sedated because of the pain, so don't worry if she wakes and talks nonsense.'

'How ill is she?' Mary asked.

The sister shook her head. 'It's a pity she wasn't diagnosed earlier. When she was first admitted there was a danger of peritonitis, but we've managed to stabilize her. Mr Harris is her surgeon. He's gone home for the night or I'd ask him to speak to you, but he'll be operating at eight in the morning. You can come in and see her before she goes to theatre if you wish.'

Mary was shocked and frightened by Vivien's appearance. Her eyelids looked puffy and violet against her pale face. She looked so fragile that Mary stifled a sob. What had they done to her baby? How could Paul calmly carry on filming while his child lay here so ill? Suddenly, as though sensing her presence, Vivien opened her eyes.

'Mummy?'

Mary stroked her cheek. 'Yes, I'm here, sweetheart, and I'm not going anywhere until you're better.'

'I called and called for you, Mummy. Did you hear me?'

'Of course I did. Go to sleep now. Tomorrow the doctor is going to make you better.'

'Will you be here?'

'Yes.'

'And when I'm better can we go home?'

Mary's heart lurched. 'Of course we can, darling, if that's what you want.'

Vivien's eyelids drooped and a moment later she was asleep again.

David was waiting for her in the corridor. 'How is she?'

Mary swallowed hard. 'Very poorly. She looks so tiny and vulnerable. They're operating at eight o'clock in the morning.'

'There's a small hotel on the corner,' he told her. 'I've booked us in there for tonight. You can be back here as early as you like in the morning.'

'Thanks.' She squeezed his arm. 'But first I want to go to Paul's flat. He has a lot of explaining to do.'

David looked doubtful. 'Are you sure you want to do this tonight? You look all in and tomorrow's going to be hard for you. You should try to get some sleep.'

But she shook her head. 'No. I've got a few things to say to him and I have to see him now.'

He walked with her to the block of flats. In the lobby he looked at her. 'Do you want me to come up with you?'

'No. This is something I have to do by myself; something I should have done long ago.' She touched his arm. 'Will you wait here for me? It won't take long.'

'Of course I will.' He pressed the lift button for her. 'But try not to upset yourself.'

It was Serena who opened the door. She didn't look surprised. 'Mary?'

'I need to speak to Paul.' Mary walked past the girl into the flat. 'Where is he?'

'He's having a meal. He's rather tired. He's been — '

'Don't tell me — filming all day. Well, I'm tired too but I can't rest until I've spoken to him.'

Serena opened a door and said, 'Paul, Mary is here. She wants to speak to you.'

A moment later Paul appeared in the doorway. He wore a dressing-gown and looked extremely irritable.

'For God's sake, Mary! Couldn't this have waited till the morning?'

'No! I want to know what happened,' she demanded. 'Vivien is seriously ill. I had a right to know. Why didn't you notify me at once?'

'You'd only have worried needlessly,' he said. 'She'll be fine. Appendicitis isn't serious nowadays.'

'The sister told me that when she was admitted yesterday they were worried her appendix might rupture,' she pointed out. 'She said she should have been diagnosed sooner. I suppose you thought more of your precious film than your daughter's health!'

'I suggest you calm down,' he said. 'Just look at yourself! Perhaps now you can see why I didn't let you know before. Serena had no business to — '

'Serena was the only person with any sense of responsibility. You might as well know now that I intend to take her home as soon as she's better.'

He glowered at her. 'Do what the hell you like. She's out of the film anyway. If you want to know, it's been a bloody disaster. The advance publicity had already gone out, saying that she was my daughter, and we've had to shoot her scenes all over again. It's thrown the budget to hell.' He turned away. 'And now if you don't mind I'd like to finish my dinner.'

Mary saw red. 'How *dare* you walk away from me!' she shouted, reaching out to grab his arm. 'Your child is seriously ill in hospital and all you can think about is how it will affect your advance publicity! You never wanted her for herself, did you? I can see that now. You saw a chance to further your career by having your daughter in a film with you and now that it hasn't worked you're throwing her aside like a piece of rubbish.'

He shook her hand off his arm and turned to look at her, his eyes flashing with anger. 'She's been an absolute pain in the neck if you really want to know. No doubt all due to your upbringing. Forever whining about everything and going on about Ferncliff and how homesick she was. No wonder I didn't take any notice when she went on and on about stomach ache. It was a case of crying wolf!'

'You insensitive brute!' Before she could stop herself she had lashed out, slapping his cheek. 'Don't think you're going to get custody of her after this.'

'*Custody?* You must be joking!' His eyes glinted as he fingered his stinging cheek. 'You're welcome to her. You can have your damned divorce too; as soon as you like. Just get out of my life and leave me alone.' He grasped her arm and marched her to the door, pushing her out into the corridor and slamming it behind her.

David didn't ask her what had passed between her and Paul. One look at her white face and tear-filled eyes said it all. They walked back to the hotel in silence and went up in the lift. He had booked two single rooms but as he opened her door for her she looked at him.

'Please — don't leave me, David. I don't want to be alone tonight.' Without a word he came inside and closed the door. She turned to him and burst into tears. 'All this is my fault. I should have put my foot down — seen a solicitor or something.'

He held her close. 'You did what you thought best. No one could have foreseen this.'

'She'd complained of tummy ache before. I should have taken her to the doctor. I should have *known*.' She looked up at him. 'What am I going to do if she — if she doesn't get through this?'

He held her away from him and looked into her eyes. 'Don't talk like that. Of course she'll get through it. Mary, listen to me. You need to be strong. The next twenty-four hours are going to be hard, but you have to be strong, for yourself and for Vivien. It's too late to speculate on what you could have done. You'd have needed second sight anyway. I'm going downstairs to get you some brandy and hot milk and then you need to sleep.'

'Will you stay with me?'

'Of course, if that's what you want.'

'I don't know how I would have got through this without you, David. I'm so grateful for all your support. It's like fate that you were there just when I needed you.'

He kissed her forehead. 'I hope I always will be.'

* * *

David hardly slept at all that night. Lying close to Mary on the single bed, he held her as she dozed, muttering uneasily in her sleep. As she stirred restlessly in his arms he could only guess at the kind of dreams that troubled her. At last he slept a little, lulled by her uneven breathing and the beating of her heart.

As soon as it was light he wakened her. 'I'm going downstairs to get you some breakfast. While I'm gone why don't you have a warm bath? It'll help you wake up. Then when you've eaten we'll go to the hospital.'

She sat up, rubbing her aching eyes. 'You look so tired. Have you slept at all?'

'I'm fine.' He smiled ruefully, rubbing his

317

chin. 'At least I will be when I've had a shave. As soon as the shops open I'll have to buy a razor and a clean shirt.' She laid her cheek against his. 'Why are you so good to me?'

He cupped her chin and kissed her. 'I don't think I need to answer that. Off you go and have that bath. I'll see what they can rustle up in the way of breakfast.'

They arrived at the hospital at a quarter to eight. A different sister was on duty, an older woman with a more formal manner. She bustled out into the corridor to meet them.

'Visiting time is not until this afternoon,' she said.

'We're here to see Vivien Snow,' Mary said. 'She's having an appendix operation this morning and I was told I could see her before she went to theatre.'

Sister tossed her head. 'Were you indeed? Well, in that case I suppose you had better see her.' She glanced at her fob watch. 'She's due to be taken up to theatre any minute though. She may even have already gone. Come this way and we'll see if you're in time.' David waited in the corridor as the woman marched ahead of Mary, her starched apron rustling. In the ward she drew the curtain back.

'Ah, she's still here. Vivien, Mummy is here to see you. Isn't that nice?' Vivien looked up drowsily.

'I promised I'd come.' Mary took her hand. 'Don't worry, darling. You'll be all better after the operation.'

'Will it hurt me?'

'No. You'll be fast asleep. You won't know anything.'

'Will you be here when I wake up?'

'Yes. I promise.'

At that moment a porter appeared with a trolley. Mary walked beside it to the lift, holding Vivien's hand. As the doors opened, the porter turned to her.

'Sorry, I'm afraid this is as far as you can come,' he said.

Mary's eyes filled with tears as the lift doors closed on her daughter.

'Nothing more we can do now except wait,' said David, coming up beside her.

As they passed the sister's office door she emerged. 'If you'd like to telephone at about midday . . . ' she began. Mary interrupted her.

'I promised her I'd be here when she wakes,' she said.

Sister bridled. 'I wish you'd asked me first.'

'She's very young,' Mary said. 'She needs me. I promised.'

'Oh well, I suppose if you promised. Come back at about eleven. She won't have come around before that.'

David took her back to the hotel with strict instructions to try to get some sleep whilst he went in search of a razor. Convinced that she wouldn't sleep, Mary lay down on the bed. Staring up at the ceiling, her thoughts were all of Vivien. She pictured her frightened little face and tortured herself with thoughts of what might go wrong. She looked at her watch and realized that the operation would be well under way by now. A moment later she closed her own eyes and fell into an exhausted sleep.

She was wakened by David, shaking her shoulder gently. 'I've brought you some coffee,' he said, setting down the tray on the bedside table.

Mary looked around; her head felt thick and heavy and her mouth was dry. 'What time is it?' She sat up. 'How could I have slept when Vivien is going through an operation?' Suddenly she remembered something. 'Mum! I meant to ring her at the beach café as soon as it was open. She must be going frantic.'

'I've already done it,' he told her. 'You were worn out. The sleep will have done you good. I said you'd ring as soon as the operation was over. Drink your coffee and we'll go along to the hospital.'

He looked fresh and clean, his face smooth and the new white shirt crisp. 'I've telephoned Thorne's head office too,' he told her. 'They're OK about our absence. I have an assistant at Cheltenham so they've agreed to let me take over for you at the Royal until Vivien is well again.'

'Oh, David, how thoughtful.' She smiled. 'And that means . . . '

'Yes, it means I'm going to be around for a couple of weeks. I hope that's all right with you.'

She threw her arms around his neck. 'It's more than all right. What would I do without you?'

'You'd have coped,' he said. 'But I'm glad you didn't have to.'

At the hospital the sister showed them both into a small waiting-room. 'Vivien is out of surgery and in recovery,' she said. 'Mr Harris will be coming down to see you in a moment. I'll let him know you're here.'

Mary reached for David's hand. 'Why does he want to see us? Do you think there's something wrong?'

He squeezed her hand. 'I'm sure it's just a formality.'

When the door opened a few minutes later to admit a tall man wearing a green theatre gown, Mary jumped to her feet.

'Please — is she all right?'

The man smiled. 'The appendectomy was completely successful, Mrs Snow, but I have to say that Vivien is extremely lucky. She was very ill when she was first admitted and if her appendix had ruptured we might have been looking at a very different state of affairs this morning.'

'I know. And I'm so grateful.'

'I know that children are prone to vague tummy aches but she must have been in considerable pain for some days. Did you not think of getting her to a doctor?'

'I — she's been staying with — with someone else. I didn't even know she was ill until yesterday.' Tears sprang to Mary's eyes. 'If only they'd let me know. If only I'd been here.'

The surgeon reached out to touch her arm. 'I'm so sorry, Mrs Snow. I didn't realize. Well, I can assure you that everything went well and she should make a full recovery very quickly. Children are very resilient.'

'Thank you. Thank you so much.'

The sister took Mary into the little room where Vivien was recovering. 'She's been a very brave little girl,' she said. 'Don't be worried by her drowsiness. She'll sleep for most of today but she'll be much perkier tomorrow.' She opened the door. 'Only five minutes now.'

Mary sat down by the bed and took one of the little hands that lay on the sheet. As she stroked Vivien's cheek she responded by opening her eyes.

'Hello, Mummy. I was dreaming about you.'

'Were you, darling? The sister tells me you were very brave and the doctor says you're going to get better very soon. How are you feeling?'

'My tummy still hurts a little bit.'

'It'll soon be better now.'

Sister's head appeared round the door. 'I thought Vivien might like to see her daddy too,' she said. 'Only to say hello, mind.'

Mary's heart lurched but it was David who walked in and not Paul. 'Sorry about that,' he said. 'She just assumed . . . '

'Uncle David!' Vivien looked at her mother. 'I thought she said Daddy.'

'I think Daddy is busy filming.'

'I won't have to be in the film with him again when I'm better, will I?'

'Not if you don't want to.'

'They can't make me, can they?'

'Of course they can't.'

'Will he be cross with me again?'

Mary glanced at David. 'No one is going to be cross with you. When you're well enough we're going home.'

Vivien smiled happily and closed her eyes.

★ ★ ★

Mary went straight to the telephone in the reception area and telephoned Dora. As she replaced the receiver and turned to leave she saw Serena coming in through the entrance. When the girl spotted them she came across.

'Mary, I'm so glad I've caught you,' she said. 'I've been telephoning the hospital and I know Vivien has had her operation. Have you seen her?'

'Yes. I don't think they'll let anyone else in today, though.'

'It was really you I came to see,' Serena said. She glanced at David. 'I wanted to speak to you. Could we have a coffee or something? There's a little café a few doors down.'

David touched Mary's arm. 'I'll see you back at the hotel,' he said tactfully.

As they sat down in the café, Serena came straight to the point. 'I've left Paul,' she said. 'I'm moving out today.'

'I'm sorry.' Mary stirred her coffee without looking up.

'Don't be. I've seen another side of him these past weeks; a side I don't like. He's controlling and utterly self-centred. If he doesn't get his own way he can be hell to live with. I don't need that.'

Mary looked up at Serena and for the first time she saw how young she was — perhaps no more than twenty, the age she had been when she and Paul had married. Perhaps that was what he wanted — someone young and inexperienced whom he could control. She had grown up quickly during the war. Giving birth and bringing up a child alone had made her self-reliant and developed her as a person. Now she realized that it was her maturity and independence that Paul hadn't liked. She smiled.

'I'm sure you're doing the right thing,' she said. 'You have all your life ahead of you and a promising career. Don't let anything spoil that. Paul certainly wouldn't.' She frowned as a thought occurred to her. 'Vivien said something about Paul being cross with her. She doesn't seem to have enjoyed filming very much.'

Serena nodded. 'To begin with she couldn't have had a worse director. Kurt Jacobson is an impatient man with a very short fuse. It's clear now that Vivien was ill and not at her best but Paul felt that her shortcomings reflected badly on him. He used to bring her home every night and make her go through the scenes again and again. I'm not surprised she didn't enjoy the experience, especially as she must have been in pain most of the time.'

As they parted company in the street, Mary thanked Serena for trying to help Vivien. 'She could have died if you hadn't intervened,' she said. 'I'll always be grateful to you for that.'

David was waiting for her at the hotel. 'I'm taking you out for lunch now,' he said. 'And then

I'll have to drive back to Cheltenham to pack a bag. I'm sure Dad won't mind if I move in with him for a couple of weeks while I keep things going at the Royal. When Vivien is discharged from hospital give me a ring and I'll come and fetch you both.'

For the first time since Sunday, Mary found herself hungry enough to enjoy food. Dora and John's engagement party seemed an age ago. So much had happened. Halfway through lunch she recalled something important that Paul had said the previous evening. She looked up at David.

'What?'

'I've just remembered. Among all the nasty things Paul said last night there was one good thing.'

'Really? What could that possibly be?'

'He said I can have the divorce — as soon as I like.'

David looked doubtful. 'Mmm. He was in a bad mood. You don't think he might change his mind when he's had time to calm down?'

'Not a chance. I shall hold him to it. It's my guess he'll want the whole thing over and done with as quickly and quietly as possible.'

David beckoned the waiter over. 'This calls for a celebration,' he said. 'I think champagne is in order.'

⋆   ⋆   ⋆

Vivien missed the beginning of term by two weeks. She confided to Dora as she tucked her up in bed the night before that she dreaded going back to school.

'It will be all right, you'll see,' Dora assured her. 'But if I were you I wouldn't mention the film or your daddy.'

Vivien shook her head. 'I won't. I don't ever want to be in a film again, Grandma.'

But next morning she clung to Mary's hand apprehensively as they approached the school. To her surprise the other children gathered round her when she arrived in the playground. The teachers had already explained to them how ill she had been and she found that all the old animosity was forgotten and she was a popular girl once more. They clustered round her, wanting to hear every detail of her stay in hospital and begging for a glimpse of the rapidly fading operation scar. It took only one day for her to settle down again, this time the kind of celebrity her classmates could empathize with.

With David back in Cheltenham, Mary missed him, but her job as manager of the Royal kept her busy and occupied. Soon after her return to Ferncliff she filed for divorce on the grounds of desertion. She heard from her solicitor soon after that Paul had not contested the proceedings and that it would be merely a matter of time before she became a free woman again.

The beach café closed its doors for the winter at the end of October and Dora settled down to the happy task of preparing for her wedding. She gathered her family together for a Sunday lunch to help with the plans. It had already been agreed that Mary would give her away and Vivien would be her bridesmaid. She planned to announce at lunch that she and John had set the date for Christmas Eve and booked St Faith's for the ceremony, but as they sat round the table at Gresham Terrace it was Erica who spiked her guns with news of her own.

'I've taken the lease on the shop next door,' she said proudly.

Dora looked up. 'Oh! Are you sure that's wise? It's not long ago that you were thinking of giving the business up.'

'Nothing ventured, nothing gained,' Erica said. 'Since the New Look came in I've more than doubled my clientele. I think the time has come to branch out.'

'So are you going to knock the two shops into one?' Mary asked.

'No, the other shop is going to be for children's clothes. And that's not all. I'm planning to put on regular fashion parades — for children as well as adults.' She smiled at Vivien. 'And I think Vivien would make a lovely little model. Do you fancy that, my pet?'

Vivien went pink with excitement. 'Ooh, yes please. Would I have to wear pretty dresses and walk up and down?'

'Of course. We'll get your hair done nicely and you can pick out what dresses to model too if you like. I thought I'd show just a couple of children's frocks during the main show — to start with anyway.'

Dora frowned at her. 'I think you're forgetting something, Erica,' she admonished.

'Forgetting what?'

'Don't you think you should have asked Mary

first? I think she's had enough of other people making her mind up for her.'

All eyes turned on Mary, who laughed. 'Of course I don't mind. Vivien isn't going to be in the pantomime this year and this will make up for it.'

'That *and* being Grandma's bridesmaid,' Vivien said. She looked at her aunt. 'Perhaps Auntie Erica can get me a bridesmaid's dress.'

Erica laughed. 'There you are! She's going to make a good saleswoman.'

Later, as Mary and her sister washed up together in the kitchen, Erica said, 'So, you're getting your divorce after all. Has David popped the question again yet?'

Mary shook her head. 'It's not easy with us being so far apart.'

'If I were you I'd chuck the job and go to Cheltenham.'

'No, you wouldn't,' Mary told her. 'You wouldn't give up your independence for a man.'

'Maybe not, but you're different,' Erica said. 'And so is David.' She smiled wistfully. 'You've got one in a million there and if you want to hang on to him I think you should snap him up before someone else does.'

Mary laughed. 'Is that my man-eating sister talking?'

Erica flicked water at her. 'Yes. And if you don't move quickly I might just be the one doing the snapping. I could, you know.'

They laughed together, but the conversation gave Mary food for thought. The situation wasn't ideal. Maybe they could talk it through when

David came home for the wedding. She'd almost lost David once. She couldn't let it happen again.

★ ★ ★

Vivien was excited about the bridesmaid's dress Erica had chosen for her. It was made from bright red velvet with a little lace frill at the neck and cuffs. She was to carry a basket of Christmas roses and holly. She could hardly wait.

There was just one thing that puzzled her and she asked David about it when she found him alone in the living-room at Gresham Terrace on the night before the wedding.

'Uncle David, you know Mummy is giving Grandma away tomorrow?'

'Yes.'

'Well, does that mean she won't be my grandma any more?'

David laughed and pulled her on to his knee. 'Of course it doesn't. She'll still belong to all of you. She'll just be Uncle John's wife as well.'

'But she isn't going to live with us any more.'

'No, that's true, but you'll still see her all the time.' He looked into the big brown eyes. 'As a matter of fact, Vivien, there's something I wanted to ask you.'

'What is it?'

'Do you think you'd like it if your mummy and I were married?'

Her eyes grew rounder. 'Oh yes!'

'Because it wouldn't mean you'd be giving her away either.'

'No. I see.' She looked at him. 'You'd be my . . .'

'Stepfather,' he told her. 'We'd be a family. I'd live with you instead of Grandma. Would you like that?'

'Yes.'

'So do I have your permission to ask Mummy to marry me?'

She nodded solemnly. 'Yes. You can if you like.'

'Thank you, Vivien.'

★ ★ ★

St Faith's, Ferncliff's fourteenth-century parish church, looked beautiful, decorated for Christmas with holly and evergreens, the candles glinting on polished brass and ancient oak. It was a quiet ceremony, gentle and moving. David was his father's best man and Mary gave her mother away. Vivien followed Dora proudly down the aisle, taking Dora's bouquet when she arrived at John's side.

As she joined her aunt in a front pew, Erica slipped an arm round her and whispered, 'There, you were a bridesmaid after all.'

Vivien smiled. 'I'm glad Uncle John didn't run away like Bob did.'

Erica took her hand and squeezed it. 'Course not. He'd never do that. He's got more sense.'

A small reception was held at what was to be the couple's house and after David had made his

330

best man's speech he found Mary and drew her away into the kitchen.

'Now that I've got that over with there's something I have to say to you,' he said, closing the door. 'This working miles apart,' he began. 'I've been racking my brain to find a way round it. But Thorne's have come up with what could be the perfect solution. There are plans to expand the Opera House, build a concert hall and maybe even a conference centre. That will mean more staff. They'll be advertising for two more managers. All you have to do is apply.'

Mary looked doubtful. 'Why should they give me the job?'

'Because you already work for them and you've proved you can do it. Besides, there's nothing to keep you here any longer, is there, now that your mother is married.'

'That's true.'

He took something out of his pocket. 'I'll let you into a secret. When I handed over the ring in church there was a tricky moment. I had to be sure I was handing over the right one.'

Mary looked puzzled. 'What do you mean?'

'I took the liberty of taking another ring with me this morning.' He held out his closed hand. 'This one — the one I tried to give you some time ago.' He took her hand and dropped the engagement ring into her palm. 'Now that you're about to be free again I thought you might agree to wear it for me. Oh, and before you say anything, I've already asked Vivien's permission to ask her mother to marry me and she thinks it's a great idea. So, will you, Mary

— will you marry me?'

She held out her left hand for him and he slid the ring into place on her finger. 'Of course I will,' she said, her eyes shining. 'Just as soon as possible.' She laughed. 'And now I think we'd better go and wave the happy couple off.'

We do hope that you have enjoyed reading this large print book.

Did you know that all of our titles are available for purchase?

We publish a wide range of high quality large print books including:
Romances, Mysteries, Classics
General Fiction
Non Fiction and Westerns

Special interest titles available in large print are:
The Little Oxford Dictionary
Music Book
Song Book
Hymn Book
Service Book

Also available from us courtesy of Oxford University Press:
Young Readers' Dictionary
(large print edition)
Young Readers' Thesaurus
(large print edition)

For further information or a free brochure, please contact us at:
Ulverscroft Large Print Books Ltd.,
The Green, Bradgate Road, Anstey,
Leicester, LE7 7FU, England.
Tel: (00 44) 0116 236 4325
Fax: (00 44) 0116 234 0205

Other titles published by
The House of Ulverscroft:

THE HAPPY HIGHWAYS

Jeanne Whitmee

Although from opposite ends of the social spectrum, Sally and Fiona become firm friends whilst working together in an aircraft factory during the Second World War. After the war ends neither can settle down, and then Fiona has the idea of the pair opening a catering business together. Whilst their new venture gets off to a good start in spite of rationing and transport problems, their personal lives are not so successful. Fiona, whose fiance died during the war, is sure she can never love again. Meanwhile, cockney Sally falls for Fiona's RAF pilot brother who she feels is socially superior. But secrets lie uncovered in both Fiona and Sally's pasts that will shape their own futures and the lives of those they love.

ALL THAT I AM

Jeanne Whitmee

After her doctor father's death in the Great War, Abigail Banks, a photographer, returns to her childhood home of Eastmere. There, Abby is reunited with her childhood friend, Sophie, and welcomed back by the poor Johnson family, who have never forgotten her father's kindness. But she also meets with hostility in the form of the hot-headed Patrick Johnson. Setting up a studio in the town, Abby finds herself encountering corruption and greed among those with influence. But she finds allies in the editor of the local paper and young Doctor William Maybury. Many battles lie ahead for Abby and she and Patrick are often destined to cross swords . . .

PRIDE OF PEACOCKS

Jeanne Whitmee

Rose, an illegitimate child abandoned by her mother and brought up by a resentful aunt in an East End pub, joins the Women's Land Army when war breaks out. She looks forward to life in the country, where she can find the sense of belonging for which she yearns. But on her arrival at Peacock's Farm she is sadly disappointed; the farm is run down, its owner a bitter alcoholic who clearly resents her presence. Determined to make the best of things, Rose gradually convinces Bill Peacock that she can help to make the farm a profitable business again. But the future holds deceit and heartbreak and there are life-changing decisions for Rose to make before she can find true happiness.

KING'S WALK

Jeanne Whitmee

King's Walk is a row of semi-detached houses built by Albert King, whose family occupies Cedar Lodge, the big house on the corner. But the war changes the lives of all who live there, whether they are working or upper class. Albert's widow, Theresa, has one son reported 'missing in action' and the other about to marry 'beneath him'. For the religious Sands family the morals of their adopted daughter bring shame. Then there is Clarice, footloose when her grandson leaves to do his National Service, who accepts a job in service at Cedar Lodge. But it is very different from pre-war days and now it will be Clarice who makes the rules . . .

BELLADONNA

Jeanne Whitmee

Hurt and betrayed, fifteen-year-old Bryony Luscombe knows instinctively that her love for Paul Blythe, heir to Brashfield Hall, is worthless. Brought up by a local wise woman in a small fishing village, Bryony's history is a whispered secret, but one which is destined to lift her from poverty. Hounded from the village on suspicion of witchcraft, Bryony is forced to seek help from a most unwelcome source. An ambitious entrepreneur, Max Randal persuades Bryony to place her trust in him. But Max has other motives and secrets of his own, and Bryony cannot afford to compromise her pride, independence — and possibly her heart — again.